THE Bitterroot DIAMONDS

DONALD F. AVERILL

INK START MEDIA
5710 W Gate City Blvd Ste K #284
Greensboro, NC 27407

THE Bitterroot DIAMONDS

DONALD F. AVERILL

Acknowledgments

Thanks to Efren Sifuentes for the initial proofreading the manuscript.

Thanks to Mary Stebbins for her editing contributions.

Chapter 1

I didn't want my car to block the packed dirt driveway that led to the old white two-story farmhouse. Creating room for someone to pass, I drove over some of the weeds at the right of the wheel grooves and parked. I didn't want to drive any closer to the building for fear of getting a flat. Who knew what was on the ground at this old vacant- looking property? I probably should have taken a chance though, since there was a fairly recent model small black pickup sitting about twenty feet from the front porch. Its tires looked fully inflated. The dusty Ford Ranger had Wyoming plates with up-to-date stickers.

My stepfather, Chief of Police of Suddenly, Montana, and my ranger mother let me use the family car, a light-green 2015 Subaru Forester, for my summer yard service business. I had accepted their conditions. I was responsible for any damage to the car while I used it and, of course, I had to pay for gas. They would continue to handle the insurance. Fortunately, the car has great gas mileage. I figured I would only have to fill up once a month for in-town driving.

Suddenly is a small compact town, population about eighteen hundred, dependent on hunting, tourists visiting the Bitterroot Forest, and the timber industry. Most of the activity takes place during the summer. December and January usually bring more than three feet of snow, but there are too many trees for skiing except on town streets.

I walked the twenty yards to the front porch, climbed five wooden well-worn steps and gave a solid knock on the screen door. I could see someone moving as I glanced through the door's shoulder-height antique glass window. The door swung open slowly to reveal an elderly woman I imagined could be my grandmother's age.

"What can I do for you, young man?"

She was a little stooped over but had a pleasant voice and nice features. I thought she might have just gotten up from a chair. Her hair was a curly mixture of gray and white. She was nicely groomed.

"I'm David Drum. My brother, Danny, told me you wanted some yard work done."

"Oh, yes. I called concerning your yard service about thirty minutes ago. I wasn't sure you would follow up. I was almost ready to contact someone else, but here you are. I'm Maud Kincaid."

"Glad to meet you, Mrs. Kincaid."

She continued, "I just returned from touring Europe for two years. I knew this place was going to look bad, but my granddaughter and I are not prepared for a job of this magnitude. The yard is mostly weeds and needles from the trees have killed the grass. I think we'll have to start over if we want a lawn."

I didn't think Mrs. Kincaid would be driving around in a pickup, her small hands had swollen knuckles and looked a little arthritic. She was a small woman and would need a booster seat to see out the windshield. Someone had to be here with her. She mentioned her granddaughter, but there wasn't any evidence of her.

"What would you like me to do? I can mow everything down to ground level, turn over the topsoil, and plant grass if you like. I can do almost anything with your yard." I looked out at the weeds, about three feet high in most places, some even taller, and waited for her reply. I had seen a single fence post at the entrance of the driveway when I arrived, but the weeds obscured any fence that might surround the property. I was surprised when I turned around and looked through the screen. Mrs. Kincaid had disappeared and in her place was a pretty blonde about my age.

"Hi, I'm Jenny Kincaid, Gram's granddaughter."

I cleared my throat and said, "I'm David Drum." Thankfully, my voice didn't crack or squeak.

"Yeah, I heard. I was coming down the stairs when you were talking to Gram. So, David Drum, what can you do for our yard . . . besides remove the weeds?"

I started telling her what options I could think of off the top of my head when Mrs. Kincaid returned and said, "Come on in, David. Have a seat and we'll talk."

Jenny held the screen door open and I squeezed past her. Her T-shirt was at least one size too small and her short shorts revealed a beautiful pair of nicely tanned long legs. She smelled great and her smile snatched my attention. She was about five-eight and very distracting. I wondered if she had ever worked as a model. She appeared to be about twenty, maybe a little older. I looked away from her and followed Mrs. Kincaid into the living room.

"Please have a seat. Can I get you something, a cold drink? I have iced tea or soda. We're making some lemonade, but it's not quite ready."

"No thank you. I just had lunch at home."

Trying to pay attention and avoid watching Jenny, I kept my eyes on Mrs. Kincaid. I had to think of mowing down all the weeds, but I did notice as I had walked across the porch that the railing needed some work, especially on the south end. It looked like some of the wood had rotted. Irregular patches of paint had fallen off.

"Well, I would like you to remove all the weeds, then we'll decide what to do with the yard. Will that be all right with you?"

"Uh-huh. I've got a weed-eater and a lawn mower. I charge ten dollars an hour or seventy-five for eight hours. I don't think it will take eight hours, though."

"I'd like to help, if it's all right with you." Jenny interjected with a pleasing voice.

I looked over her shapely figure dand I had to warn her. "Do you have some jeans and boots? Debris gets flung up from the weed-eater and mower and will injure unprotected legs."

Nodding, Jenny said, "I'll change and join you outside." She quickly moved across the room to the stairway, took two steps at a time and was gone.

Mrs. Kincaid said, "Okay, David. Let's see what you can do. I'll look out and watch your progress occasionally. Don't worry if you see me watching from a window. I'm a curious sort."

I made it out to the Forester without tripping, trying to get Jenny's naked body image to dissolve from my brain. I pulled out the weed-eater and inserted earplugs. I hadn't thought to ask Jenny if she had some ear protection, but my mind was a little frazzled. I don't know why I was so taken by Jenny; Megan and I were steadies.

Megan, my next-door neighbor, was gorgeous and I had known her for almost my entire life. We were planning on attending the same university, probably Montana State in Missoula. I had to keep my grades up so I could apply for scholarships, I didn't want my parents to support me while I attended college. Megan didn't feel that way; her dad, Bruce Isaacs, was the president of the local bank and pulled down a hefty salary.

I had just started the weed-eater when Jenny came out the front door. I heard the screen door slam shut, muted by the motor's noise. She was now dressed appropriately for yard work and still sexy. I gave her a thumbs up and smiled. "Do I pass inspection?" she asked over the idling engine noise.

"Yes, Private. Grab a rake. It's in the back of my car." Watching her walk away, I tried to imagine she was Megan, they both had a sexy walk, although they couldn't help being sexy, they just were. But I wasn't sure about Jenny, I had only known her for ten minutes. I sighed, revved the engine and started cutting weeds along the driveway.

I had cut a swath about twenty feet long and looked back to see what Jenny was doing. The rake was leaning against the car and she was poking her fingers in her ears. I shut off the weed-eater and walked over to her.

"Don't you have any earplugs?" I asked.

"No. Can't you get a muffler for that thing?"

I shook my head, "Earplugs are much cheaper. Plugs are in my glove box. Climb in and get a pair."

I watched as she rummaged through the items under the dash and found a small paper container with a set of foam rubber plugs. I was amused when she tried to stuff one of the plugs in her right ear without rolling it to a smaller diameter. Obviously, she had never used ear plugs before, or at least not the kind I had.

I let the weed-eater slide to the ground and said, "Let me show you how to put them in."

"Okay. You do one and I'll do the other." She tossed me the container and moved her hair to expose her right ear. "Show me." I rolled the plug between my thumb and index finger until it was small enough to slide into her ear canal. When I touched her skin to insert the compressed plug into her ear, my heart skipped a beat.

"Oh! That tickles."

She let her hair drop back to her shoulders and I watched her fumble with the other plug. She did all right.

I pointed at my mouth and mouthed a few words but didn't make any sound. She responded by nodding and yelled at me. "I can't hear anything!"

I laughed when she heard herself yelling. She grabbed my right arm with both hands and punched my shoulder. "That wasn't funny!" She pretended to pout.

"I couldn't help it. I think you need your gullible level checked. You'd better watch out around here, most of us have a wicked sense of humor. You've lived most of your life in a city, right?"

"Yeah, St. Louis."

"But your truck has Wyoming plates."

"Grandmother has a home in Cheyenne. This is the old family farmhouse."

"So, what brings you to Suddenly?"

"My parents thought I needed a change in environment." She seemed to be implying what's it to you. "Can we get back to work?" Jenny's smile had disappeared, and she started raking the downed weeds, pulling them onto the driveway.

I took the hint and restarted the weed-eater.

I hadn't thought of where we were going to put all the debris; mostly dry, dead vegetation, but the driveway would do as a temporary location. As I began leveling the waist high growth, I decided we would transfer the rubble to a tarp and load it into Jenny's pickup. Then, I'd show her the local dump.

We had worked for nearly an hour before I noticed Jenny had dropped the rake and vanished. I had to stop shearing off weeds because the machine had run out of nylon cord. I shut off the engine and walked back to the Forester to check the back seat where I had put the package of replacement nylon, but it wasn't there. At first, I thought that Jenny might have moved the container, but she hadn't been in the back seat when she got the earplugs. I must have left the extra nylon at home on the garage floor next to the gas can.

My frustration ruled for a moment. I was going to have to drive back home and get the spool of nylon but the extra trip would just waste twenty minutes of work time. I decided to begin using the lawn mower. Clearly, this job was going to take more than one day; I'd bring the cord tomorrow. I'd rewind the spool tonight at home.

I opened the cargo door and lifted out the lawn mower. As I set it on the ground, I heard Jenny calling.

"David!"

I couldn't see where she was, so I started walking toward the front porch. I walked fast thinking Jenny needed help with her grandmother. I stepped out from behind the pickup and saw Jenny leaning over the rotten porch railing. "Come in for some lemonade. Take a break!"

"Don't lean . . ." was all I said before the railing gave way and Jenny fell off the porch on top of the dislodged and broken wood. I heard a snap and thought it was one of the balusters breaking, but when I saw Jenny lying there moaning, obviously in pain, I figured she might have broken her collarbone or maybe a rib. It had been about a four-foot drop and she had landed awkwardly.

I rushed to her side looking for a sharp piece of wood that might have penetrated her skin but couldn't see any blood or obvious broken bones.

She wasn't trying to get up but rolled to her back off the broken railing and onto the dirt and cut weeds. She was in obvious pain, but I couldn't see any injury. She was holding her left arm against her body.

"I heard and felt something snap. Can you help me up?"

"Sure." I grabbed her around the waist and lifted to her feet. "Where's the pain?"

"My left arm and shoulder. Don't touch my left arm, I think something's broken."

"It might be your collarbone," was all I could think to say. "I'll take you to the hospital for x-rays."

She was staring at the ground and said, "I feel a bit nauseous. Don't stand too close, I don't want to barf on you."

I almost laughed, but said, "Don't worry about that. These are my work clothes."

She gave me the semblance of a grin and said, "You wouldn't like the smell."

With my hand on her right shoulder to steady her, we walked slowly to the pickup and she leaned against the passenger door for support.

"Rest here a minute. I'm gonna tell your grandmother that I'm taking you to the hospital. She'll be worried if we suddenly disappear."

I jumped to the top of the porch and rapped on the screen door. "Mrs. Kincaid!"

"Just a minute," came from the back of the house. "I'm in the kitchen." It took her about ten seconds to get to the door. "What is it?" She uttered, nearly out of breath.

"I think Jenny has a broken collarbone. I'm taking her to the hospital for an x-ray. Do you want to come?"

"Oh dear," she gasped. "Yes, of course. Let me get my things."

"Do you have a bath towel; in case she gets sick? We'll take my car; the ride will be less bumpy than in the pickup."

I had never seen an elderly woman move so quickly, but she was back in what seemed only a few seconds carrying a light-blue bath towel and a small purse. I helped her down the steps and we carefully ushered Jenny into my car. With Mrs. Kincaid buckled in back, I drove over the heaps of weeds to the street. We were at the hospital Emergency Room in less than five minutes. I ignored the speed limit, but there wasn't much traffic. I wasn't worried about getting a speeding ticket anyway, I felt it was a real emergency.

Chapter 2

The emergency entrance to the hospital hadn't changed much since a year ago when I was there with my mom when she broke her ankle. Judging from the faint odor, the back wall of the hospital had been painted recently.

I helped Jenny out of the front seat, taking care to avoid her left arm. Mrs. Kincaid slid out of the back seat without assistance and headed into the hospital ahead of us at a brisk pace. Jenny walked slowly, holding her left arm to her side with her right hand, grimacing slightly with each step.

Megan was the first person I saw inside. She grabbed the intercom phone at the ER desk and paged Dr. Rennick. Nurse Berg was next on the scene and helped Jenny into a wheelchair.

Clearly agitated, Megan pulled me aside. "Who's the blonde, and why are you with her?"

I was surprised by her accusatory tone.

"I'm working out at the old farmhouse on River's Road and Lincoln. It belongs to Mrs. Kincaid." I pointed to her and said, "She hired me to clean up her yard. Jenny, her granddaughter, was helping me. She leaned on the porch railing, it gave way, and she fell to the ground on top of the broken wood. I think she broke her collarbone."

"So, this Jenny chick is living there? And she just volunteered to help you?"

I had to smile at Megan, she was jealous!

"She was raking weeds and took a break to get us something to drink. Jenny is Mrs. Kincaid's granddaughter from St, Louis."

"So, she's just visiting?"

"I guess. All she said was that her parents wanted her to have a change in environment, whatever that means." I shrugged innocently.

Dr. Rennick called out, "Megan, would you bring the portable x-ray unit to ER2?" Mrs. Kincaid and Jenny were in ER2, obscured by blue curtains.

Megan said, "I'll be right back, David. Don't go anywhere. We aren't through."

That was the first time Megan had acted like she was my drill sergeant. I wasn't going to move farther than across the hall to a chair. I had to take the Kincaids back home following the hospital visit. But that got me thinking. I wondered if Mrs. Kincaid was able to drive the Ford Ranger or was she dependent on Jenny for transportation. If Jenny had a license from St. Louis, Missouri, she was certainly capable of driving that little pickup.

Megan came down the hall pushing the x-ray machine and maneuvered it into ER2. The curtain was opened briefly, and I had a brief glimpse of Jenny without her shirt but facing away from me. All I saw was a white bra strap, bare skin and long blond hair around her shoulders. I couldn't look away.

When Megan reappeared, I snapped out of my fantasy.

"You were right, David. She's got a broken collarbone. Doctor Rennick is going to tape her and give her a sling that will immobilize her arm." Megan looked at me skeptically, "She won't be helping you any more for several weeks. Were you thinking of hiring her to help you with your summer jobs?"

I laughed and reached out to gently stroke her left arm. "No, Megan. She volunteered to rake the debris into the driveway as I cut down the weeds. We had earplugs and hadn't talked for more than a minute." I looked into her eyes to make sure she understood I was being serious. "I'm curious though, how old is she?"

Megan didn't answer immediately. "I can't discuss anything about a patient, but she said she would be a senior this fall. She's going to be at Forest Hills with us this fall."

"Jeez, I thought she was in her twenties, out of high school. The boys are gonna go crazy this fall; two beautiful senior women."

"You think she's beautiful?" Megan pounced on that word; I had walked full force into that one. I blinked and said, "Well, you're a ten and she's at least a nine and a half."

"You said beautiful, David." Megan challenged me, clearly not ready to let this go.

"My mistake. She's very pretty, you are beautiful." I tried charming her. I smiled and she started laughing.

She shook her finger at me, "You'd better watch it, buddy."

Dr. Rennick called from behind the curtain. "Megan, please bring me some more tape from ER1 and get some ice water. Miss Kincaid is thirsty."

Megan squeezed my arm and said, "I've got to go back to work. You can wait for the Kincaids in admissions. You should probably move your car out of the ER access lane, an ambulance might show up."

"Okay, see you later. We'll talk after dinner. Oh, how much longer will they be?"

"About thirty minutes. Dr. Rennick is about finished. Nurse Berg will be giving them instructions and Jenny will be discharged. She'll be in a wheelchair."

We turned in opposite directions and I listened to Megan's footsteps as we departed. I followed her orders and drove around to the front parking lot. I considered driving home to pick up some more nylon trimmer line, but I thought I'd better tell the receptionist that I'd be back in about ten minutes if the Kincaids finished in the ER and were looking for me. I was walking to the hospital entrance when Mrs. Kincaid came out the automatic front door. That door reminded me of Wal-Mart in Butte.

"We're ready to go, David. Doctor Rennick is very efficient and a very nice man. I've never met a doctor quite like him." She was impressed with Rennick's care.

"Will Jenny need help to the car?"

"Nurse Berg is bringing her along in a wheelchair; hospital policy I guess." She kept glancing through the thick glass entrance doors, expecting Jenny any second.

We waited by the door and when the wheelchair came from the entranceway, Nurse Berg said, "Be careful with our latest patient, David. Avoid any of the bumpy roads you usually drive on. This girl needs some TLC. The Kincaids are our newest residents, so treat them kindly." The nurse and I guided the chair to my car, and I opened the doors.

We got Jenny into the passenger seat, although she didn't need much help.

"Miss Kincaid, no more taking headers off your porch." Nurse Berg teased as she stepped away from the car. As an afterthought, she said, "David, I told her all about you, so treat her right." She snickered as she turned and walked toward the hospital door.

I felt a little flush of embarrassment as I climbed in the driver's seat. I glanced at Jenny, "Ready?"

As I started the engine, I thought about Mrs. Berg's comment. Where did she get the idea that I drove on bumpy roads? Oh, Megan probably told her of the dirt roads we used when I taught Meg to drive a stick shift. I made sure my passengers were buckled in and drove them past the Isaacs' and my homes so they could see where Megan and I lived.

Danny was outside flying our drone and Spectrum was lying in the sun on the porch with Suzy, a few feet away. I beeped the horn as we drove by and Danny waved. I was relieved when he didn't give me the finger. The dogs didn't even move, they were taking a sun bath and were probably sound asleep.

As I took the most direct route to the Kincaids', Jenny asked, "Megan told me that you guys have the same father. Why are you dating your sister?"

I was distracted from driving for only a second, "What?" I gave Jenny a fleeting glance and shifted my eyes back to the road. I gave her a clue, "There's no blood relationship."

"But Megan told me you two have the same father." Jenny's statement was almost a question.

I didn't know whether to laugh or explain, which resulted in a kind of snort. In my rearview mirror, I saw Jenny and Mrs. Kincaid look at each other in amused confusion. Megan and I were going to talk about this tonight.

"Remember what I said about the people of Suddenly having a wicked sense of humor? Megan told you the truth, but I think I'll let you figure it out. I'm not giving you any more clues."

There was a second of silence before Jenny said, "Hey, that's not fair." She raised her voice, "You can't just stop there. What do you mean you have the same father, but are not blood related?"

I smiled mischievously, "No more hints. Use your brain."

Mrs. Kincaid said, "When we were in the hospital, I heard that your stepfather is the sheriff of Suddenly and your mother is a forest ranger, but she's expecting."

Jenny reacted, "Aha, a clue!"

"That's right. Mom is pregnant and has started maternity leave, but I don't think she'll take all the time allowed. She really likes her job."

"So, you think she'll soon return to work?" Mrs. Kincaid inquired.

"Oh, yeah. Danny and I will be changing lots of diapers after she goes back to work. I might have to take a class: Babysitting 401. That's a class for seniors."

"Good practice for you, David. When you and Megan get married, I bet you'll have several kids."

Jenny was acting like Megan and I were more than an item. We had never talked about getting married except in vague terms. We hadn't planned that far ahead. I glanced at Jenny and she was smiling, trying to get me to react to the suggestion of a large family. I was unsure how to reply.

"Have you and Megan decided on a wedding date?" Jenny asked sweetly.

Jenny had decided two could play the game. I didn't show any emotion and said, "We haven't set a date yet. I'll make sure we send you an invitation. What would you get us for a wedding gift?"

"It wouldn't be anything very expensive, maybe a book about how to tell a joke."

Mrs. Kincaid started laughing. Jenny and I joined in and I almost missed the turn to the Kincaids' house. Jenny was a quick thinker. She was going to be fun to have around school.

I drove all the way to the porch so the ladies wouldn't have far to walk. It crossed my mind to offer to carry Jenny into the house, but I was sure that proposal would generate some strange reaction from her. I imagined she would suggest I wanted to practice carrying a woman over the threshold and into the master bedroom. My biggest fear was that it would somehow get back to Megan. When I shut off the engine, I said, "Let me get the door for you, Jenny. I don't want you to jar your collarbone."

"Dr. Rennick gave me a prescription for pain pills. I hope I don't have to use many of them. I hate being on medication. He told me I might have to use the pills for a few days and call him at the hospital if I run out. But he gave me enough for a week." She shook a plastic bottle so I could hear the pills rattle.

As I opened the passenger door for Jenny, Mrs. Kincaid opened the back door and struggled slightly to get her feet placed securely on the ground. When I heard her door slammed shut, I knew she could take care of herself.

I latched onto Jenny's right arm to help her slide from the passenger seat. She was moving cautiously, probably expecting to feel a sharp pain, but apparently, the pills were doing their job.

When she had both feet planted securely on the ground, she said, "Thank you."

"You're welcome." That's when I jumped in with both feet and offered to carry her into the house, but she surprised me.

"Thanks for the offer, but I'm probably too heavy for you to carry me that far."

What I had imaged her doing was in my mind only. I was slightly disappointed. In the past six months since football season ended, I had grown two inches and put on nearly twenty pounds of muscle. I weighed in at one hundred eighty-eight pounds. I wanted to try out my new physique plus what normal male would pass up the chance to carry a gorgeous eighteen-year old into her house.

I walked alongside Jenny and guided her to the sofa in the living room. It was still covered with a white sheet. It had fold marks though and It was probably covering dust and holes made by critters while the house was boarded up. I guided her into a comfortable position and placed a light blanket over her legs.

Mrs. Kincaid joined us and said, "Sit down, David. We prepared some lemonade for you before Jenny decided to fall off the porch."

I adjusted a couple of magazines on top of the coffee table as I tried to hide my grin.

"Grandma! You make it sound like I planned to break my collarbone." It's going to ruin my summer. The doctor said it would take from six to twelve weeks to heal. What am I going to do for three months? I can't help with yardwork." She was getting emotional and I was feeling sympathetic. What would I do if my collarbone were broken?

Mrs. Kincaid said, "I'll get the glasses and the pitcher." She hustled off to the kitchen.

"Do you have any hobbies?" I asked. I was trying to think of something Jenny would like to do that could keep her mind active but wouldn't require much physical effort.

Mrs. Kincaid returned with a little serving cart with glasses and iced lemonade. She poured the glasses nearly full and handed me one. I passed mine to Jenny and Mrs. Kincaid gave me a second glass nearly overflowing. She was a little unsteady, making the pitcher look very heavy, as she poured the lemonade.

Jenny and I both took long drinks and came up for air. Jenny answered my question but first stated, "You'll think my hobby is dumb, but I'll tell you anyway."

I was pleased that she would confide in me and I was prepared to listen closely. "Okay, tell me about your dumb hobby."

"Promise you won't laugh?" She seemed to want a guarantee.

I held up three fingers and crossed my heart. "Scout's honor."

"I like designing jewelry and clothing, but I'm not a very good artist. My boyfriend said I should quit playing with paper dolls. I felt like breaking his nose when he said that."

"Well, I don't think it's dumb. I'll bet you have pretty good artistic skills."

"I don't think so. My stuff doesn't look like what's in magazines."

"Look, the things in magazines are done by pros using computer graphics or photography. Mrs. Silverton could give you some tips; she's the art teacher. She does design work for people doing home renovations and she also helps with flower arrangements for weddings. You should sign up for her class in the fall. I think Megan is going to. Maybe you guys could work together on a project."

"Wow. She sounds amazing!" Jenny's outlook had quickly reversed course.

"Thanks, David. I'll talk with Megan about it. Do you want your earplugs back?" She began fumbling in her pocket to retrieve them.

"Nah, keep them for future use." I grinned, "Wait until you hear my lawn mower." I looked out the side window at what I had left to chop down. "I'd better get back to work before the weeds grow back. Thanks for the lemonade and don't bump your arm." I smiled and went back outside. The lawn mower was sitting there waiting for me to put it to use.

I walked the area I was going to cut and didn't find anything that would damage the blade, so I inserted my ear protection and started the engine. I had removed the collection bag and the mower blew the chopped weeds out the side. It didn't take long before I began to sneeze. I stopped pushing and got a dust mask from the car. With the dust mask in place, I continued cutting, walking through the dust and debris cloud.

The mower ate the weeds in two-foot wide swaths, so I was making good progress from the side of the house to the property boundary when I hit something. The mower quit and I knew from the abrupt metallic sound, I would undoubtedly have to change the blade, perhaps get it straightened and sharpened. Perplexed at what I had run over, I started to flip the mower over, but at first I began kicking the downed weeds that littered the ground. Damn, I was irritated. I hadn't seen any rocks when I walked the area earlier.

Chapter 3

66 David! Are you all right?"

Jenny had yelled at me from the porch, almost from where she had tumbled earlier. I had dropped to my knees and was in the process of flipping the mower over when I heard the yell. I yelled back, "I'm okay. I hit something with the mower and I'm trying to check the damage. I think I ran over a rock."

"You're sure it wasn't your foot?"

I laughed. "No, it wasn't my foot. What are you doing out here? Go in and rest."

"I heard a noise and then the mower noise was gone. I had to check on you. Grandma wanted to know also."

"I think I'm going to quit for the day. I'm out of trimmer cord and I'm sure the mower blade is damaged. I can't mow if it's out of balance. I'm done for today."

Grandma says to keep track of your time. "Tell us when you leave."

"Okay, I'll let you know."

Jenny went back in the house and I turned the mower in its side. I watched for gas to leak from the top of the tank, but no drips appeared. The gas was probably getting low when the mower shut off. The sharp edge of the blade was dented, and the bar slightly bent, but it wasn't anything I couldn't repair. What had I hit? I had walked the area before and hadn't seen a rock big enough to cause a problem.

I put the mower and weed eater back in my car and shut the cargo door. My evening was determined, unless Megan had something she wanted to do. There was a new movie showing at the Big Screen Theater. It could be a late night. Still curious about what rock I had run over, I walked near the fence and kicked the clumps of butchered weeds away from the path I had made.

It wasn't a rock, it was a terra cotta lawn ornament, an ugly looking turtle minus its head. The figure was half covered in dirt and moss with clumps of grass and weeds holding it in place when I tried to kick it out of the way. I dug my boot under the edge and lifted. The ceramic figure flipped over and I picked it up. Then I glanced around and found the decapitated head. A fairly clean cut had severed the neck. I held the two pieces together to create a damn ugly turtle and I wondered why it was out here by the fence. Why wasn't it on the porch, or near the overgrown garden area behind the house where I could have seen it?

I decided to confess to Mrs. Kincaid that I had broken the turtle and that I would pay for the damage. I hoped it didn't have any sentimental value or was expensive to replace. I knocked on the front door screen. Jenny was lying down on the sofa reading a magazine.

"Is that you, David?"

I think the sun was reflecting off the hardwood floor and she couldn't see who was knocking.

"Yeah. Is Mrs. Kincaid there? I need to show her what I ran over."

"I want to see," she dropped the magazine and sat up. "Grandma! David wants to talk to you."

"No need to yell, dear. I'm not hard of hearing. Just a minute; I'm mopping the kitchen floor."

I heard the sounds of a mop being placed in a bucket and Mrs. Kincaid came to the door wearing an apron and rubber gloves.

"Why didn't you invite him in, Jenny? It's hot out there."

"Sorry, I was asleep. I didn't think."

"That's all right, I'm very dirty. I was on my way home. I'll be back tomorrow with my equipment repaired. I wanted to show you what I ran over."

Mrs. Kincaid said, "Was it a rock?" She brushed a wisp of gray hair away from her eyes, scratched behind her left ear, and frowned.

"It wasn't a rock. I hit a turtle out in your yard and cut off its head. I can take it home and glue it back on. It's a clean break; I think I can fix it."

Jenny laughed as she came to the door, "You can't glue a turtle's head on, it's dead. Just bury it."

"You don't understand, Jenny; it's made of clay. It's a lawn ornament." I grinned when I realized she thought the turtle had been real. She had never seen it.

Mrs. Kincaid shook her head. "I never liked that old thing, I thought it was gone, hauled off with the trash. I haven't seen it in years. Robert told me when he passed on, I should give it to his old friend Mat Ortner." Her eyes grew distant as she remembered her loss.

"Who is Robert, Mrs. Kincaid?"

"My late husband, Robert Patrick Kincaid. He passed about eighteen months ago. I tried to find Mathew, but he is no longer with us either. He had a heart attack and died about a year ago."

"I thought I'd better pay for it, I broke it." I was relieved it wasn't important to her.

"Oh, heavens no," she chuckled. "You can have the ugly thing, David. Maybe your mother can put it in her flower bed. If you want to take it home, that's fine. Otherwise, toss it. It will probably end up in the trash anyway. Good riddance!"

"Okay, thank you. Maybe my mom will like it after it's repaired. It might remind her of a pet turtle she once had."

"Well, do what you want with it. We'll see you tomorrow?"

"Yes, ma'am, about ten o'clock. I'll bring my lunch and work all afternoon."

Ten seconds later, I was on the road home planning repairs to the mower and getting the weed eater prepared with a full spool of nylon cord. As I pulled into my driveway, I remembered Megan would probably be over to discuss the day's affairs.

I didn't know whether to look forward to seeing her or dread having some type of confrontation about Jenny.

I sat there for a moment before realizing I had to unload the mower, so I backed out, turned around and drove in reverse to the garage and unloaded. I spent over an hour straightening the mower blade, sharpening, and rebalancing it. It was after five o'clock when I removed the trimmer line spool and wound it with new nylon string. Reassembly took another five minutes and the weed eater was ready to go. I reloaded the car, so it was ready in the morning.

"David! Better wash up. Scott brought home KFC. We have soft ice cream for dessert."

"Okay, Mom, I'll be right in."

When I got in the kitchen, Scott had his arms around Mom and was giving her a kiss. Mom's hands were supporting her stomach from "sagging to the floor" as she put it.

We were in the middle of dinner when Mom said, "I had an ultrasound today and you boys are going to have a little sister."

Danny and I made brief eye contact. Our eyebrows raised; the news had abruptly added realism to what we had considered an it. It was now a girl.

I didn't know what to say but I calmly asked, "Have you picked out a name yet?"

Danny quickly said, "I suggest Brunhilda."

Everybody laughed at his joking proposal.

After I wiped the grease from my lips and the tears from my eyes, I commented, "Come on, Danny, be serious for once. Make a real suggestion."

"All right, Suzy Two. We have a dog named Suzy, so Suzy Two." He had a sly smile.

"Mom, you and Scott had better pick a name. Danny has no realistic idea. Whatever you choose will be great by me."

Mom looked at Scott and grinned. I think they had already picked out a name for the new member to the family, but they didn't divulge their choice. We'd just have to wait.

After the soft ice cream, I said, "I had an unfortunate thing happen today at work. Well, actually two things happened." I looked around. I had their attention. "I spent about an hour in the ER." Mom looked very concerned. I continued, "Mrs. Kincaid's granddaughter, Jenny, fell through a rotten porch railing and broke her collarbone."

"Oh no! Is she okay?" Mom had probably recalled her broken ankle last year and was genuinely concerned.

"She's sore right now. She's frustrated that her summer plans have been ruined."

Scott commented, "That's understandable. The Kincaid property has been becoming an eyesore. I understand it has been vacant for a couple of years, David. I was out there several months ago and wondered when the windows were going to be broken out. You'll be helping to liven up the place. Could use some paint, too."

"Tell us about the granddaughter," Danny requested, but it was more of a demand. He was always checking out new females and kept his eyes open for young female tourists. I knew he had plans to show new girls around town.

"She's too old for you, dude." I glared at him. "She's my age and will be a senior this fall."

I changed the subject. "The other thing that happened was I hit a turtle with the lawn mower and cut its head off." Unfortunately, I was grinning, and Mom knew I had only divulged part of the confrontation with the turtle.

"All right, David, tell us the real story." Mom had leaned back and crossed her arms over her expanding belly.

"It's a lawn ornament, and I spent an hour in the garage straightening and sharpening the mower blade. I'm going to epoxy the turtle's head back on, but I want to ask if you would like to put it in the garden; it's kind of ugly." Mom was smiling and she looked at Scott.

"I don't think I can arrest you for anything, David. That kind of wildlife is not protected. You're in the clear. Now, if it had been a real turtle, the law would require that you make turtle soup and donate it to a family in need. Of course, we'd have to give it a taste test." Scott looked serious, but I knew he was holding back a smile.

Danny snickered, "What law is that, Sheriff?"

Scott answered, "It's a sheriff's decree, just passed by the lawman."

"There's no such thing; that's garbage." Danny couldn't be misled.

"I want to see this so-called headless turtle. Show it to me." Mom stood up slowly and started toward the garage. I ran ahead, opened the garage door and turned on the light. The body of the turtle was still covered with dirt, but Mom could easily see what it was.

"Well, you were right about it being ugly. I wonder where it originated. No artist sculpted this thing, unless they were trying to replicate something that lived through the apocalypse. It's had some genetic modifications; that's for sure. It takes years for that much moss to accumulate. Mrs. Kincaid told you she didn't want it?"

"Yeah. I'm going to epoxy the head on and give it a coat of brown paint. Do you want me to put it in the garden? It might scare away rabbits and turtles that would eat our vegetables."

"Go ahead and fix it, David. If we don't like it, we can always toss it. The price was right. I have to go back in the house to use the bathroom." Mom waddled back to the house. I opened a bench drawer looking for the epoxy.

Danny had been watching Mom and me as we evaluated the turtle. He said, "Bring that thing out in the yard and I'll hose it off, it might not be so ugly without the earthy makeup."

"Now that's a good idea."

I dropped the two pieces on the lawn, and Danny squirted them with the garden hose. A minute later, the dirt and moss were gone. I dried the clean pieces with the towel I had brought from the workbench. Danny picked up the head, I grabbed the body, and we returned to the garage work bench.

When Danny tried a dry fit and with the head, the turtle didn't look that bad. He put the head on the bench and said, "Epoxy,

Doctor Drum."

I laughed. He does say some funny things.

"David?"

I heard a voice I'd recognize anywhere. I could see her reflection in the garage door window. She was walking up the driveway toward the garage, her head turned, searching for me in the backyard.

"In here, Meg. I'm in the garage with Danny and a turtle." I had to smile because she had no idea what I meant by a turtle. I stepped outside and waited for her to join me. I gave her a kiss and said, "Come and see what I have. I hit it with the lawn mower over at the Kincaids'."

She followed me toward the garage, frowning as she took baby steps, not knowing what to expect. She held onto the doorjamb with her right hand and swung her head into the garage with her other hand raised to protect herself. I guess she thought I was going to pull a fast one and make her look silly. We joke with each other so often; I wasn't surprised at her caution.

"What is that?" She saw the ceramic lump on the workbench but didn't recognize it as a turtle, especially when it had no head.

"It's a turtle from the Kincaids' yard. I'm getting ready to glue the head back on. You can help me. Danny has something to do in the house." I gave him the you're not wanted look and he left saying, "Yeah, I'm working on a 1,000-piece jigsaw puzzle of a pink elephant in a bedroom."

Megan picked up the turtle's head and held it on the body so she could see the shape of the original figure. She raised her eyebrows and glanced at me. "It's not something I would pay money for. What are you going to do with it?"

"I'll see if this epoxy works and go from there. If the epoxy holds, I'm going to paint it."

"You're going to glue it back together?"

"Yeah. I was just getting ready to mix some epoxy, when I heard your voice."

I started unscrewing the cap on the tube of resin when Megan suddenly said, "Wait, there's something in there, in the turtle's body. Look, it's shiny. What do you think it is?"

I looked but didn't see anything out of the ordinary. I pulled the portable lamp arm closer to get increased light where Megan was pointing. Then I saw it.

"Boy, you've got good eyes."

She laughed and said, "Better to see you with."

I grinned and shook my head, but she had gotten my attention. She had seen something.

I pulled out the shallow top drawer under the bench and picked up a nail set used for small brads. Megan handed me the tack hammer and I grinned, "Thank you nurse."

We tapped at the ceramic, chipping small pieces of clay away. Meg suggested the shiny object was a ring. My first guess was a washer of some kind, but Megan was more imaginative; she was sticking with her guess that it was a ring.

I removed bits of ceramic for about thirty minutes before Megan said, "Let me work at it for a while. Aren't your fingers getting sore?"

"Okay. I'm gonna get us some pop. What would you like?"

"Orange, please." She picked up the tools and began where I had left off.

I brought back two cans of pop and two cereal bowls of soft ice cream. I had two plastic spoons in my pocket, but I didn't let her know. Megan had made significant progress while I was gone. The object was a ring, just as she had expected, but we still couldn't see if there was a stone mounted.

I put the orange drink on the bench with the ice cream and she said, "How am I supposed to eat the ice cream?"

"Use your tongue and lick it." I couldn't help grinning and she held out her hand for a spoon which I pulled from my pocket and stuck in the vanilla treat like a flagpole.

"You are so bad, David."

Chapter 4

When we finally got the ring free of the turtle, the pop cans were empty and so were the bowls of ice cream. Megan's hunch had been correct, the turtle had eaten a ring. We tried to rub off the ceramic traces from around the stone, but it was a losing battle. Meg and I were both afraid we would damage the stone if we chipped away too vigorously.

"Could that be a real diamond?" Megan asked.

"I've never seen one that big. I bet its cubic zirconia. Why would a real diamond ring be inside an ugly ceramic turtle almost buried for years in Suddenly?"

"Mrs. Kincaid didn't know about the ring or she never would have given the turtle to you, David. Let's take it down to Leo's Jewelry in the morning. Mr. Grinberg will be able to tell us all about it."

"Good idea. I'll pick you up at nine o'clock, unless you have something else planned."

"I was going to get some clothes laundered, but I'll do that tonight. Sweet dreams." Megan gave me a kiss, turned, and walked across the grass toward Isaacs' back door, the slider leading to the kitchen.

When she was about halfway to her house, I yelled, "Dream about diamonds! Good night!"

I picked up the ring, doused the garage lights and went in the house.

"Mom?" I hollered from the kitchen.

"In here, David." Her voice came from the living room. Apparently, Danny had gone to his room and Scott and Mom were sitting on the sofa. Mom was leaning against some pillows and her bare feet were in Scott's lap. Scott was massaging her ankles. Mom looked at me, "What were you and Megan tapping on in the garage, a bird house?"

I laughed, "We weren't making anything. We found something inside the turtle. Megan discovered it and we were trying to get it out of the clay without breaking it."

"What did you find?" Scott looked away from the TV and had that policeman's questioning expression, as he continued working on Mom's swollen ankles.

"A diamond ring, but it's probably a fake."

Scott held out his hand, "Can I take a look?"

I reached in my pocket, put my right index finger through the metallic ring and held it in place with my thumb. I dropped the ring in Scott's outstretched hand and knelt beside the sofa next to Mom. Scott moved so they could get a better look with the light from the floor lamp.

"Hmm. This was inside the turtle? It sure looks like a real diamond. Did you shine a black light on it?"

Mom and I looked at each other, shrugging, not knowing what a black light would reveal.

"Yeah. It was embedded in the clay. We just found it an hour ago. Megan and I are going to take it to Leo's tomorrow and see what he says. We don't have a black light, do we Mom?"

"Nope. Do you have one, Scott?"

"There's one at the department. I could go get it."

"That's all right, I'll find out at Leo's." I asked, "What does a black light show?"

"A real diamond turns blue," Scott replied. He grinned at Mom, "Leftover facts from my FBI days."

Mom said, "Hmm. I'd better check my engagement ring." She laughed and pushed Scott with her foot. He grabbed her foot, tickled the bottom of it and wouldn't let her pull away.

Mom started laughing and said, "Quit, Scott, you'll make me wet my pants."

"If you guys are going to wrestle, I'm going to bed. Tomorrow's going to be a long day."

As I started up the steps to the second floor, Mom said, "Good night, David, I hope that's a real diamond. Some day you can give it to Megan."

Scott added, "Good night and good luck at the jewelry store. Maybe Grinberg will buy it. Don't buy anything too expensive with the money. Save your money for college."

Scott was almost always a source of constructive advice.

My alarm woke me at 8:00 a.m. I could hear Megan's voice and I thought I was dreaming since it sounded far off, but strangely in the house. I dressed quickly and went downstairs. Her voice got louder as I approached the kitchen and when I got to the dining room, I saw her sitting on a bar stool talking to Mom. They were both nursing a glass of orange juice. I entered the kitchen slowly and stood quietly beside Megan with my hand on her shoulder.

"Good morning, David," she said without looking away from her glass.

"Morning, ladies. Did you sneak over during the night, Megan?"

"Sure did. I wanted to see that ring. I'm thinking it came from a box of cereal or Cracker Jack; it can't be real. The stone must be some type of cheap plastic."

"You're full of it. They don't put toys in those packages anymore, do they Mom?"

"Good morning. I haven't kept up with those things for a long time. I've been wondering how that turtle swallowed that ring. It had to have been put there before it was fired at high temperature."

"Yeah, that's right." I looked around. "Where's Scott?"

"He got up early and went to the office. He had to make a call to the FBI in Washington, D.C."

I finally had to ask, "Meg, why are you here so early? Aren't we going to Leo's in an hour?"

She gulped the last of her orange juice and snickered, "I didn't want to be late; I know how you are about being punctual." She grinned at mom. "No, I couldn't sleep. I kept thinking about the ring. Where is it? I want to give it a closer look."

I pulled the ring from my pocket and handed it to her.

She volunteered some new information. "Mom and Dad left early for Butte to catch a flight to St. Louis. Dad had to be at a meeting of independent banks. He's the vice president of the organization and I didn't want to go; too boring."

"So, you're home alone. We can have a sleep over. I'll bring my shorts with hearts on them, we'll watch a late show and have some popcorn." I tried to keep from laughing but it didn't take more than a couple of seconds.

Mom said, "You will not!"

Megan and I burst out laughing. I moved away so Mom wouldn't hit me. She might have thrown a wet washrag at me if one had been handy.

Mom said, "You can stay in our guest room over the garage if you like, Megan. How long will they be gone?"

"Three or four days. They'll be back on Friday; maybe Saturday. Could Suzy stay with me during the night? She likes me and I would be fine with her around. Her bark would scare off anyone."

Mom turned toward me, "What do you think, David? Could you fix a place next door for Suzy to eat and sleep?"

"No problem, we can put her bed and bowls in the Isaacs' mudroom. You'll have to take her outside for a bathroom break before you go to bed though, Meg. Just let her out in the backyard for a few minutes. Ah, on second thought, don't worry about that, I can do it for you."

Megan was agreeable, "Just knock on the slider at about 9:45. I go to bed at ten. You'd better not forget."

"Me? My mind's a steel trap."

Megan decided to stay and talk with Mom as I ate a bowl of cereal. While Mom and Megan continued gabbing in the kitchen, I changed into my work clothes. I would go to the Kincaids' after we visited the jeweler. Meg helped with the dishes and carried the laundry basket to the washing machine so Mom wouldn't mess up her back. Mom seemed to be getting bigger every day, but it was probably just the appearance when she was standing beside Megan. Meg looked like a model in anything she wore.

Leo's Jewelry was a ten minute drive away. I had my lawn equipment in the back of the Subaru ready to continue work at the Kincaids'. When Meg got in the car, she took a big sniff and scrunched up her face.

"Ah, the fragrance of dead grass and weeds. What a joy." And then she giggled.

"Yes, my dear, better than alcohol, bleach, and vomit in party boy's cars. Remember, I'm earning money for college the best way I can in Suddenly." I opened the windows for fresh air.

Megan slid over next to me and kissed my cheek. "I'm just kidding, I don't mind. Some of the fumes at the hospital almost make me gag."

I countered, "Fumes from the bathroom make me gag. I never eat in there." I grinned although that wasn't entirely true. We both knew there was a little truth in what we said, but it was shrugged off without ill will. We had teased each other nearly every day since we were able to talk.

Traffic on Main Street was almost nonexistent at nine in the morning. I didn't have to look for a parking spot, I just pulled up to the curb and we hopped out. Meg went in the jewelry store first, the bell above the door announcing our presence.

Mr. Grinberg's voice came from behind the glass counter, "Be right with you."

He was on his knees, arranging some items on the bottom shelf below some antique watches displayed on the top shelf of the counter. I couldn't remember ever seeing the man before; I had never been in the jewelry store.

A few seconds ticked off before he struggled to his feet. He was about the same height as Megan, had a full head of gray hair and wire-rimmed glasses adorned his round face. He was a little skinny. "What a nice-looking couple. Are you looking for a ring?"

I took what he said seriously, "No, sir. We found a ring and wanted you to tell us if it's a diamond." I fished it out of my pocket and handed it to Mr. Grinberg. He mashed his lips together and frowned. "It's kind of dirty. Where did you find this, buried?" He focused on the ring and stone and scratched his left cheek with his thumbnail. He laid the ring on the countertop, said, "One moment," and disappeared behind a light-green curtain to the back of the shop. He returned with a lens, a shallow box of hand tools that looked a bit like something a dentist would use, a tiny electric drill, and a black light.

Megan and I watched intently as Leo performed a variety of manipulations on our ring. When he turned on the black light, the stone turned blue. Megan looked at me, covered her mouth with her hand and said very quietly, "It's a real diamond, David."

Goose bumps attacked my back and arms; something I had never experienced before was happening. I reached out to Meg and grabbed her hand.

While Leo spent about ten minutes cleaning the ring, Megan looked at necklaces and earrings and I inspected watches. Leo then went to his computer at the end of the front counter. He was being very businesslike, not showing any sign of excitement.

We couldn't see what he was doing on the computer, but after about five minutes, he came back to us and said, "Do you want the good news first or the bad?"

"The good news," Megan said immediately. I had to agree.

"You've got a 2.85 carat diamond worth about twenty-four thousand dollars, maybe a little more. That's a beautiful stone."

I was shocked. "Really? That much?"

Megan said, "Holy cow. That's incredible!"

I had calmed down a little and had to ask, "What's the bad news?" What could be bad about that?

Mr. Grinberg scanned our faces and said slowly, "It's a stolen gem."

I was having a difficult time believing what he said. "Stolen? How do you know?"

"Well, I cleaned the dirt and claylike material from the setting and checked the girdle, that's the edge where the diamond is attached to the setting. I found a laser identification number and checked the stolen gems website. The diamond was part of a 1997 shipment to New York from Antwerp, Belgium."

I swallowed hard. "Geez, Mr. Grinberg, should I report it?"

"I already have, David. I sent a message to our sheriff's office and to the insurance company. Your stepfather will keep the diamond locked in his safe until the agent arrives to claim it. My little safe is not as secure as the one in the courthouse."

"You know who I am?"

Leo smiled, "I follow the sports in the paper. And you must be Megan Isaacs. Your picture was in the paper with David's, taken at the prom a few weeks ago. I'm sorry I kidded you when you came in. I didn't really think you were looking for a ring. I thought it was amusing when you showed me the ring you found."

I hadn't paid much attention to what Mr. Grinberg had said, being so interested in finding out about the ring. "That's okay, Megan and I spend a lot of time together."

Leo held the ring up and said, "I didn't give you all the good news. You will be getting a ten percent reward from the insurance company, about twenty-four hundred dollars. That's after the investigation has been completed, of course. No telling how long that will take. It might be months from now."

Megan and I looked at each other and smiled, then she hugged me and said, "That's going to be a big help for your college fund; you won't have to do as many yards as you thought. If some scholarships come through, you'll be in great shape for your first year in college."

"Sounds awesome, doesn't it? Now I need to find some more lawn ornaments to hit with my mower."

Megan laughed, "Yeah! I wonder what a giraffe or an elephant would have inside, or a hippo!"

I grinned, "I think my mower would have a hard time cutting the head off a hippo. A hippo would ruin my mower." I glanced at the grandfather clock against the far wall and realized I was going to be late at the Kincaids' if I didn't get Megan back home in the next five minutes. "C'mon, Meg, we've got to go. Thanks for all the help, Mr. Grinberg."

Megan started for the door and I was right behind her. She waved at Leo as we rushed to the car. When we got home, I parked next to the side kitchen door. Mom appeared at the door, handed me a sack lunch and said, "Cut lots of weeds, David, and Megan, come in and tell me all about your trip to Leo's."

As I got back in the car, I saw Megan and Mom laughing when Meg entered the house.

Chapter 5

om had saved me about ten minutes by making me a lunch. As I drove to the Kincaids', I wondered if she had tried to pull something on me. I was thinking that she and Megan were laughing about something she put in my sandwiches. I usually made two, so she had a couple of opportunities to mess with me. She might have included a lemon with a note to make myself some lemonade or a sweet pickle instead of a dill. Since Mom and Scott were married a year ago, Mom had become more relaxed. I think she was more at ease now that she was not the only bread winner in the family, and she was seriously in love with Scott. When Dad died, I think she thought she would never find love with anyone else, but after almost five years, she did.

Jenny was sitting on the front porch steps when I arrived. The Ford was still sitting in the same place as yesterday; apparently it hadn't been driven. The broken railing hadn't been moved either. It was probably too heavy and awkward for Mrs. Kincaid and Jenny wasn't going to risk further injury by trying to move the twisted heap of splintered wood.

Jenny waved to me as I got out of the Subaru and opened the rear door. I yelled to her, "Good morning, how's your injury?"

"Not too bad, I've only used two of those pain pills."

I removed the weed-eater and walked over to where I had left off and set it down against the fence where I had struck the turtle. I had decided to tell the Kincaids' about the diamond. I thought it would be better to let them know right away, rather than keep it secret. I went over to the porch to see what Jenny was working on. It looked like she was drawing something in a sketchpad. She had colored pencils and charcoal in a cigar box. Her right index finger was blackened.

"What are you working on?" Before she had a chance to answer, I grinned and said, "Did you hit your finger with a hammer?"

"No, I cleaned the fireplace with my index finger."

I replied, "Awesome. From the looks of your finger I'll bet you did a very good job." Our joking was reminiscent of Megan's and my verbal sparring.

"If you promise not to laugh, I'll show you one of my creations. It's not finished but I think you'll get the idea." She opened her sketch book and what I saw surprised me.

It was a picture of Romeo and Juliet and was beautiful. In my opinion, she didn't need any instruction from a high school art teacher.

"Wow, that is really good, Jenny. You are really talented. I'm not an art critic, but I've never seen anything like that done at school. Mrs. Silverton would be happy to have you in her class. She would have to search her art books to find something to teach you."

"Thank you, but I know I still have much to learn. Did you get the turtle repaired?"

That gave me the chance I needed. I was wondering how to tell the Kincaids what Megan and I had found. "Not yet. Megan and I were about to glue the turtle's head back on when Meg spotted something; it was shiny and looked out of place. We spent about an hour removing it from the turtle's body."

"What did you find, a turtle's egg?" She grinned.

Nonchalantly, I said, "No, a diamond ring."

"C'mon, David, no joking. What did you really find? Was it a message in a tiny bottle? You know, two can play this game."

"If you don't believe me, call the jewelry store. Mr. Grinberg will tell you what we found. Megan and I took it to him, and he told us it was worth twenty-four thousand dollars, but it was part of a stolen shipment from Belgium. He turned it over to my stepfather."

"Why would he give it to your stepfather?"

"There's a secure safe in the courthouse. I think an insurance investigator will be here tomorrow or the next day; he'll want to talk to your grandmother."

Jenny turned toward the front door and yelled, "Grandma, come here. David has something to tell you." She tossed her chalk and pencils in the cigar box and said, "Would you please help me up?" She closed her sketch book, shut the cigar box, and extended her right hand so I could help her stand. "Let's go inside and sit down with grandma. I don't want her to faint." She was finally convinced.

I wished Megan were with me now; I had never been with anyone that fainted. Maybe Jenny would know what to do if her grandmother passed out. I followed Jenny inside, and we watched Mrs. Kincaid come down from the second floor. She was holding the railing and watching each step, descending slowly. When she was on the hardwood first floor, she looked at us and said, "What is it, David? Do you want to be paid for the work you have completed? I thought I would give you a check when you finished everything."

"Oh, nothing like that. I have to tell you what I found in that turtle you gave me. There was a diamond ring inside. It's very valuable, but it's from a nineteen-ninety-seven shipment from Europe to New York that was stolen. Mr. Grinberg, the jeweler at Leo's, found that out this morning and told my girlfriend and me that an insurance investigator would be here soon. The investigator will want to talk with you."

"You think I had something to do with a diamond theft?" Mrs. Kincaid was becoming a little indignant. Her hands were clasped together, and she had stiffened her posture. "Well, I don't know anything about it. It's all news to me. I wonder if my husband knew there was something valuable in that ugly turtle." She shook her head and scratched the back of her neck. "An insurance investigator will be here tomorrow?"

"That's what Mr. Grinberg said. Maybe the day after."

Mrs. Kincaid asked, "Will you be sure to be here to explain how you found the ring?"

"Sure, I've got a lot more work to do on your yard. I'll fix the porch railing, too, and I can get some of my friends to paint your house, it sure needs it."

"I don't want to spend that much on this old house, David."

"It won't cost a cent, Mrs. Kincaid. There is a reward for the diamond. That's more than enough to paint your house and repair anything on the outside."

"But David, that is your reward money, you don't need to spend any of it on this old building of mine."

"How long will you and Jenny be living here, Mrs. Kincaid? I think Jenny would like to have a nice-looking place to live, don't you?"

Mrs. Kincaid appeared to be a little bit uncomfortable with what I said, so I wound it up with, "Maybe It's none of my business, so if I'm out of order, I apologize."

"No, young man, you are correct. I knew there were a number of things to do here, but when I returned, I was just overwhelmed. With my limited resources I didn't think much could be done to make the old place livable again."

"Okay, make a list of things you would like to have done and I'll see what I can do by myself. I'll get some of my friends to help me and we'll get your property looking respectable. Can you think of anything right now?"

She thought for a moment and perked up. "Well, yes. That old windmill hasn't worked in forever. It needs to be taken down and the hole plugged; we have city water service now. Maybe the wood could be cut up and used for firewood. During the winter, we could use the fireplace for extra heat if we get snowed in. A fire always lifts one's spirits, especially around Christmas. Could that be done?"

"Not a problem. As soon as I finish with the weeds, I'll take that tower down and use some of the wood to fix your porch railing." I glanced at Jenny and said, "That way Jenny won't fall off and break her other collarbone."

I grinned at Jenny and she said, "If I didn't have a broken bone, I'd slug you for that crack. It appears you and grandma are ganging up on me."

"I think your grandma and me just want you to be more careful around here until things have been repaired." The conversation ended with silence for what seemed at least a minute. I felt a bit uneasy and decided to get to work.

I turned toward the door. "I'd better get busy. I'll expect a wish list from you tomorrow, or if you have time today, you can make a list before I finish up this afternoon." I went out the front door, jumped off the porch to the ground, walked to the weed eater, put on my dust mask and started the engine.

It took almost an hour to knock down all the weeds inside the fenced area of Kincaids' yard, and another thirty minutes to rake everything into a pile. Then I investigated the structure of the windmill and discovered it was going to topple easily. All the metal parts had already been removed and some heavy bricks covered the hole.

I walked around the house looking for an electrical box but didn't find one. I would need a hand saw and a shovel from home. Then it occurred to me that cutting the upright timbers of the windmill to fireplace-size pieces would be too time consuming and tiring with a handsaw. I decided to bring a skill saw and an extension cord tomorrow. If the wood is really rough, I figured I'd use a chainsaw to make firewood out of the timbers.

The sun was directly overhead when I quit for lunch. Sweat was running down into my eyes and I wiped my face with my T-shirt removing dust and water. I felt the beginnings of sunburn on the back of my neck; I had forgotten to apply sunscreen earlier at home when I heard Megan's voice downstairs, so I expected to suffer a burn before the day was over.

I needed fluid so I gulped down an orange soda and crawled into the shady cargo space of my car. I got comfortable and opened my sack lunch expecting a surprise from mom, but she hadn't done anything weird to my sandwiches as I had imagined. After the first sandwich, I ate a big juicy dill pickle and started on a carrot stick when my thoughts of tearing down that old windmill were interrupted.

I heard Jenny's voice, "David? Where are you?

"I'm in the rear of my car, in the cargo area."

She stepped around the mower and ducked to avoid hitting her head on the raised cargo door. "Oh, there you are. Grandma and I wanted to ask you to have lunch with us, but I see you're already eating."

"Thank you for the invitation, but I'm just about ready to get back to work. Do you have any more lemonade?" I swallowed what was left of the carrot stick, and it scratched on the way down. I had swallowed too soon, blinked my eyes and reached for the Thermos, usually full of cold milk. I tried to clear my throat and Jenny said, "I interrupted your eating, sorry. Come with me, we have some more lemonade. That's Grandma's and my favorite summer beverage."

I swung my legs out of the car and walked with Jenny into the house. I noticed the table was set for three. Their invitation hadn't been planned at the last minute. I wondered if it had been Mrs. Kincaid or Jenny that had thought to invite me for lunch. I'll probably never know, kind of a stupid thought.

Mrs. Kincaid was standing at the table. I knew I was in for some more questions about the diamond. She sat down as I approached the dining area.

"He's already eaten, but would like some lemonade, Grandma."

Mrs. Kincaid pointed at the chair at the head of the table and said, "Sit." She reached for the pitcher and poured me a glass full of cold lemonade. When she had nearly filled the glass, a couple of ice cubes plopped into the glass almost causing an overflow.

"Oops, that was close." Mrs. Kincaid laughed and said, "We should have asked you to lunch sooner, David."

"That's all right, thanks for the invite. I like your lemonade. I usually eat in my car and get right back to work. It's nice to have someone to talk to."

Jenny smiled, "We'll do better next time."

We talked about disposal of the weeds and I told them about the supervised burning the fire department carried out during the rainy season, which was in June. They were in luck; a burning was planned for the upcoming weekend.

"If you trust me with your pickup, I'll transport the weeds and get them taken care of."

"That would be awesome! I'll go with you and supervise," Jenny Laughed.

"Okay, I'll bring a pitchfork and come over Saturday. When would it be convenient?"

Mrs. Kincaid shrugged her shoulders when she looked at Jenny. It was up to Jenny.

"When do they burn?" Jenny quizzed.

"All day from nine in the morning until five o'clock."

"I usually sleep in on Saturdays. How about 1:00 p.m.?"

"Sounds good to me. Why do you sleep in? You don't need any beauty sleep."

There was a moment of silence and then, "Thanks, David. I'm trying to rest my collarbone." She glanced at her grandmother and saw she wasn't watching. She gave me a wink.

I smiled and said, "Thank you for the lemonade, I'd better get to work. Too much fun and I'll be a poor young man." I excused myself and went outside, surprised that nothing about the diamond had come up. I went to the backyard to take a closer look at the windmill to decide how I wanted to fell it. Due to the age of the timbers, I was thinking if I cut one of the four supports, the tower might fall in that direction, but to be sure, I would cut through the two supports farthest from the house. I decided I would tie it to a far tree to be sure it wouldn't topple in an unusual direction and strike the building. I had never cut down a tree, but the windmill couldn't be too different.

I shook one of the supports and the entire structure creaked and groaned, it was ready to come down without much intervention. If Danny wasn't doing anything, I'd have him come for assistance. For five bucks, he'd be happy to help.

I started for my car and heard someone drive up and park. As

I came around the corner of the house, a white Toyota Prius was parking directly behind my Subaru, blocking me from backing out of the driveway.

A short bald guy in a wrinkled light-brown suit was trying to extract himself from the driver's seat. He sat for a moment with his feet hanging in the air and then slid to the ground. Reaching back into the car, he grabbed a black business case and slammed the door.

Chapter 6

"Hey! You've got me blocked in. I need you to move your car." I hoped my tone of voice showed my irritation.

"I should only be a few minutes, sonny. Keep your shirt on." His short legs began moving almost like those of an old-fashioned wind-up toy. He climbed the porch steps with some effort and rapped on the wooden-framed screen door.

I heard Mrs. Kincaid say, "What is it, David?"

The chubby little man said, "It's not David, it's Cyrus Whitmore. I'm an insurance investigator for Euro-Atlantic Insurance Agents. I would like to talk to Mrs. Kincaid, if she is available."

Mrs. Kincaid pushed open the screen door, forcing the investigator to step backward. He took a look back, to be sure he wasn't going to tumble off the porch. He seemed to have noticed the broken railing. She came outside, wiping her hands with a towel, and said, "I'm Mrs. Kincaid. What is this all about?" She saw me and motioned for me to join her on the porch.

"As I said, I'm Cyrus Whitmore, representing Euro-Atlantic Insurance. It seems a stolen diamond was found on your property. I would like you to answer a few questions. Do you mind if I come in?"

"No, I don't mind." She held to screen door open and he entered. I was right behind him. "You should probably talk to David; he found the diamond."

"In good time. The diamond was found on your property. Is that correct?"

"No, that is not correct."

Cyrus stared at Mrs. Kincaid as if she were lying and said, "That does not seem to be the case. Are you trying to hide something?"

Jenny had joined us and said, "My grandmother does not lie. David found the diamond in his garage."

Mr. Whitmore asked, "Do you mind if I record this conversation?" He pulled a small digital device from his suitcoat pocket and pressed a red button on the side of the matchbox size silver object.

We agreed to the recording and I said, "Let me tell you what happened."

He looked at me, "You're David, right?" I nodded. "All right, go ahead."

Mr. Whitmore started writing in a small notebook as I talked. I could tell he wasn't writing in English and decided it must be shorthand or some foreign language.

Whatever it was, he was very adept at it and scribbled, with no hesitation, as I talked.

After I completed the story, he asked, "And where is this friend of yours; this girl Megan?"

"She works as a candy-striper at the hospital in the afternoons during the week. Sometimes she goes in on Saturday if they have something for her to do."

"I'll need her to corroborate your story. It seems a little far-fetched to me."

I laughed. "You think I made that up? Wait until Megan tells you the same story; you'll apologize."

"We'll see." He turned away from me. "Oh, Mrs. Kincaid, I need to get your husband's name, age, birthplace, and such from you. This investigation is going to take some time and resources. David, I would like you to show me the turtle and the tools you used to retrieve the ring. I need to photograph the evidence."

"If you want to follow me, I'll take you to my place and show you what you need. I'm finished here today, but I'll work here tomorrow." I glanced at the Kincaids so they would know I would be returning to take down the windmill and pack the pickup with the weed refuse.

Mr. Whitmore squeezed into his car and backed out of the driveway so I could do the same. I told the ladies I would come back tomorrow at nine o'clock with my brother and some tools. I loaded my equipment into the Subaru and drove back home with the white Prius following closely behind; sometimes too closely.

I parked on the street and let the agent pull into the driveway. I guessed Mom had been in the kitchen and she must have seen a strange car park next to the side door. I saw her look out the front window and notice me getting out of the Subaru. She came out the front door, let Spectrum out, gave me a brief wave, and pointed at the Prius. Her palms were up wondering about the stranger.

When I was nearing the porch I said, "Hi, Mom. He's an insurance investigator from Chicago." I laughed, "He wants to see the turtle." Danny had followed Mom out the door and we watched Spectrum put his paws on the driver's window of the strange car and bark. Mr. Whitmore lowered the passenger side front window a couple of inches and called out, "Will the dog bite?"

I felt like telling him the dog was vicious, but instead I replied, "He's very friendly, he might lick you to death." Mom laughed and Danny called Spectrum.

Whitmore cracked the door open, gradually worked his feet to the concrete using the door as a shield from Spectrum, and cautiously exited his car. He approached Mom and extended his hand, "You must be Mrs. Drum." Mom shook hands and replied, "I'm Mrs. Wilson, David's and Danny's mother. I've remarried."

Danny whispered to me, "He must smell like bacon; Spectrum is sure interested in him."

I chuckled, thinking his head looked like a volleyball with ears. I was reminded of

Tom Hank's movie. I walked past the Prius and said, "I'll show you the turtle, Mr. Whitmore. It's in the garage."

The agent tagged along, and we went into the garage. I flipped on the overhead light and pointed at the carcass. "Last night I was getting ready to glue the head back on when Megan noticed something shiny. I used a small nail set and hammer and chipped out the ring. It was close to the surface of the break. We took it to Mr. Grinberg, the jeweler, this morning. I didn't think you would arrive until tomorrow."

"When I heard that a stolen gem had been recovered, I caught a direct flight to Butte. I like to get on these things as quickly as possible. Nothing from that shipment had been recovered in the last fifteen years except a small diamond in an engagement ring in Boston. The company was pleasantly surprised, so they sent their most experienced agent."

I watched with increasing interest as Mr. Whitmore turned the turtle over and began taking close-up photos of each ceramic foot. I wondered what his interest was in the feet. Megan and I hadn't noticed anything out of the ordinary on the extremities, but we hadn't taken the time to look. We were only interested in digging out the ring.

Whitmore turned the turtle's body right-side-up and took one last photo. He didn't bother with the head. He leaned against the work bench and began scanning through his recent photos, spending most of his time squinting at those of the feet. He motioned for me to look over his shoulder, so I stepped closer. He nodded as if those four photos meant something as he showed me the pictures of the feet.

"Look closely at the third picture." He scanned through them again and stopped on the close-up. "Do you see it?"

"See what?"

"The number seven." He zoomed in and I could see a faint number seven. Then he took a list from his pocket and pointed at the seventh item. It was a description and the value of the diamond Megan and I had found. "The stone you found is the seventh diamond on the list."

"Do you think more diamonds are hidden in lawn ornaments?"

"I was going to ask you if you knew of anyone else in this little town that had lawn decorations like this turtle; maybe not a turtle, but something similar like squirrels, rabbits, that kind of thing. How long have you been cutting lawns?"

"Just a couple of weeks, since school let out for summer."

"All right, I need to go back and talk with Mrs. Kincaid. Why don't you come with me? I'll drive."

I thought for a couple of seconds. Megan wouldn't be back from the hospital until around five, so I said, "Okay, but I have to tell my mom where I'm going."

"Right. I'll back my car out and wait for you. Hurry up."

I stuck my head up to the front screen door and peeked in. Mom was lying on the sofa reading a book. "Mom, I'm going with Mr. Whitmore to see Mrs. Kincaid. I don't think I'll be very long, maybe an hour at the most."

"Okay, David."

I jogged out to the Prius and hopped in the front passenger seat. Mr. Whitmore stepped on the gas and squealed the tires when he turned at the corner. He seemed to know the shortest way to the Kincaids'. Why he was in such a hurry, I hadn't a clue.

"You're lucky Deputy Doureline or my stepdad didn't stop you; the town speed limit is twenty-five, not forty."

"I'm not used to driving in these small bergs, son. Thanks for the info. I'll watch it next time." His driving was not something to admire unless you wanted to see a doll's bobble head flop around.

"Why did you want to get here so fast?"

"You never know when a perpetrator will run."

I laughed, "You think Mrs. Kincaid had something to do with the theft?"

"Not necessarily the old lady, but her husband might have had something to do with it. She might have known her husband's role in the heist. She might know something and doesn't realize it."

We jerked to a stop behind the pickup and I got out easily. I waited for Whitmore to extract the car from around his inflated waist. Jenny was on the porch sketching as before.

"Hi, Jenny. I'm back with my sidekick." I grinned and she laughed.

"I guess Mr. Whitmore wants to talk with Grandma."

"You know it! We're hot on a diamond hunt."

Whitmore had caught up with me and held his notebook. "Miss Kincaid, I'd like to ask your grandmother a question." Whitmore's forehead was sweating, and he had pulled a handkerchief from his jacket pocket. He dabbed his forehead and glanced at Jenny's work. "Very nice sketch."

"Thank you." She didn't try to get up, turned her head and yelled, "Grandma! He's back!"

A couple of seconds later Mrs. Kincaid pushed the screen door open and walked out carrying a folding chair. She opened the chair and sat down. "What is it, Mr. Whitmore." Her demeanor had changed significantly since our earlier visit.

He cleared his throat and requested, "I would like the names of your friends in Suddenly that your husband knew when he lived here."

"You mean from 1997 until he passed? I'm not sure I can remember all those families, but I have lists of names and addresses we mailed Christmas cards to. Will that suffice?"

Whitmore mopped sweat from the top of his head and replied, "I suppose that will have to do."

"It will be a minute; the box is in my bedroom closet. David, could you please help me? Mr. Whitmore and I are at a disadvantage, we're too short to get things from the closet top shelf. At my age, I don't want to climb on a chair."

"Sure. I won't be embarrassed by anything I see, will I?"

Jenny giggled, "Hide your dirty undies, Grandma."

"Oh, hush." She shook her head. "I have two teenagers out of control." She slapped my arm playfully. "Come on, David."

I smiled and followed Mrs. Kincaid into the house, down a short hallway and into a back bedroom. I expected to see unopened boxes and piles of clothes scattered around the room, but the bedroom looked like an efficiency expert lived there. When Mrs. Kincaid opened the closet, nothing fell out; it was very neat. Mrs. Kincaid was on my admiration list.

"It's the box up there; the one with the gold top. Try not to spill anything." She pointed to a box on the shelf about a foot above her clothes rack. Another box was on top of the gold one, so I stretched and held one box while pulling on the desired one. It slid out easily and I handed it to Mrs. Kincaid's outstretched arms.

"Thank you, David. Let's go back out on the porch."

"Do you want me to carry the box for you?"

Mrs. Kincaid smiled, "No, it's not very heavy; it's mostly full of memories, but thanks for asking."

The agent vacated the chair when we arrived on the porch and Mrs. Kincaid resumed her former position with the box on her lap. She removed the top carefully, leaned it against a chair leg and pulled out a manila envelope marked 2012. She looked at the investigator and said, "This is the last Christmas we were in Suddenly. We moved to England in February of that year. All the names and addresses are in there."

The agent accepted the small package and said, "May I see the 1997 list?"

Mrs. Kincaid flipped through several envelopes and found the oldest and thickest which was labeled 1997. She handed it to the agent and said, "The lists get smaller as the years go by. Friends move away, don't keep in touch, or in more and more cases, pass on. I've marked on many of the names if they are no longer with us."

Whitmore undid the clasp on the envelope and cards, letters, and a lengthy list; the entire contents, emptied into his left hand, but as the materials began to overflow his small hand, he pressed the paper items against his chest. I reached out to help him and caught several old Christmas cards.

He said, "You can keep the cards and letters, I just need to look at the list."

Chapter 7

Whitmore put on some reading glasses and quickly scanned the list of names and addresses. He reached into the breast pocket of his jacket and then began reading the list.

Jenny glanced at me and frowned, "What did he just do?"

I said, "A recorder; he's not writing anything down."

Whitmore said, "That's all for 1997." He put the list in the manila envelope and handed it to me. "You can replace the cards and letters." He asked Mrs. Kincaid for the 1998 list, which she handed him, said, "Thank you," and repeated the procedure he had carried out with the 1997 envelope. He continued the routine with each envelope, completed with the 2012 list and returned the manila enclosures to Mrs. Kincaid.

"Thank you, Mrs. Kincaid. That should be all the information I need. Will you be leaving town in the next week?"

She placed the lid on the box and looked up at the agent. "No, we have nothing planned. The only place I need to go is the market, I need to buy some food."

I offered, "I can drive you to get groceries."

Whitmore said, "No, you're coming with me, David. When we're through you can help them with groceries. You told your mother you would be gone about an hour. That hour has expired, let's go. You can return in your car."

I almost said no to Whitmore, but I decided not to rile him and moved toward the Prius. I turned to Jenny and whispered, "I'll be back in a little bit."

As we started back home, Whitmore withdrew the small recorder from his breast pocket and spoke to me, "Open the glove box and take out the laptop. There's a small cable in there, too. Connect it to the recorder and plug it into the port on the left side. Open the computer and press the download icon. It's on the top right corner."

I followed his directions and leaned back in my seat.

Whitmore parked on the street behind my car and as he shutoff the engine, the laptop chimed, and a little red window appeared in the center of the screen blinking DOWNLOAD COMPLETE.

"Do you have a table in back where we can spread out?"

"Spread out?"

"Yes. I have a Suddenly city map I'd like to lay out flat on a table so I can see the streets and mark the addresses I obtained from the Christmas cards. I want us to check each of the locations for lawn ornaments. Have you seen any objects like the turtle around town?"

I shook my head. "Nope, but I've only mowed a few lawns since I started my service last week. I didn't see anything like the turtle in any of those places, but I wasn't looking for anything like that."

"Hmm. I can't go around searching through properties in Suddenly. I'd get picked up for trespassing."

"Same here, and my stepdad is the sheriff. He and my mom would get pissed."

I looked at Whitmore, thinking I almost called him Wilson. I grinned when an idea popped into my head. Danny could use our drone to look around the properties and nobody would even know we were checking for lawn ornaments. Danny would surely want a fee for doing the work. All I have to do now is find him. But I had promised Jenny and Mrs. Kincaid I would be back to go shopping. Danny would have to wait.

Apparently, Whitmore had been watching my facial expressions.

"What are you thinking, David?"

I didn't want him messing with my brother unless I was there to supervise, so I didn't mention my idea. "I need to go back and help the Kincaid ladies get some groceries. Why don't you mark the map to indicate the places we need to search? I'll be back in an hour and we can try something I just thought of."

Whitmore frowned and then must have decided not to press his luck. "All right but tell your mother I'm out here looking at the city map."

I passed through the house, told Mom what I was going to do, and that Whitmore was in the back yard with his work spread out on the picnic table. She hardly paid attention, briefly looked up and resumed reading. Something in her book sure had corralled her thoughts.

Jenny and Mrs. Kincaid were sitting on the porch steps when I pulled in their driveway. I parked directly behind the Ranger pickup so they wouldn't have far to walk. I hustled to the passenger side and opened the front and back doors. Jenny had changed her work clothes and had on an oversize plaid shirt, probably from her grandfather's wardrobe, gray jacket and light-blue slacks. Except for the plaid shirt, she was overdressed for grocery shopping but damn, she looked nice.

As she carefully buckled herself into the front seat, Jenny turned to me. "I thought you had forgotten us; it's been over an hour." I wasn't sure whether she was teasing me or actually irritated, but then she giggled.

"Sorry, but that insurance guy wanted my help. I left him in my backyard working with the city map and the locations of your grandparents' old friends." Winking at Jenny, I said, "There's no way I would've forgotten you. Sometimes I wish I had a clone so I could be in two places at the same time." I wiggled my eyebrows and made her laugh.

Mrs. Kincaid interrupted, "Should I give you two a moment alone?"

Jenny gasped, "Grandma! He has a girlfriend."

I guided Mrs. Kincaid into the back seat and watched her latch the seatbelt. She was able to pull the door shut without my assistance. I hated shutting the door on someone's foot or ankle. I slid into the driver's seat and looked at Jenny. Her belt was twisted, so I reached behind her, straightened it and made sure it locked in place. She had on a touch of perfume which I couldn't miss. I glanced at her and said, "Ready?"

She smiled, raised her eyebrows and said, "We're ready, let's get out of here." Five minutes later, I pulled into the parking lot at Lightman's Grocery. Inside, we wove through the aisles with two carts, following Mrs. Kincaid; I pushed one and Jenny was able to shove the other cart with one hand and an occasional hip bump to keep going in a fairly straight line. I lagged behind and every once in a while, got alongside Jenny when her cart was filling faster than mine. Mrs. Kincaid knew how to shop; she was practically buying one of everything. The cupboards out at the house must be almost bare but not for long.

Another customer, moving in the opposite direction wanted past, so I let Jenny get ahead of me a couple of cart lengths. When the lady had passed me, I raced to catch up. I was almost even with Jenny and she turned into me. The collision had to be on purpose.

I started laughing as I kept the cart from toppling over. "Hey, this isn't NASCAR! Did you get a cart pusher's license?"

Jenny giggled, "No, I just have a learner's permit."

"Well, I think you need supervision until you have more experience."

"Will you two quit playing? We came here to shop. Can you think of anything else we should get, Jenny?" Mrs. Kincaid glanced at me and frowned, then looked at Jenny and the two nearly full carts. "This is going to cost a fortune. Could you have your mom invite us over for dinner sometime, David?"

"Grandma! You can't ask to be invited to David's home."

I had to laugh, because I didn't think Mrs. Kincaid meant it as it sounded.

"Oh, my. That's not what I meant. I want to meet your parents and younger brother, but I don't want to invite them over to our place until the house and grounds have been cleaned up. I'm sure I can find some small jobs for your brother. Maybe he could start painting the house, especially on the southern side; it's pretty weathered."

"I'll mention it to him and see what he thinks. If I tell him about

Jenny, I know he'll want to come over." I grinned and gave Jenny another wink.

Jenny glared at me. "He's too young for me, David. Didn't you say he was only thirteen?"

"Danny has been a little awkward when talking to girls and I thought you might give him some tips about dating. I'm sure he'll be interested to talk to you. Mom has kind of given up; she's too removed from kids his age to give him advice about the opposite sex. Scott, our stepdad, admits to never being a lady's man and didn't date much because his work with the FBI demanded most of his time."

"Well, since you put it that way, maybe I can give him some tips."

"Great! He'll be coming over with me tomorrow to take down that old windmill tower. I'd have you help, but I don't want you to mess up your injury."

"Okay, you two, let's check out and get back home. Do you think your car will hold all this stuff?" Mrs. Kincaid wasn't serious; she just was trying to break up Jenny's and my blabbering.

We arrived back at the Kincaids' about twenty-five minutes later and I unloaded thirteen sacks of groceries. I carried in the stuffed bags while Mrs. Kincaid and Jenny remained in the kitchen filling cupboard shelves. After the last bag was empty, I excused myself and returned home.

Whitmore had moved into the dining room table and mom was helping him locate the addresses in the city map. She was describing the yards when he asked about the families that lived there. There were a few names mom didn't recognize, and I wasn't much help. I only knew the names of people that had kids in school and a few of the elderly who were big complainers about random noises.

Danny came in the house about fifteen minutes after I arrived. I followed him to his room where he was changing clothes. He peeled off his sweaty T-shirt, dropped it on the floor, flopped onto his bed, and slid off his shorts. He looked up at me and said, "What's going down, David?"

"I have a job for you for tomorrow. I'm taking down an old windmill and I need your help."

"I'm gonna take a shower. Let me think about it."

"C'mon, Dan, it's either yes or no. It's a paying job and you'll get a big surprise, free of charge. You have something else planned?"

"Yeah. Jimmy and I are gonna to throw a football around and go over to his place and lift weights. We're both going out for football in September."

"Okay, but you're going to miss out on something special, plus I was going to pay you five bucks to help me. It'll take about five minutes. I guess I'll have to have her help me."

"Her?"

"Forget it. I'll have Megan come with me. She's not busy in the morning and I don't have to pay her anything to help. Megan met the new girl at the hospital." I turned away and went back downstairs to find out what Whitmore had planned after locating positions on the map.

Mom was back on the sofa with her book and Whitmore was texting someone that I guessed was his superior.

When he looked up at me, he seemed a little guilty, like he had been caught in the act. He turned off his phone and said, "I need to find more lawn ornaments. I think I'll discover more of the diamonds in them. Do you think you could help me?"

"I was thinking about it earlier. My brother and I have a drone fitted with a camera. We might be able to fly over the locations and check for ceramic animals. I don't think Suddenly has an ordinance against drone flying, but I'll check with my stepfather."

Whitmore's expression changed from one of frustration to delight when I mentioned that we had a drone. "Great idea, David. I wouldn't have to set foot on those properties; a flyover might be enough to detect objects of interest. Could we start the searches tomorrow?"

"I have the morning already planned. I'm going to take down the Kincaids' windmill. You could help me with that, and we could start the flyovers in the afternoon."

"I don't know if I'd be much help. I don't have any work clothes and I'm not very handy with tools. I've been dependent on my brain, not my brawn, for most of my life."

"It wouldn't require much. All you'd have to do is pull on a rope; I've got some gloves you can use. I was going to ask my girlfriend to help, but you can do her job."

Whitmore glanced at his hands probably thinking if he did anything but pound a keyboard, his hands would suffer the disgrace of manual labor. I watched his cheeks wiggle and then he answered, "Sounds like a deal. What time do you want me at the Kincaids'?"

"I'll meet you there at nine o'clock. That will give the ladies a chance to get up, get dressed, and eat breakfast before we start work."

"All right. I'll do some computer work this evening and be ready for physical work in the morning. I'd better check in at a motel and get settled."

Mom had been listening and said, "Mr. Whitmore, you could . . ."

I shook my head at Mom, and she stopped in mid-sentence. I guessed that she was going to offer our apartment above the garage to him. I had a feeling he would be around for another week, maybe longer, and I didn't want him mooching off us. Mom didn't need anyone else to care for at this stage in her pregnancy.

"Yes?" Whitmore said.

"It was nice meeting you. Have a good evening."

"Glad to have met you and thank you for the help with the map, Mrs. Wilson. Good day."

Chapter 8

Danny came downstairs and quizzed mom, "How's the baby doing today?"

"Just fine." She rubbed her stomach which looked like she swallowed an inflated soccer ball. "What do you guys want for dinner?" She closed her book after marking it with an envelope from some junk mail, sat up and commented, "Mr. Whitmore is a fairly nice gentleman, but he can be a bit abrupt. He says exactly what's on his mind. Do you think he can be of much help, David?"

"Oh, he'll be all right. I just need someone to pull on a rope. Danny boy is going to be busy tomorrow. He'll miss out meeting Jenny. But maybe he'll be better off. He might embarrass himself drooling at the sight of a pretty girl."

"That was your surprise? Meeting a girl? Give me a break, David." Danny rolled his eyes.

I snickered and said, "She's beautiful, Danny. Wait until you see her; you'll be telling all your buddies about the gorgeous new chick in town." I gave Mom a wink.

"Whitmore and I will need the drone tomorrow afternoon. If you want to pilot it, I think Whitmore will pay you for your time. Depending on the flight time, he'll probably give you ten bucks an hour."

"I'll do it but remember there's only a one-mile radius for controlling the drone. The live TV reception needs house electricity. We can't take it just anywhere. Let me know the time and I'll have it set up in the back yard."

"No problem. Whitmore will be here with you observing and I'll be at each site to tell you where to investigate each property. We'll use our walkie-talkies for giving directions. I have a feeling we won't find anything, but I'll get an idea where to peddle my lawn service; a little bonus."

I glanced at mom. She had put down her book and was waiting for Danny and me to quit gabbing.

"Okay boys, what do you want for dinner?"

Danny plopped down on the sofa and said, "How about some KFC? You won't have to do anything, and Scott can bring it home."

"That's okay by me, Mom. We've got pop in the fridge and ice cream in the freezer."

Megan ate dinner with us and recapped the afternoon's activities at the hospital without mentioning any names or maladies. I went over what I had done at the Kincaids' and what Whitmore and I planned for tomorrow.

Megan mentioned, "Mrs. Laird saw you at the market with Jenny and her grandmother. She said you seemed to be enjoying yourself bumping carts with Jenny." Megan was fishing for more info from me, so I cooperated.

"Yeah. Jenny pushed her cart into the side of mine. At first, I thought it was accidental because she was only using one arm, but I realized it wasn't unintentional after all; she was just messing with me. Her grandmother told her to quit fooling around. Mrs. Kincaid almost bought out the store. After that, I took them home, helped unload groceries, and came home."

Mom saved me by changing the subject, "Were you all right at home with Suzy last night, Megan?"

Megan smiled and said, "Sure, I slept on the sofa with her. She's a really good companion; she kept my feet warm and only got up once to get a drink of water. I could hear her slurping out in the kitchen."

"I think Spectrum missed her. I heard him walking around during the night; probably wondering where Suzy had gone." Mom was a lite sleeper these days.

Scott said, "Yes, I heard him moving around too; his nails were clicking on the hardwood floor. When something changes, he wanders from room to room trying to solve the latest mystery, where is Suzy? But I think he's used to changes people make. When I was gone for several days at a time on cases, he didn't seem to get too upset. I think he knew I would be back; at least that's what they said at the kennel. He did get excited when I picked him up after returning from my trips."

While we were all gathered, I remembered to ask Scott about drone flyovers.

"Is there any ordinance in Suddenly about flying a drone over properties other than our own?"

"Good question. I'm not aware of anything that has passed the town council in the past couple of years, but I haven't had time to read everything that Sheriff Howell had put into files. He kept fairly complete files on ordinances. I'll check for you tomorrow morning and let you know. When do you plan on using the drone?"

"Tomorrow afternoon. We're going to the Kincaids' in the morning. Then, Mr. Whitmore, Danny and I want to use it to investigate some neighbors' yards for other lawn ornaments that might contain stolen diamonds. Didn't Mr. Whitmore talk with you when he came to Suddenly?"

"Uh-huh. He came by the office and introduced himself. Said he was an insurance agent on the search for stolen diamonds but didn't say how he was going to investigate. I'm not sure how I feel about you boys being involved. I'd like you to keep me informed, David."

"Okay. I'll tell you all about tomorrow's activities at dinner. So far, Whitmore hasn't gotten very excited about anything, but I think Mrs. Kincaid doesn't much care for him. I'll try to find out more about him when we're looking over neighbors' yards. I'm wondering what he'll do if we discover something in someone's yard. Maybe he'll knock on their door and try to buy it, something interesting could happen."

It rained during the night but by morning the sun was out, the humidity was up and by 9:00 a.m. the temperature was more like that of an early spring day than one of summer vacation. By noon I wouldn't need a jacket and the only reminder of the rain would be wet boots and a little mud stuck to my soles.

Mr. Whitmore was waiting for me at the Kincaids'. Fortunately, he hadn't parked in their driveway; probably didn't want to have to take his vehicle to the car wash. I pulled into the property but stayed on the grassy area I had mowed. Whitmore got out of his car and began walking toward me before I had stopped my Subaru.

"Morning, David. What have you got planned for taking down that tower?"

"Good morning, Mr. Whitmore. Did you take physics in school?"

"Physics? No, I took a year of chemistry, but I don't remember much of it. I took history, business and math. I took a year of woodshop in ninth grade; built a birdhouse."

"Well, that's all right. We'll work together and I'll show you something new. I brought about 150 feet of rope and an axe; that's all we'll need."

I popped the cargo door on the Subaru and gave Whitmore a fifty-foot coil of Nylon rope. I stuck my arm though the hundred-foot coil, grabbed the axe and we started toward the windmill behind the house. When we were standing at the foot of the tower, I tried to shake it. It wiggled slightly but was sturdier than it looked. I gazed up at the top, grinned and said, "Want to climb up there and attach the end of my rope?"

"You're kidding, right?" He frowned and continued, "I have trouble getting on an eight-foot ladder. This thing is at least thirty feet high."

"Yeah, I was joking. I'll climb up and secure one end of the hundred-foot rope to the leg farthest from the house. When I drop the rope, you can tie the shorter rope to the middle of the longer one."

"So, we'll each have a rope to pull?"

"No, you're going to pull the tower down all by yourself."

"Seriously? I'm not very strong."

"You can do it. I'll show you how."

There was plenty of cross bracing on the tower and climbing was easy. When I got near the top, I tied my rope and tossed the coil in the direction of a tree that would anchor the other end. Whitmore was right, the windmill was at least thirty feet high at the bottom of the top planks. Luckily, I didn't need to get on top. I couldn't see above the planks because of the overhang.

I yelled at Whitmore as I started down the tower, "Approximate the center of my rope and tie yours to mine. Tie it so it can't come loose or slip." I was confident that the longer rope would reach the trees on the outside of Kincaids' fence and after checking Whitmore's knot, which he had tied expertly, I played out my rope to the fence. Whitmore had followed me and watched as I vaulted over the fence.

"You expect me to do that?"

I laughed. "No, I want you to hand me the end of the longer rope. You don't need to come over here." I thought he was going to be pissed off, but he wasn't.

"If you want me over there, I'll get in my car and drive around the fence." He grinned. He did possess some humor.

As time passed, I was gradually beginning to like Whitmore. He was more amusing than his regular demeanor suggested. "Okay, the next step is to secure the rope to something that won't move; that's a tree trunk, near the ground."

"Not a fencepost?"

"Nope. A fence post might pull out of the ground and then I'd have a fence to repair." I found a tree that was directly opposite the house from the tower, pulled the rope tight and secured it around the tree at ankle height.

"All right, what's next, young man?" He didn't know what I was doing, but he seemed interested.

"Time for me to use that axe. I'm going to cut through the two tower legs that are closest to us. Then you carry out the next step;

pull down the windmill."

Whitmore frowned. He still hadn't realized that he was going to pull on the shorter rope; the one he had tied to the middle of the longer one. I took a whack at one timber and realized they were not going to severe easily; they were made of hardwood. Just the exterior of the wood looked rotted. I pretended the tower legs were trees and changed my method of attack.

It took twenty swings before there was just a sliver of wood remaining to cut. I moved to the other leg and took a whack, same thing. I dropped the axe in the dirt and leaned against the timber. I was out of breath; it wasn't necessary to hurry, so I walked over to Whitmore and explained what his next move would be.

"Okay. If I understand, when you yell, timber, I pull on the short rope?"

"That's the plan. You'll have to pull hard and don't let up until the tower tips over. If it doesn't come down when you pull, I'll join in and it will topple with both of us pulling."

As I walked back to pick up the axe, I heard some tapping on an upstairs window. I looked up and saw Jenny wave to me. Her smile was contagious. I smiled back and returned her wave. The axe made easy work of the second timer and it was ready with only fifteen blows. I yelled, "Timber!" and moved away from the tower.

It creaked and groaned but didn't want to topple. I could hear the wood fighting to stay in place as I joined Whitmore. I slipped on my gloves, grabbed the Nylon rope and we both pulled. Whitmore was watching the tower as it began to tip away from the house.

"It's going to tip, David, I can see it's almost ready to fall over."

I jerked on the rope, heard wood splintering and then silence, until the tower impacted the ground with a loud crash, throwing up a cloud of dust and debris. The cross bracing kept the tower from collapsing on itself, so I was going to have to do a lot of disassembling. Mrs. Kincaid told me she wanted the timbers cut into firewood lengths. The two remnants of the legs I had nearly severed with the axe were still stuck in the ground. I'd have to dig them out, but they were only buried about a foot in depth and the ground wasn't too hard.

Whitmore was untying the ropes and coiling them, something he had begun voluntarily. He gave me the coiled fifty-foot rope and said, "I'll let you untie the rope attached to the tree. I undid the end on the windmill."

I smiled, "Thanks, Mr. Whitmore. I know you don't like fences."

He laughed and responded, "Yeah, short fat people balk at fences. That's a reason to have tall thin acquaintances with them."

I jumped the fence as before and removed the rope from the tree. As I coiled the rope, I noticed what appeared to be a rock that hadn't been there before. I used the last few feet of the rope to tie the coil together and kicked the rock over. It wasn't a rock. It was a ceramic frog.

"Hey, Mr. Whitmore, I found another lawn ornament. It's a frog." I picked it up and handed it to Whitmore who had hustled over to the fence to see what I had found.

He immediately flipped it over and pulled out his camera. "Here, David, hold it for me so I can get a good photo. Don't move." I must have wiggled 'cause he said, "Can you steady yourself against one of the fence posts?" I did like he asked, and he took three pictures.

"Let's ask one of the ladies for some water so we can wash the bottom of the figure; the pictures aren't very clear."

"We don't need to bother them; I've got some water in my car."

I tossed the coils of rope in the cargo area and got a bottle of tap water from the console. Whitmore held the frog upside down and I doused it with water. He fished a handkerchief from his pants and rubbed the frog's feet clean. I had to hold the frog one more time for new pictures.

Whitmore began inspecting the figure, squinting, closing one eye and looking at each frog foot. "Two numbers, David!" Whitmore looked at me, glanced at the feet again and said, "Three and four."

Chapter 9

The bright sunlight was making it difficult to see the numbers, but with Whitmore's guidance and the shade of Kincaids' porch I detected the numbers on the hind feet.

Jenny stepped out on the porch when she saw we were puzzling over what she thought was a rock.

"What have you found, David?"

"Hi, Jenny. I think we have found two more diamonds; they're in this ugly frog lawn ornament." I flipped it over so she could see the ceramic amphibian.

"You're right. It is ugly. Are there numbers?"

"Uh-huh, three and four."

"What do those correspond to on the list?"

Whitmore had gone to his car to get the list from his other clothes folded in the back seat. He climbed into the seat and pulled the list from his pants pocket.

"I saw the old windmill fall over. How did you know how to do that with the ropes?"

"Physics, my dear Watson."

"Oh, Holmes; I am flabbergasted by your brilliance." Jenny's eyes danced and her smile was lighting up my morning.

"Sorry about my Sherlock imitation. I remembered a physics problem about moving a car with a rope and applied it to the tower. It worked. I think the frog was on top of the windmill, but no one could see it from below or even from the second-floor windows."

"Think there are any other things that might have come down with the tower?"

"Something else could have. I need to walk the area and search for more animals, but they might be under the timbers. I'll have to watch for them as I clean up the wood. I have to make those old timbers into firewood, too. Your grandma's request."

"I'd like to help, but I'm a little afraid I might trip and fall."

"Yeah, your balance is off with only one arm free. Ask your grandmother where she wants the firewood stacked. I'll start on that tomorrow. This afternoon, Whitmore, Danny and I are going to do some snooping with our drone to look for more ceramic yard creatures in town. My stepdad doesn't think there's any ordinance against flying over neighbor's property."

"Don't come peeping around here unless you want me to shoot it down with my twenty-two rifle."

"Better watch out. It's against the law to shoot a gun in the city."

"Gotcha, David. Grandma's yard is outside the city limits. This was farm country at one time and never became part of the town."

I hadn't realized we were outside the city limits.

Whitmore came toward the porch smiling. He sat down on the second step and said, "If stones three and four are in the frog, we've recovered another sixty thou in diamonds. Where can we chip away at the frog?"

"I don't have any tools except the axe, and we can't use that."

"I know where Grandpa's tools are; I'll show you. Follow me."

Jenny took us around the house to a side door which was probably the quickest way to the windmill in the old days. The steps to ground level had been removed but she reached up and twisted the doorknob.

"David, give me a boost."

I interlaced the fingers of both hands to provide a step and she pushed open the door and stepped into the house. I grabbed the doorjamb and half-pulled and half-jumped into a small room.

Whitmore was watching Jenny and me from ground level. I hadn't offered him a boost; I didn't want to injure my back. He seemed content with being an onlooker.

Jenny and I were in a mud room. There was a work bench with wooden boxes of tools stacked on the floor. She pointed at the boxes and said, "Dig in. You can use anything you want. I don't know what half that stuff is."

She was right when she used the word dig. The top boxes were full of doorknobs, hinges, pieces of galvanized pipe and greasy rags. I set them on the floor and behold, a box of tools appeared with hammers, bags of nails, screws, and washers. I found what I needed on the very bottom: nail sets, punches, and chisels for both wood and concrete.

"Boy, your grandfather must have been a pretty good handyman."

"Grandma said he fixed almost everything himself. Did you find what you need in there?"

"Uh-huh. It won't take much, just a hammer and a chisel should do."

I picked out a ballpeen hammer, two chisels for concrete and a small nail set for use in tight places and jumped to the ground: a drop of about three feet.

"I'm going around to the front. You'll work out there, right?" She closed and locked the door before I could answer.

Whitmore had already started around the house before I said anything. I shrugged my shoulders and followed him with the tools in both hands. I was imagining what we would find in the frog. Would there be two diamonds or nothing?

Whitmore had set the frog on the porch and was getting a tarp from the trunk of his car. I put the tools beside the frog and used some of the wood from the broken porch railing to create a hard surface for pounding. Whitmore recognized what I was doing and spread the tarp on a relatively flat area a few feet from the porch steps. I retrieved two pair of goggles from the Subaru, put on one pair and gave Whitmore the other. We didn't need any ceramic fragments in our eyes that would require hospitalization.

I flipped the frog over on the tarp, placed a chisel on the belly between the hind webbed feet and whacked hard with the hammer. The frog broke into three large chunks, but I couldn't see any unusual signs on any of the surfaces. Whitmore and I inspected the broken pieces and agreed; nothing.

"Go for the head, David."

I laughed, "Okay, certain kill!" I didn't bother with the chisel; I used the riveting part of the hammer and gave a crushing blow to the ceramic. Two thimble-sized pieces tumbled away from of the outer larger intact pieces. I glanced at Whitmore and handed him one of the small chunks. He asked, "Think there's something in there?"

"Could be." I picked up the other piece and tapped lightly with the hammer. One irregular edge separated, and a metallic reflection of sunlight caught my eye.

"Got something!"

Jenny had come close, dropped to her knees and said, "Can I see?"

"Sure." I gave her the piece and she rotated it between her thumb and forefinger of her good hand.

She was disappointed. "That's not very big."

"I think there's something bigger inside that chunk. More clay has to be removed. Let Mr. Whitmore take a look while I operate on the piece he has."

Jenny and Whitmore exchanged objects and she handed me the one she was given. The piece was rounder than the one I started with and I tried to hit it dead center with the chisel, but not too hard. It cracked open like a nut and the seed inside popped out as neat as could be, a beautiful slightly-blue diamond. I handed it to Jenny, and she held it up to the light.

"That is gorgeous! I hope I have a diamond like it some day; maybe in an engagement or a wedding ring." She looked at it a little longer, smiled and handed it back to me. I wondered what was going on inside her pretty head.

I grinned. "You'll have to find a rich man to marry." I held it so it sparkled in the sun. "This stone is worth about thirty-thousand dollars. I have to agree with you, though, it is really beautiful. The insurance company is going to love getting it back."

I glanced at Whitmore who was holding his hand out. He had a little pouch on the ground ready for the stone which I dropped into his cupped small chubby palm. It was the first time I noticed his small hands. He tossed the encased diamond to me and said, "See if you can get that one cleaned up. It seems to be in some type of setting."

I tapped it with the hammer a few times and it cracked open almost like the other one had, but Whitmore was right; the diamond was in what looked like an earring to me. I laughed and said, "This one must be for someone with only one ear."

Jenny laughed too, "Or maybe an athlete that only wanted one ear adorned. Do you wear earrings at school?"

I laughed and said, "If I did, I don't think I'd have many friends. Jewelry on a man in a conservative town like Suddenly would cause the wearer major peer problems. It just isn't done."

Jenny grinned, "You could start a new trend, David. Some of my male friends back home wear earrings."

"You know, you're pretty sneaky. I'm going to have to be very careful about what I say around you. You might spread the word that I'm going to wear earrings. So, if you think I'm ignoring you sometimes, you're probably right."

Jenny laughed again, "Geez, David, I didn't think you would be worried about what I say."

"No, just cautious. I do have a reputation to protect."

Whitmore cleared his throat, "I hate to break up this dual of wits, but let's go out and search the ground around the windmill. Maybe we'll find something else to crack open." Whitmore slipped the two stones into his little pouch, poked it into his breast pocket and buttoned the flap.

Mrs. Kincaid appeared on the porch as we got up and started for the backyard.

"Have you found something?"

Whitmore changed direction and walked toward Mrs. Kincaid. "We've found two more diamonds. They were encased in a clay frog. We think it was on top of the windmill."

"Oh, my. Why would these things be on our property? I don't understand it at all. I still don't think Robert was involved. He would have told me."

"I don't want to alarm you, Mrs. Kincaid, but I think your husband must have known about these things."

"But he was an honest man, Mr. Whitmore. I'm sure Robert didn't know there were diamonds hidden in the lawn ornaments. I just can't believe it."

Whitmore scratched his head above his right ear and said, "Maybe one of his old buddies knew about the diamonds. Can you think of who that might be?"

"Hmm. He knew a lot of young men from the army when he was in Vietnam. Maybe one of them had something to do with this."

"Well, please think about it and let me know if anyone comes to mind. We're going to continue searching your backyard to see if anything else fell from the windmill."

The three of us walked to the backyard to begin searching the area. Jenny was looking near the downed tower's timbers and I had scaled the back fence and was clearing the area with a rake. Whitmore watched as Jenny and I checked the ground around the fallen windmill. Agent Whitmore observed us for a few minutes before asking, "Have you come up with anything new?"

I answered, "Not yet. How about you, Jenny?"

"I haven't seen anything but dirt and weeds, no wildflowers even; nothing of interest. Do you really think there might be something out here?" She looked at her feet and frowned, "My shoes are getting filthy."

"Sorry about that. I should have told you to put your boots on."

"It's not your fault, David. I should have thought about it before coming out here. This whole yard is a disaster."

Back on the front porch, Mrs. Kincaid was sitting in a yard chair reading. Beside her was a TV tray holding four glasses and a large pitcher of lemonade. Whitmore aimed right for it as he struggled up the front steps.

He opened his folded handkerchief and dabbed his sweaty face. "We didn't find anything more, Mrs. Kincaid."

She closed her book and let it slide from her lap to the porch floor. She spoke to all of us, "I thought you worker bees might like something to drink; it's awfully dusty out there."

"Thank you, I'm sure we all can use a drink," I said as I brushed off my pants.

Jenny stomped her feet on the porch steps to rid her shoes of some of the dust and debris. She waited as Whitmore filled two glasses of the icy-cold liquid and gave one to Mrs. Kincaid. She thanked him and he handed the pitcher to Jenny. Jenny took over pouring duties and filled two more glasses. She handed one to me.

"Thanks, Jenny."

"You're welcome. Grams and I were glad to see that old windmill taken down. When will you be able to cut it up?"

I took a sip of lemonade and replied, "I'll try to get to it tomorrow. This afternoon will be spent with my brother and Mr. Whitmore. We're going to scan the yards of people that exchanged Christmas cards with your grandparents."

"What do you mean, scan the yards?" She was confused by the word scan.

"We have a drone with a TV camera. We're going to fly above the properties and look for more lawn ornaments."

"Awesome. Will you show me how to fly the drone?"

I smiled. "Sure, as soon as you can use both hands."

Chapter 10

Jenny suggested, "If I came with you, I could approach the property owner about something in their yard. My smile might be better than yours."

Jenny had made a good point. She would be less intimidating than either Whitmore or me. It was an awesome idea and she would be more fun to have around than just Danny and Whitmore. Mrs. Kincaid could come over and visit with mom while the rest of us investigated real estate with the drone. I think mom would enjoy talking with Mrs. Kincaid and she might learn something that would provide help to locate other diamonds.

Jenny was still waiting for me to answer. I glanced at Whitmore and then at Jenny.

"I think that's a good idea. You're cuter than we are, and the property owner would have sympathy with a young woman with a broken collarbone."

"We'll be down the street watching so nothing can happen to you."

Jenny snickered, "Hey, I'm a big city girl, I know my way around. You don't need to worry about me."

"We'll be watching anyway, just to make sure. We need a signal so we can come running if something goes wrong. You can turn toward us, and wave and I'll be on you like a wet T-shirt."

Jenny frowned and replied, "I hope not, I'm not into wet T-shirts. But I know what you mean."

"I'll be back for you at one o'clock. Is that all right with you Mrs.

Kincaid? Do you want to visit with my mother?"

She was smiling and didn't need to answer, but she gave a quick reply, "Yes, I would enjoy that. I haven't talked to any townspeople since I came back home, except you and the people at the hospital. I'd like to meet your mother, brother and your stepfather, too, if he's available."

"He's usually at the office or in his cruiser all day and home for dinner. I'm sure you'll get to meet him before long. I'll come pick you up after lunch."

As Whitmore and I walked together toward our cars, the agent said, "Jennifer likes you, David, but don't you have a steady girlfriend?"

"Yeah, my next-door neighbor; we grew up together. We plan on going to college together and after that, we'll get married."

"And you'll return to Suddenly?"

"Maybe, we haven't planned that far ahead."

We parted with Whitmore going to his car and I checked to make sure the cargo door was shut on my Subaru before I climbed in and drove home. I hated to see that red door open icon light up on the dash and have to get out and slam the cargo door. Whitmore drove off quickly, exceeding the speed limit by at least five mph. He was slowing down in town. I didn't know where he was going; he took a different route than I did. He was probably going to a nice restaurant for lunch. According to Scott, expense accounts were pretty handy when travelling. The FBI had provided numerous meals and lodging for him over the years.

Mom was in the kitchen making sandwiches when I got to the house. Danny was outside hooking up the TV set to receive from the drone so we would have it ready to go following lunch. After saying hi to mom, I opened the slider and told Danny that Jenny and Mrs. Kincaid were coming over after lunch. Mom heard what I said.

"David? You invited the Kincaids over without consulting me?"

"I'm sorry, but it just kind of happened. Jenny said she wanted to help with the drone flyovers and her grandmother would be home alone, so I thought Mrs. Kincaid could come and visit with you. She said she wanted to meet you. They don't have a phone hooked up yet, or I would have called you."

Mom was quiet as she looked at me, continued with a sandwich, cut it in half diagonally and said, "Well, all right. It's not like I'll be entertaining a bridge club or a meeting of the PTA, and I won't have to fix them anything to eat. I'll have to comb my hair and fix my face. Do you think Mrs. Kincaid will dress up?"

"No, Mom, she's a grandmother and you always look great, even when pregnant, no matter what you wear."

"How old do you think she is?"

I grinned, "About your age, maybe a little older." A second later, I caught the wet washrag Mom threw at me. She almost got me in the face.

Mom said, "David, she must be twenty years older than I am, at least."

"You know I was just kidding; you're pushing forty though."

"Thirty-eight, young man."

I moved slowly over to mom and put my left arm around her shoulders. "You still make great sandwiches, Mom."

"Well, thank you. You'll know when I become too feeble to carry on my kitchen duties."

"How will I know?"

"The refrigerator and the cupboards will be empty. Call your brother so we can eat and get ready for company. Are you going to pick them up?"

"Uh-huh. Whitmore will be here at one o'clock and he'll want to get right to work. I'll go for the Kincaids at twelve forty-five. Danny and I will help you clean up as soon as we eat, okay?"

"Sounds like a plan." She kissed my cheek and tousled my hair. She hadn't messed up my hair like that in at least five years.

The ham and cheese sandwiches, potato chips, and milk were downed in less than ten minutes, then we spent about thirty minutes helping mom clean and organize. I vacuumed the living room floor and hid my dirty clothes in my bedroom closet. The array of magazines was gathered up by Danny and stacked on the bottom shelf of the coffee table where mom could get at them easily when lying down on the sofa.

Mom had gained weight with the baby coming, but other than the stomach bulge, she didn't look any different. She hadn't expanded noticeably around her butt and her face looked the same as always. I knew better than to ask her how much she weighed, though. She went in the bathroom and came out wearing different clothes; she had changed from an old sweatshirt to a loose white blouse and wore dark-blue pajama pants that had a string-like belt for easy expansion. She still wore slippers.

She looked at the clock in the kitchen and reminded me, "You have to leave in five minutes, David. Don't be late."

"I know, Mom. Thanks. I think you're going to like the Kincaids. Try to remember names of residents of Suddenly that were acquainted with them back in the 1990's. It might be important to Whitmore. I think Mr. Kincaid, Sr., Jenny's grandfather, might have been involved in something his wife knew nothing about."

When I pulled into the Kincaids' dusty driveway, I saw Mrs. Kincaid and Jenny waiting on the porch steps. The porch had been cleared and I assumed they had locked the doors. Jenny helped her grandmother to her feet, and they arrived at my car as I opened the passenger doors. I helped Mrs. Kincaid in the front and Jenny hopped in the back behind the driver's seat.

"Take us to your home, James." Jenny ordered from behind me. I glanced at Mrs. Kincaid and she smiled.

I replied, "The horses have been fed and watered, miss. It will be but a few minutes. I expect you will have a pleasant ride."

As I started the engine and selected drive, Mrs. Kincaid said, "Sounds like you two have regressed in time about two hundred years."

I glanced across at Mrs. Kincaid and saw a big smile, but I wasn't really sure what it was a result of. She had just fastened her seatbelt without help and that could have been the reason, but I felt more confident that it was due to Jenny's and my banter. I stopped at the street, looked both ways and stepped on the gas. Jenny was laughing quietly.

Five minutes later we were getting out of the car and I ushered the two women into the house through the front door. Mom and Danny were in the kitchen, coming into the living room to meet the Kincaids. I made a quick introduction and as expected, Danny couldn't take his eyes off Jenny. She noticed his attention, too. I glanced at her and she winked. Danny was an easy mark for Jenny. I was fairly sure she remembered what I had mentioned about Danny before, but I didn't want to insult her by reminding her what I had said.

Mom asked Mrs. Kincaid to sit on the sofa with her and they started gabbing. I looked at Danny and grabbed his shirt to start him outside to the backyard. I gave him a little shove to get him moving faster. Jenny and I followed.

Whitmore had arrived and was waiting, sitting at the picnic table. He was strumming his fingers on the tabletop and appeared frustrated. It was only a couple minutes past one o'clock.

"Ah, you're here. Let's get to work. Show me how this drone system works, boys."

Danny took over the controls; he had put in more flying time than I had, so his experience would speed up the searching. He said, "Let's do something close so we don't discharge the batteries before we look over a property. Give me an address, Mr. Whitmore, so I can take the drone over there. You can stay here and observe on the TV screen. Make it close by, I don't want to walk very far. David will have to take me to places farther away than a couple of blocks."

Whitmore laid the map of Suddenly on the table and pointed at an address only a block away. I knew the Winthrop family. Their son was a friend of dad's and had fought in the forest fire that dad had died in; but Allen had made it out alive. After the fire, he moved to a small town in Utah where there were few trees, mostly arid desert. He worked for a mining security company. "That's the Winthrops', Danny."

"Yeah, I know. I'll operate the drone from the corner where they can't see me. After I scan the property, I'll be back."

"Can I go with you?" asked Jenny.

"Ah, sure." Danny looked a little flustered but seemed to shake off the uneasiness when Jenny spoke. He picked up the drone and controller and set off down the street. Jenny had to walk fast to catch up. "Not so fast, Danny! I can't run." He turned and waited for her to join him. They disappeared around the corner and in a couple of minutes the TV flickered, and we could read Winthrop's house number easily.

Whitmore asked, "Can't he fly the drone from here?"

"Nope. A drone pilot has to see the 'copter at all times; it's called LOS, line of sight. We have to follow the rules."

"There's lots of rules that don't seem to apply to anybody but a small minority, but I guess that's life. Someone is always trying to make everyone happy all the time, but it doesn't work. Hey, there's an animal in the grass. What's that?"

"That's a squirrel, a live one. See, it just moved."

"Yeah. Damn rodents. I bet they're all over the place in Suddenly. Just like rats in the city."

"But you've got to admit, Mr. Whitmore, they're cuter than rats."

Whitmore didn't respond, he was watching the TV screen very intently. "There's something! It looks like a rabbit." He put his figure on the screen and I verified what he was seeing. It was a ceramic rabbit in a vegetable garden; crouched with its ears along its back like it was eating. "The drone is hovering right over it. Do you think Jenny will try to find out more about it?" Whitmore was excited, his eyes were opened wide, but he only gave me a cursory glance and refocused on the screen.

"I hope not. She should wait until we can watch what happens when she goes to the door. I told her what the procedure was going to be. I hope she doesn't do anything on her own, but she might surprise us. She thinks she's a tough city kid and can handle any situation."

Danny guided the drone across the yard from front to back and slowed to survey the garden area. He could see a grayish lump and thought it might be something to scan. Jenny saw it too, and suggested Danny pilot the drone closer so we could get a good look. The sound was very clear, we didn't need to use the walkie-talkie.

"Circle around it, Danny, so the guys can get a close-up view. I wonder what it is, just a rock? I want to go over there and see what it is; do you think David would mind?"

"Un-huh. You'd be trespassing. You'd better wait and talk with him before you go marching onto the Winthrops' yard. I don't see a sign that discourages solicitation though. Mrs. Winthrop probably likes to talk with people coming to the door. Those people are pretty old and don't have many visitors. Their relatives live in other states.

Jenny reacted, "That sounds perfect for me. I'll go to the door and talk with them after we go back to your place and meet with David."

Chapter 11

There wasn't enough energy remaining in the drone battery to fly over another property until the power supply was recharged, so Danny flew the 'copter to David and Whitmore as he and Jenny returned home. He landed the drone on the picnic table and shut off the motors.

Jenny was excited about going back to the Winthrops' to ask about the form they had seen in the garden. "We thought the object was a rabbit, but we couldn't see enough to make sure."

"It's a rabbit all right." Whitmore said. "Let's go see if the property owners are home. Do you know what to look for, Jennifer?"

"Un-huh, but if the bottom is covered with dirt. I'll need to wash it off and dry it to see if any numbers are present on the feet."

"I'll give you a squirt bottle of water and a couple of paper towels," said David.

"I'm going to start recharging the battery while you guys check out the rabbit, okay?" Danny was removing the battery from the drone.

"How long will that take, a couple of hours?" Whitmore was getting anxious for more positive results. I could tell he wanted the property searches to be continuous, no delays.

Danny was relaxed and didn't care what Whitmore thought or said. "It will take about a half-hour to get a full charge. Go do your thing and you won't notice the time delay."

I couldn't have said it better. When did Danny become so smart? We were doing Whitmore a favor, so he had little reason to complain.

Jenny took the water bottle from me and I folded the paper towels and stuck them between her sling and her shirt. She looked at me and grinned, but I wasn't sure what the grin was for; maybe she was proud of how Danny had handled Whitmore, or maybe she was happy to be helping us.

We walked to the corner of the block one street over to Ash where the Winthrops' front yard abutted and stopped beside a hedge that offered a good observation point. Jenny didn't lose a step when Whitmore and I stopped. I wondered what Whitmore was thinking as he watched her cross the street and walk to the front door, which was only one step above the level of the grass. The sidewalk up to the porch was made of pavers or old bricks, I didn't know the difference.

When Jenny turned to step on the pavers, I decided to join her. I hadn't talked with Mrs. or Mr. Winthrop for at least a year, maybe longer. I couldn't remember exactly. But when Whitmore and I were watching on the TV screen, I noticed the Winthrops' grass needed mowing. I might get a job out of this.

"Jenny! Wait! I'm coming with you."

She stopped, made an about face and waited for me.

"What's wrong? Changed your mind?"

"No, go ahead. I want to ask if I can do their lawn. We'll make up a story about the rabbit. Tell whoever comes to the door that we're curious about the rabbit. Where did they get it? Your grandmother could use one in her garden, couldn't she?"

"Oh, that's right. She wants to replace the turtle someone destroyed with his lawn mower." We both laughed as we approached the door. Jenny knocked and we could hear some talking inside. We heard something unintelligible from voices and then very clearly, "Just a minute."

The door opened slowly, and Mrs. Winthrop appeared wearing an apron over her house dress. I could smell what I thought was chicken soup. She pushed her glasses back on her nose and said, "I know you; you're David Drum." She glanced at Jenny and asked, "Now who is this pretty young woman? My gosh, are you hurt?"

I answered, "This is Jenny Kincaid. She's visiting her grandmother, Maud Kincaid. Maybe you remember the Kincaids; they have a two-story farmhouse on the outskirts of town."

"Oh, sure. I heard that Robert passed away not long ago. Maud and I used to belong to the same bridge club. Gosh, it's been years since I played. The members began passing away and the rest of us lost interest, seeing them go like that. But what can I do for you youngsters?"

Jenny asked, "We were wondering where you got that rabbit lawn decoration. Do you remember where it came from?"

"Oh, sure. Your grandfather gave that to us about twenty years ago. It's seen a lot of wear; it used to be painted, I think."

"Could we look at it, Mrs. Winthrop? I'd like to get another one for my grandmother." Jenny sounded convincing.

"Oh, I don't think you can do that. Robert told us the figure was unique and we should keep it a long time. It might be valuable someday. It was made in Vietnam."

"Do you mind if we look at it? I used to have a pet rabbit and always loved its ears and white tail."

"I don't mind, dearie. Go right ahead and look. It's a little dirty, though."

Jenny grinned and held up the squirt bottle and paper towels. "We came prepared, Mrs. Winthrop."

"Go ahead and take a look. I'll meet you out there. There's a clay pig somewhere around the garage, unless Eddie ran over it with the car." She chuckled, "He named it Bacon. Eddie doesn't drive much anymore, neither do I; our eyes aren't what they used to be. Bacon isn't very big; he's a pot-belly pig about this long." She held her hands up about a foot apart. She chuckled, "I always thought he was kind of cute."

We had turned the rabbit over and were washing off the feet to remove the dried mud when Mrs. Winthrop joined us. She asked, "What are you looking for on the bottom of the rabbit?"

Jenny had knelt on the ground and looked up, "We were

wondering if there was a serial number on the bottom; maybe a manufacturer's name."

"Oh, I don't think you'll find anything. Vince said the ornaments were made by a pottery family; they usually made dinnerware and ornamental bowls for flowers. He said they only made one of each object; specifically, for certain American servicemen. Corporal Owens brought about a dozen of them back on a troop ship."

I had to find out who Corporal Owens was. "Was Mr. Owens here in Suddenly some time ago?"

"Yes, I believe it was back in 1998. Three of my Eddie's Vietnam buddies had a reunion and each of them brought mementos from their war experiences. Vince and Lloyd both brought some of those lawn ornaments. Steve Rogel brought me a big bouquet of flowers; he was a really nice man, but never married."

"Lloyd? Who was Lloyd?" asked Jenny.

"Let me see." Mrs. Winthrop cocked her head to the side and thought for a few seconds. "Oh, yes, Lloyd Berry was his name. His wife Genevieve came with him. They were from New Jersey. They've both passed, but their daughter, Barbara, is still living. I think she lives somewhere in Michigan; she's a teacher of the deaf."

Jenny and I inspected the rabbit very closely and didn't find any indication of a number. After giving the rabbit a good bath and a second inspection, we returned the ornament to its original position at the edge of the garden. The next step was to find Bacon; he must be camouflaged or hiding under something so we couldn't see him from the drone.

I turned toward Mrs. Winthrop, "Do you know where Bacon might be? We don't see any other lawn ornaments around." Jenny and I had scanned the yard and hadn't come up with anything that looked like a pig. We both mistook a good-sized river rock for the pig but couldn't detect anything else that might be an ornamental clay porker.

"Let me ask Eddie if he's seen the damn thing. He's got a bad knee and is resting today. I'll be right back." Mrs. Winthrop went in the back door and left it ajar. We could barely hear them talking.

Jenny said, "A pig could be stuffed full of diamonds. Don't you think?"

"Could be." I smiled, "I had a plastic piggy bank once, but it never was full of coins. I used to take a table knife and slide the pennies and nickels out through the slot; every so often a dime would tumble out. Danny and I bought gum and candy with the proceeds." I laughed, "I wasn't thinking of saving for college back then."

"Yeah, you'd about have enough for one meal now. You'd need a very big piggy for all the loot you need these days. I've never thought about college, but I'd really like to go to art school."

The back-door hinges squeaked as Mrs. Winthrop reappeared smiling. "Eddie said he buried the pig. He didn't want to hit it and throw the car wheels out of alignment."

Jenny laughed, "So the pig is looking for truffles?"

I had to laugh, and I added, "It works for the underground. That pig is smuggling foreign lawn ornaments across the Canadian border, claiming they are looking for lawn work."

Mrs. Winthrop didn't think my sense of humor was very good. She frowned and asked, "Don't you want to know where Eddie buried it?"

My smile faded and I said, "Sure, Mrs. Winthrop. Where do we dig?"

"Eddie said stand at the corner of the garage farthest from the house and walk three steps west and seven steps north. That's because our house number is 307."

"Very clever. I'll get a shovel from home and be right back."

Mrs. Winthrop said, "We have a shovel in the garage that you can use. The pig isn't very far down, only about a foot or so. I'll get you the shovel."

Eddie Winthrop had wrapped the pig in a plastic bag before he dropped it in the hole and covered it with dirt and sod. I was careful to lift the top layer of grass up so it could be replaced without leaving a bare spot or a depression in the yard. Jenny unwrapped the clay figure carefully so it could be rewrapped and reburied after we inspected it.

We didn't have to wash it off; it was very clean. The plastic grocery bag from Safeway had protected the little pig from weathering. Jenny flipped the fat piglet over and we checked the bottoms of the feet but didn't find any indication of numbers there or anywhere else on the clay figure. We had struck out. We repackaged the pig and stuck it back in the hole. When I replaced the grass and tapped it down with the shovel and my feet, no one would notice we had just dug there.

I put the shovel back in the garage and thanked Mrs. Winthrop for letting us look at the clay figures. "Would you like to talk over old times with Mrs. Kincaid?"

She didn't respond with any enthusiasm. "We were always opponents in the bridge club, I didn't know her very well. It was nice to meet you, Jennifer. Tell your grandmother hello for me. Maybe I'll see her sometime."

As we began to back away from the Winthrops' home and move toward Whitmore, I said, "Let me know if you need your grass cut. I'll give you a special rate. Here's one of my cards." I gave her one of my business cards and we said goodbye.

Whitmore was sitting on the curb out of sight of Winthrops' and I believe he had fallen asleep. He moved surprising fast when we approached him and when he stood, he almost lost his balance, stepping backward to regain his equilibrium.

"Well, what happened? You sure took long enough."

Jenny didn't like his attitude, nor did I, but having grown up in Suddenly, I probably had more patience than the city girl. If it had been a cold winter day, I would have seen steam rising from her entire body. If she hadn't had only one arm functioning, I could see her slapping Whitmore silly. Before she had a chance to give Whitmore a blast of blue air, I said, "We had to take the time to build a reasonable story to explain our interest in the lawn ornaments. We found one that was buried; we couldn't see it from the drone camera."

Jenny had calmed down. She took a deep breath and said, "We

checked the rabbit and a potbellied pig but couldn't see any numbers on either one. However, Mrs. Winthrop gave us several names that weren't on the Christmas cards grandma had."

"And you think they might be the source of the clay figures?" Whitmore was extracting his miniature recorder from his shirt pocket. He stood there waiting and we gave him the names Mrs. Winthrop had mentioned to us.

"They were army buddies from the Vietnam war. They came here for a reunion in 1998. Some of the clay ornaments were presents from them, at least the rabbit was. We're not so sure about the little pig."

"But you said there weren't any numbers on either one?"

I nodded and said, "That's right."

"Well, I think that took us for a wild goose chase. Let's go back and scan another property. There's got to be more figures with diamonds in them. We're too early in the hunt to give up."

Chapter 12

I was disappointed that we hadn't found any numbers on the figures we had checked, but Whitmore was the most frustrated of our threesome. He was anxious to get video from another property so he walked as fast as his short legs would carry his plump body. Watching him walk ahead of us reminded me of a commercial where a man was rushing to the post office to get his tax return mailed before the deadline. Jenny and I smiled at each other knowing he was generating a sweat.

Jenny commented, "I hope he put on deodorant this morning."

"I guess we'll find out in a couple of minutes."

When Jenny and I arrived in the backyard, Whitmore was seated at the picnic table checking his pulse and wiping perspiration from his face. He had overdone the short trip back from Winthrops' but his face was expressionless. He seemed in control.

Danny looked up from the battery charger and the fueled drone and said, "The drone is ready to go, where is the next field of battle?" He glanced at Jenny and me and then Whitmore.

Whitmore wiped his forehead once more and unfolded the city map stored in his jacket pocket. He scanned the marked X's and jabbed his finger down on the next closest property to our home. It was the Randolphs', five blocks away: two blocks east and three blocks south, a knight's move. Mr. and Mrs. Randolph were noteworthy residents; they owned and ran the Dairy Queen restaurant, a beehive of activity for high school students. But they aren't elderly, they're only a little older than mom, maybe in their mid-forties. I told Jenny who they were.

"Jenny, why would your grandparents send a Christmas card to the Randolph family?"

"Maybe their parents would be about the right age?"

"Yeah. I'll bet that's it. Good thinking."

She grinned, "Thanks. I'm not just a girl with a sling."

I chuckled, "That's for sure."

Whitmore had turned on the garden hose and gotten a drink. He soaked his handkerchief and rubbed it over his bald head. After wringing out the hanky, he stuffed it in his pants pocket. Jenny and I almost laughed when we saw the appearance of a wet spot on the front of his trousers. He didn't care. He headed toward his car and said, "C'mon, Danny, I'll drive you over there. David, you and Jenny watch the monitor and take notes if you see anything interesting. C'mon, bud, let's get that thing in the air." He motioned to Danny and Danny followed him to the rental.

Jenny stood next to the bench seat of the picnic table and turned in a circle looking at the tall pines and firs. She heard a bird's call and asked, "What kind of bird makes that song, David?"

"I'm pretty sure that's from a mourning dove, unless Danny is playing tricks on us. It's also called a turtledove. They're pretty common around here."

"I've only heard a couple of different birds in the city, just pigeons and sparrows, and they seem to crap on everything. Kids go around and shoot them with BB guns and once in a while the kids shoot out a window, the cops show up and the BB guns disappear to come out another day. I think they shoot out the windows on purpose.

"I'll show you an eagle and some hawks someday, but we have to go out to tower seventeen or farther out to twenty for sure. We'll take some binoculars and see where they nest. You afraid of bears?" I was trying not to grin by biting my lower lip, but I had to turn away to prevent her from noticing the beginnings of a smile.

"Bears? I've only seen them at a zoo, never in the wild. Have you seen many around here? I mean in town?"

"Actually, no. Only a few reports have been made in the last few years. Mom and another ranger tranquilize them and release them twenty miles out. I was just trying to see how you'd react. When we go out in the woods, we always take a rifle or a tranquilizer gun with us. Unless they're pretty hungry, bears stay away from people. But you can't outrun a bear. Don't even try."

Jenny was a little irritated about my teasing, so she became quiet and stared at the TV screen. I should have kept my big mouth shut. Danny accused me of being a know-it-all, but when dad died, I felt I had to take over and learn as much as possible. I expected a reaction from her that mimicked one from Megan, but Megan grew up in Suddenly, not in a large city. Their life experiences were completely different.

All of a sudden, the screen flickered, and we could see Danny operating the drone control panel, the drone above his head and moving away. Whitmore was out of the picture, probably sitting in his car sweating up a puddle.

"Jennifer, your grandmother wants to go back home. Are you ready?" It was mom calling from the slider in the kitchen-dining room area. I almost cussed but caught myself just in time and kept my trap shut.

Jenny said, "Just a minute, Mrs. Wilson." She looked at me and said, "What are we going to do, David?"

"I've got an idea, keep watching. I'll be right back." I ducked into the garage, grabbed an old VHS recorder and a blank tape and hurried back to Jenny. I plugged in the unit, attached the cable to the TV and pressed the on switch. The TV flickered and then settled down as the recorder started doing its job.

I grabbed Jenny's hand and tugged her toward the house. I thought Mrs. Kincaid was in a hurry the way Mom called Jenny.

"Hey! Don't rip my arm off. I can walk, you know."

I let go of her hand when she protested my efforts to get her in the house. "I'm sorry, I was under the impression that your grandmother was in a hurry to get back home."

"I don't think you know how strong you are. You might cause

me to wear another sling." She grinned, knowing I hadn't pulled that hard.

"Please excuse my rough treatment. I forgot you were such a fragile woman."

"Just you wait, David. When I get back the use of my left arm, I'll show you how fragile I am."

Mrs. Kincaid was sitting in the living room when we got in the house. She looked at us and said, "Ready to go, Jen? I think your mother is ready for a nap, David. I've talked all the energy out of her for at least a day." She stood up and straightened her skirt.

"How's the project going? Is Mr. Whitmore still trying to run the show? I haven't heard any of his mellow tones today."

I had to smile when she said mellow tones. She was more than generous describing his voice that way. "Danny and Whitmore are surveying another property with the drone. The TV images are being recorded. We'll look at the results later."

"David, I need some eggs. After you take the Kincaids home, pick up two dozen eggs for me."

"Okay. Tell Danny I'll be back in about thirty to forty minutes. Is there anything else you need?"

"No. I'll have Scott get some things for me at the drug store. I don't want you to be embarrassed." She smiled as I left the house with the Kincaids.

We had just reached the corner to turn toward the city limits and the Kincaids' when I thought it would be a good idea to show them the Dairy Queen location.

"Would you ladies like some soft ice cream? I'll buy." I glanced at Mrs. Kincaid and she nodded, "Yes, that would be nice."

"What made you think of that, David?" Jenny poked me in the back and said, "Now my mouth's watering. I'm going to get fat because of inactivity. I hope my collarbone heals fast."

"Don't worry, you won't get fat until you start having kids." I pulled into the drive-through lane at Dairy Queen. There was one car ahead of us; I didn't recognize who it might be. The license indicated the vehicle was from Idaho, probably vacationers.

The Idaho car pulled forward and I pulled up at the window and gave my order to Mary Lynn, a classmate; she'd be a senior this fall, too. She leaned forward, "Hi David, what can I do ya for today?"

"Hi Mary. I'd like three large cones, please."

"Coming right up, just a sec." She turned away from the window.

Someone had driven in behind us and was honking. I wondered what their problem was and looked in my rearview mirror. It was Megan, my girlfriend, in her dad's old jeep. Megan had been using the jeep for two years, primarily for going to the hospital and driving to and from school. I couldn't remember ever seeing her dad drive the jeep since I showed Megan how to use a stick shift. That had been a riot for me.

Megan was getting out of the jeep and coming toward me. She wasn't wearing her usual Candy Striper uniform. She was dressed in a set of yellow scrubs; she looked delicious. Leaning in my window, she gave me a peck on the cheek. "Who's your date?" Winking at Mrs. Kincaid, "I don't have anything to be jealous of, do I?" Then Meg saw Jenny in the back seat. "Hi, Jenny."

"Hi, Megan. You aren't working today?"

"Slow day. I mopped some room floors, stocked supplies, and that was about it. We're waiting for David's mom to come to have her baby." She smiled and poked my shoulder. "The nurses told me to take some time for myself. I'm on the way home. Were you at David's talking with his mom?"

Jenny nodded but Mrs. Kincaid replied, "I wanted to meet Mrs. Wilson, with the baby coming soon and David working at our place so much. I have a feeling it will be another boy."

"Order's up!" Mary was reaching out of the drive-up window with the cones in a paper tray made to dispense four cones. I handed the tray to Mrs. Kincaid.

Megan stepped aside and quietly said, "I need to talk with you, David. See you tonight?"

"Sure. I'd invite you to dinner, but I think Mom is tired and wants to rest this evening."

"That's all right. I'm going to pick up a burger and shake. How about eight o'clock?"

"Sounds good. See you after dinner."

Mrs. Kincaid passed the tray to Jenny who waited for me to pull ahead and out of the drive-up lane. I glanced in the rear-view mirror and could see Jenny watching me get back on the road to her house at the edge of town. I knew what she was going to say.

"Can you drive and eat a cone at the same time?"

"I can multitask with the best of 'em, but only at low speed." I reached back over my right shoulder with my left hand and Jenny placed a cone in touch with my fingers so I could grip it. "Thank you. Very cleverly done."

"You're welcome, James. Please take us home now or you will be dismissed."

"Yes ma'am."

Mrs. Kincaid raised her eyebrows, shook her head and said, "Here we go again." We all laughed as we licked away at the soft vanilla ice cream.

I drove directly to the Kincaids', pulled up behind the pickup and let the ladies out.

Jenny leaned into the passenger window and said, "You're coming over tomorrow, right?"

"With my chain saw. I'll bring some extra earplugs for you and your grandmother; the chain saw is pretty noisy. See you at nine o'clock."

I watched Jenny help Mrs. Kincaid up the porch steps and then I took off to pick up the eggs Mom wanted. The side trip and longer route home to Kincaids' had taken almost an hour. Danny and Whitmore were waiting at the picnic table when I got home.

Danny was discussing the use of the drone's control panel showing Whitmore some drone maneuvers.

Chapter 13

Danny waved at me when I parked in the driveway. I waved back and went into the house to deliver the eggs. I stuck the cartons in the refrigerator and rinsed the remnants of ice cream off my fingers before going to talk with the troops.

"Have you looked at the tape?"

Danny was quick to answer, "Yeah. We didn't see anything but grass and weeds; no lawn ornaments."

"Did you use your ground penetrating radar?"

"Sure did. We found an old Indian burial site."

"Okay, boys. Enough kidding around." Clearly disappointed, Whitmore rolled up the town map. His frown showed his frustration with the negative results of the search of the Randolphs' property. "That's all we're going to do today. Tomorrow, I'm going to take the day off from physical activity and do some thinking. Thank you for your help. Can we start again on Saturday, day after tomorrow?"

I looked at Danny and he gave me a thumbs up. I answered Whitmore, "I have to help the Kincaids on Saturday morning, but I'll be free in the afternoon."

"Can't you help them tomorrow instead?"

"I am, there's a lot to do there. I'm cutting that old windmill tower into firewood. Don't worry, I'll be looking for anything that might have fallen under the timbers."

Whitmore bit his lower lip, picked his nose with his stubby left little finger and said, "If you find anything, let me know. I'm staying at the Shady Lake Motel, cottage three."

Danny and I watched the agent shuffle to his car and drive slowly away. Danny said, "He sure likes to give orders. I bet he's already thinking about what to have for dinner. I don't like him."

"Has he given you any money for your time and the use of the drone?"

Danny scowled, "Nope, nothing. Not even a real thank you."

"If he doesn't come up with some bucks, don't worry, I'll pay you from the finder's fee I get. Be sure to keep track of your time spent."

"I'm doing that. I'll ask him about it next time we use the drone. If he doesn't give me some money, I'll tell him no more flights."

"If he doesn't cough up some coin, tell him he'll have to deal with the sheriff. He knows our relationship with the local law."

Danny smiled and said, "Good idea, bro."

As eight o'clock approached, I was getting the chain saw ready for the morning's work at the Kincaids'. I checked the oil and made sure I had enough gas in the three gallon gas can. I saw Megan coming out the slider at her house and walking toward our backyard. When she came through the gate to our yard, I said, "Just a minute, Meg, I've got to put this stuff in the garage. Take a seat at the table."

I put the saw and the gas tank together on the workbench and smeared some Goop on my hands to clean off the oil and dirt. Wiping my fingers on a clean rag, I glanced at my pretty neighbor. Megan didn't seem to be herself, kind of withdrawn. She sat there and didn't make eye contact, not even attempting to give me a kiss. I sat down beside her and put my arm around her shoulders. She turned her head to look at me and cleared her throat.

"I'm not sure how to tell you this," she began.

"What is it? Has something bad happened to your folks?"

"No, they'll be back tomorrow. It's not about them. How are you and Jennifer getting along?"

"Does this involve Jenny?" I knew Megan might get jealous and I was worried she wanted to break up. "We're just friends, Meg, that's all. I'm helping them clean up their property; I'm getting paid for a job. I need money for college and I've only got one year until I start college, you know that."

"That's not what this is about, David. It's about what just came up at the hospital."

"Has Dr. Rennick been hitting on you? Do I need to have a man-to-man talk with him?" I teased.

"No, David. That wouldn't happen." She was not in the mood to joke.

"Why not? You are gorgeous, and guys are going to hit on you everywhere you go."

"Thanks, but that's not a problem with Dr. Rennick." She thought for a moment and then continued, "Besides, he's gay."

"You're kidding. How did you find that out? Did he tell you?" I was genuinely shocked, but maybe I shouldn't have been. It isn't that unnatural these days.

"The nurses were talking in the break room and I overheard them."

"So, what did you want to tell me?" I couldn't figure out what she was trying to say. Megan was usually not hesitant about anything.

"Dr. Rennick told me he would support my attending medical school when the time comes to apply."

"Okay, but that's four years from now, isn't it? Don't you schedule the MCAT after your junior year in college? That's a long time from now, four years."

She nodded, "But he thinks I should do my undergraduate work at a more prestigious university than those in this area; like the University of Washington or one of the California schools, maybe USC or Stanford. He said with my grades and a couple of great recommendations, I would be accepted into the undergraduate program and I would have a very good chance to be approved by their medical schools. But I've been thinking, what if I lose sight of my goals in the next four years?"

My mind was getting so stuffed with Megan's train of thoughts, I felt like a balloon being filled with air and I might pop if anything else was added for me to think about. I didn't know what to say, I just sat there kind of numb. It took me about twenty seconds to digest what she had said.

"Well, if you go out-of-state to college, I won't be able to go with you. I can't afford out-of-state tuition. I can barely afford in-state costs; maybe junior college for a couple of years and I'll have to get a job and work part time. Mom doesn't have the money to support my education and I don't want to ask Scott for help. With the new baby, they'll have more than enough to think about as far as money is concerned."

"But what about the money from the recovery of the diamonds?"

"Maybe I'll get ten percent for that first one, but after that, Whitmore comes into the picture and I might not get much from further finds. I don't want to apply for student loans. Repayment might get out of hand and I don't want the government on my case for years to come."

"But you could get an athletic scholarship, couldn't you?"

"I'd have go as a walk on. Look, Megan, I'm not that good, I'm more of a Rudy than a full ride jock."

Megan and I sat in strained silence for what felt like hours, but was probably less than a minute, before she totally switched gears and said, "Want to come over and watch a movie with me? I'll fix some popcorn."

I wasn't in the mood for a movie; what Megan was saying meant she wanted to break up. After she had told me her change of plans for the near future, I didn't have any energy to even think about our relationship. I still had a job to do at the Kincaids' through Saturday and then I wanted to continue to work with Whitmore. Plus, I was still looking for anyone else that needed yard service. I looked away, "I don't think so, not tonight. I'm too tired; I'd fall asleep during a movie. Good night Megan."

"Night, David. Will I see you tomorrow?"

"Maybe. I'm working for Mrs. Kincaid in the morning."

Megan turned toward her house and slowly walked away from

me. She didn't look back as she normally would have done. She went in through the slider and closed the drapes. I felt like she was walking out of my life after all these years. We had made plans for our future together, but it struck me that those ideas had completely changed. I guess I really hadn't known what she wanted for her future. Perhaps it wasn't in the cards. I should have realized that we might reach a turning point where we would take different pathways after high school. Dejected, I got up from the picnic bench, went upstairs to my bedroom and hit the sack. Tomorrow was another workday. I needed sleep.

Morning came too fast. I had laid in bed for nearly an hour before I was able to drift off and then I dreamed of being in a fight, wrestling with someone on the ground in the front yard. I woke up early in the morning and discovered I had kicked off my sheet and blanket. I dozed until mom called me for breakfast at 7:30. I could smell coffee, pancakes and a hint of maple syrup. I heard Scott's cruiser start and back out of our driveway when he left for his courthouse office. I stretched my arms and legs, dressed in an old pair of jeans, my work boots, a T-shirt, and a yellow sweatshirt. It was going to be partly cloudy and cool this morning; good working conditions for cutting up windmill timbers.

I told mom about my talk with Megan and she responded with what I thought was a very insightful comment. "Becoming a doctor is a very difficult course of study and takes an enormous amount of discipline, David. When Megan discovers what she will be giving up to become a doctor, she might change her mind, but you have to let her discover those things by herself. If you really want Megan in your future, you both have to work toward your own desires. For example, are you sure, at this point in your life, that you want to become a veterinarian?"

"Jeez, I think it's too early to know, Mom; I've got four years of study ahead before I have to decide. I might even change my college major before I graduate."

"There you go; things happen you can't predict. If we could see into the future, many things would be different." She drank some orange juice, rinsed the dishes in the sink and rubbed her protruding belly. She saw me looking at her and said, "You know, a year ago, I didn't predict this." She pointed at her big belly and laughed.

I laughed with her and said, "But it wasn't a big surprise, either."

"No, but plans don't always turn out as expected." I could tell mom wanted to ask me something, so I kept my eyes on her as she watched me pick up my dirty dishes.

"How are you and Jenny getting along? She's a very pretty young woman, don't you think?"

"Un-huh. We're doing fine. I like her, but I've been with Megan for a long time and I don't want to foul that up." I didn't know how to put my feelings about Megan into words, especially after what Meg had said last night. Should I just forget about her and start shifting my activities and thoughts to Jenny? I guess I should let things happen and not try to force anything one way or another. Right now, I need to concentrate on making money for college. I only have about fourteen months until I'm a freshman again. I have a lot of work and huge decisions ahead of me.

When I arrived at the Kincaids', I couldn't tell whether the ladies were up, so I quietly unloaded the car. I sat in the front passenger's seat lazily scanning the property until I noticed activity in the house; the living room curtains parted a few inches so someone could glance outside. Jenny emerged from the front door a few seconds later and waved.

I tapped my pants pocket to be sure I had ear plugs with me and got out to greet her. She was waiting on the top porch step smiling as I walked toward her. "We're up; just finished breakfast and ready to go. Why didn't you come to the door?"

I pulled the package of plugs from my pocket and said, "I didn't want to wake you up. I didn't see any motion in the house."

"We've been up for more than an hour. Grandma has been opening shipping boxes and we've been talking about what color we want the house painted. I suggested light blue, but she likes yellow. What do you think?"

"I'm kind of afraid to say. I don't want anyone to blame me if you hate the color. I want to maintain neutrality, if that's possible." I grinned and handed Jenny the ear plugs and said, "I like blue though, as long as it isn't too dark; with white trim?"

Jenny opened the bag and peered inside. "Thanks for the plugs. I'll give a couple to Grams. Are you going to start work right away?"

I nodded, stepped away from the porch and started back to the car to get the chainsaw and the gas can. "Don't come around the house and sneak up on me. The chainsaw is dangerous. I don't want to be surprised while I'm working." When I got to the car, Jenny was no longer on the porch. I hoped she heard what I said.

When I got ready to start the saw, I realized I hadn't gotten instructions about where to stack the firewood. I decided a platform next to the back mudroom door would be handy. I estimated the space the stack of wood would occupy and started the saw. The two by four braces from the two timbers tilted above ground were laid next to the back door and I went back to the car to get a hammer and a handful of large galvanized nails.

In about ten minutes the elevated stand was constructed. It wasn't much to look at, but it would keep firewood off the ground away from bugs and mice and be easily available from the back door. The platform from the top of the windmill would serve as a cover to keep rain and snow off the firewood. It wasn't ready to be moved yet.

I went to work on the two timbers that jutted into the air, cutting them into fireplace length pieces. Once completed, I shut off the saw and started stacking the cut wood on the stand I had built. That's when I was interrupted.

Chapter 14

"David? Oh, there you are." The feminine voice wasn't Jenny or Mrs. Kincaid, it was Megan. I glanced toward the corner of the house and saw Megan coming into sight. What was she doing here? I was so surprised I didn't say anything, not even hello, but I noticed she was wearing work clothes with her hair in a bun and cowboy boots covered by jeans. She was within a few feet of me when I said, "Hi, Meg. What are you doing here?"

Her smile vanished as she planted her feet in the dirt. "I came to help you; I know Jenny can't work with only one good arm. Don't you want me here?"

"You surprised me, that's all. I didn't expect anyone to help. I was just thinking of what I would do next. Of course, you can help me. Do you have some gloves?"

She surprised me again; reached behind to her back pockets and pulled out worn leather gloves, dangled them so I could see them clearly and slipped them on.

"Come over here." I walked to the closest timber lying in the dirt and said, "I'm going to lift this off the ground and I want you to push some boards under it to keep it in the air." I dug my hands under the timber and lifted the four-by-four about a foot off the ground. Megan quickly slid three chunks of two-by-four under the timber and I set it back down. "Perfect, good job." I picked up the chainsaw and suddenly turned toward her. "Do you have any earplugs?"

She frowned, "No. Do I need them?"

"Yes. You can get in my car and listen to the radio while I use the chainsaw. It's going to be really noisy for about fifteen minutes. I'll come and get you when you can help stack more wood." I waved her away, she turned and walked around the corner of the house. I had no idea whether she would do what I said. Maybe she'd just drive away.

It took me a little longer than I had estimated to cut the wood. I shut off the saw and walked to my car. Megan's jeep was parked behind my car, but I couldn't see her. Maybe she had gone inside the house. At least the noise would be somewhat muffled inside. I popped the cargo door and lifted it as high as it would go. Surprise! Megan was laying on the blanket behind the rear seats, asleep. She hadn't used the radio.

I touched her ankle and said, "Hey, sleeping beauty, it's time for work."

She jerked her leg back from my touch and rolled to her knees. "I'm ready, I was just resting my eyes. Watch it, I'm coming out."

I backed off as Megan slid out feet-first to the ground, straightened her pants and said, "Let's go. What are we doing?"

"I've cut the support legs into short pieces and they need to be stacked on the stand by the backdoor. We'll work together; a little teamwork."

Ten minutes later, we had the wood in a reasonably tidy stack and Jenny leaned out the back door, apparently to check on me.

"Oh, hi Megan. I thought I recognized your car out front. Did David ask you to help him today?"

"No, he didn't know I was coming out here. How's your shoulder?"

"Feels better every day. I think I'll be able to take this sling off in another week or so."

"Make sure you get enough calcium in your diet. How are you doing with your design work?"

"I've been a little lazy the last few days, but David and I are going to load the truck with weeds and take them to the burn location tomorrow. I was going to help look for lawn ornaments today, but

Whitmore is taking a break."

"Yeah, David told me."

"Hey, Megan, give me a hand." I was pulling the windmill platform toward the stacked firewood, dragging the six-foot square of wood across the ground where the windmill had fallen. I had stopped about halfway and was adjusting my gloves which were slipping off.

Megan looked up at Jenny and said, "The boss calls, I'd better go."

Jenny stepped back into the house. She yelled, "Be careful!" and shut the door.

Megan grinned and I figured she was reflecting about Jenny's comment. I waited, holding the platform edge about waist high as Megan approached. About a yard from the platform, she extended her hands to grab the edge of the wooden structure, but she tripped.

I anticipated Megan's face coming in contact with the elevated wood and I assisted gravity, forcing the platform to the ground with an energetic push. It was too late for me to catch Megan, but she had extended both hands, one striking the ground and the other hit the platform as if she was doing an awkward pushup.

"Oh!" She exclaimed, falling clumsily to the ground in the small cloud of dust. I quickly picked her up by the waist and turned her around to face me.

"Are you all right?"

"I think so. I don't think I broke anything. I tripped on that damned rock." She pointed about ten feet back toward the house. "I'm not used to these boots and I stubbed my toe."

I glanced where Megan had pointed but didn't see a rock. I thought she had just been clumsy and caught her boot on an uneven mound of soil where weeds were growing. "I've got some antibiotic ointment in the glove compartment. Are you bleeding anywhere?"

Meg was examining her hands for traces of blood as I walked back to check the ground where she had tripped.

"No blood, but I think I bruised a couple of fingers on my left hand. I'm not worried about breaks in skin, I've had enough shots to protect me from nearly every disease known to man." She waved both hands to show me there wasn't any blood and smiled.

I slid my right shoe over the spot where Meg had caught her foot and felt something hard. "There's something here, Meg. You weren't being clumsy. Get my hammer, let's dig this thing up. I don't think it's very big."

"Don't you have a shovel?"

"There's one in the car, but the claws on the hammer will do what we need." I was on my knees pushing away loose soil when Meg returned with the hammer and handed it to me. "Thanks. Whatever this is, I think it was driven into the soil by the weight of the dead windmill. I'll bet that old structure weighed at least half-a-ton."

She commented, "We sure got a lot of firewood out of it. I wonder how long that wood will last during the winter."

I took a look at the stack and replied, "Less than a month if they use the fireplace every day. A fireplace is not very efficient for heating purposes, but it's good for mood and for roasting marshmallows." I grinned and started pulling away the dirt around the object in the ground. I had dug down about three inches when I realized the object was made out of clay like that of the turtle I had struck with my mower. Normally very calm when others get excited, I felt my pulse quicken.

Quickly trying to free it, I couldn't get a good grip and had to break away the dirt on opposite sides, then dig a couple of inches deeper. I put the hammer down and grabbed with both hands and gave a hard yank. A fist-size wad of dirt came flying up, showering Megan and me with dust and small dirt clods. I almost fell backwards when the earth released the clay object. It was a life size clay dove with light-blue wings and a yellow beak. When Megan saw what it was, she started laughing and I joined in. We had exhumed a clay bird.

She held out both hands, "Can I see?"

I handed the bird to Meg and said, "I'm giving you the bird."

She giggled, "Oh! You are such an idiot, David. That was really dumb."

We laughed together as she cleared dirt off the bottom of the bird and spit on the clay surface, then wiped it clean with the bottom of her sweatshirt.

"Look, David! Numbers!" Her hands were shaking as she held it in front of my face. I had to push it back about a foot and hold it still to focus on the marks. The numbers five and six, plain as day, were scratched into the bird's belly.

"That makes numbers three through seven accounted for. Whitmore's going to be excited."

"We're going to have to smash the bird to get the stones out. Should we show the bird to the Kincaids? Maybe Mrs. Kincaid will recall seeing this thing before."

"Good idea, Megan. I wonder if anything else was mashed under the windmill when it fell. Maybe I should rent a rototiller and turn over all the soil in the backyard."

"Why not have Whitmore do that? He's getting off easy having you and Danny doing all his work."

"But he's supposed to be paying us, Meg. He's the boss."

"Yeah, well you should be the boss. Let's ask Mrs. Kincaid if she knew there was a clay bird somewhere in her back yard."

"Let's walk the area first; see if we can trip over anything else." I grinned at Megan and she stuck her tongue out at me. We took our time, slowly inspecting everything that looked like it might be hiding something, but we didn't find anything even remotely suspicious. Only remnants of grass and weeds growing out of the dried-up soil remained. Our boots were covered with dirt and greenish stains from the dying plant life.

Megan carried the dove and I grabbed a piece of firewood. We walked around the house to the front door and knocked on the jamb. The door was open, and we could hear the hum of an electric fan through the gray wire mesh. Cool air was being drawn into the house; the sun hadn't been high enough to start the early afternoon heating. That's another thing I liked about living in the mountains; the cool morning air was refreshing, except in the middle of winter when it was so cold it hurt to breathe.

"Just a minute, David. I'll be right there." Jenny was calling from the kitchen or dining room; I couldn't tell which, a wall obstructed my view. I heard some background noises of drawers opening, closing and the rattling of pans.

Jenny suddenly appeared at the screen door; her head wrapped in a large brown bath towel. "Hi, guys. It looks like you found something. Is that a bird?"

I nodded and said, "I dug it up using a claw hammer. It was buried underneath one of the legs of the old windmill. I think it was on the top platform and fell off when we pulled the windmill down. Then it was shoved into the ground."

"So, David, you found it and gave Megan the bird?" She grinned and Megan reacted, "Don't go there, Jenny. David already did that." We all laughed. "You know, you and David have the same sense of humor, but it's on crutches. I think I'll make you two an appointment with the joke doctor."

I was still grinning when I asked Jenny if she had a plastic bag we could use. She frowned but turned and went down the hallway toward the kitchen. It took her at least a minute before she returned carrying a plastic bread bag. The towel had disappeared from her head and so had her blond hair. Jenny was now a brunette.

"Hey, what happened to your blond hair?"

She opened the screen door and gave me the bread bag. "I got tired of the blond look and wanted to get back to my original hair color. I was going to shave my head, but grandma told me not under her watch. People would think I had cancer or ringworm or some other disease. I got tired of touching up the roots; two-tone hair is not a good thing and a waste of time." She smiled and said, "What did you want the bag for?"

"The bird has numbers five and six on it, so I thought it would be a good idea to keep all the bits and pieces together until we find the two stones. The bird flack might carry away the diamonds, then we'd have to search for the missing stones."

"Huh, good idea. When are you going to break the bird?"

"Right away. Come out and watch, if you're not busy." Megan

and I stepped off the porch and I dropped the chunk of wood to the ground to have something solid to pound on. Meg put the clay bird in the bag, and I withdrew the hammer from my belt. We waited a few seconds for Jenny to join us. We all knelt around the bag and I tapped with the hammer until I could see the bird was breaking up. An onlooker would probably think we were trying to start a fire or drive a nail into the piece of wood. Who would think we were looking for two diamonds?

Chapter 15

Megan was leading a cheer, "Find the eggs, hit that bird, don't save anything, not even a turd."

I laughed and said, "And you think my jokes need help. Was that some of your hospital humor?"

"You'd be surprised at what nurses say when they think no one is listening. I won't repeat some of their stuff; it's pretty bad."

Jenny suddenly grabbed my right arm before I struck another blow with the hammer. "Look, there's one of them!"

"I see it! Let me get it out of the bag." Megan held the bag steady with her left hand and slid her right-hand fingers slowly into the plastic bag, being careful to avoid disturbing the contents. She squeezed a small chunk of clay between her thumb and forefinger and pulled her hand from the bag. A small portion of a sparkling diamond could be seen; clay still covering about eighty percent of the stone.

Jenny and Megan took the small popcorn looking piece of clay to the porch and began scraping away the clay with Jenny's pocketknife. I continued fracturing the large chunks of the broken bird watching carefully for any sign of a sparkle. I looked up occasionally to see if the girls were making any progress. Mrs. Kincaid had joined them on the porch and seemed to be making suggestions as to how to remove the last bits of clay adhering to the diamond. I kept working on the remnants of the bird in the bag.

I continued tapping on clay morsels for about five minutes before I discovered the other diamond. The ladies looked up when I exclaimed, "I found it!" I followed Megan's method of picking the desired object from the debris and wrapped it in my handkerchief. I considered taking the stones to Mr. Grinberg to have the clay removed from the surface of the diamonds because I was pretty sure the girls hadn't had much success cleaning the first one found. I walked over to the porch and was a little surprised at the progress they had made. Most of the clay was gone from the shiny stone.

"Thanks for the help, ladies. Can I buy you lunch?"

Mrs. Kincaid was the first to reply, "Why don't we all eat here. Jenny and I have plenty of groceries and I can make a mean sandwich, French bread, several cheeses and a salad. We can have lemonade, tea, or coffee to drink."

Jenny and Megan stood up, straightened their clothing and helped Mrs. Kincaid to her feet. I said, "Your lunch sounds better than hamburgers and the company is great, although I'm outnumbered three to one. After lunch, I want to show Mr. Whitmore what we've found. He'll be excited to see two more diamonds. His commission will take another leap."

I glanced at Megan and asked, "When do you have to be at the hospital?"

Megan was already going into the house behind Jenny, who was following her grandmother. I fell in line behind the women.

"I need to be there at two o'clock today. There's a rep from an instrument company to show everyone how to operate a new patient monitor system. It's a wireless system, state of the art like Wi-Fi. Dr. Rennick got a grant to test the new equipment at a small hospital setting."

Mrs. Kincaid and Jenny were in the kitchen retrieving things from the refrigerator when Megan and I caught up. We helped transfer things to the dining room table and Mrs. Kincaid encouraged us to start making our own sandwiches. I finished my second sandwich as the ladies were still working on their first. I slowed down, drinking lemonade and tried to contribute to the conversation but without much success.

Megan commented when she noticed I had stopped stuffing my mouth and was listening to the ladies' small talk. "You were really hungry. There's still some food remaining; make another sandwich." She grinned as Jenny and Mrs. Kincaid chuckled.

"No, thanks. I've had enough. It's hard work running that saw for nearly an hour. I felt like I'd been through a three-a-day football practice. You should try it sometime; you could build up some muscle for fighting unruly patients and doctors."

I wiped my mouth with a paper napkin and finished off my lemonade before I asked, "Who's going with me to report to Whitmore? He's staying at the Shady Lake."

Jenny was the first to react, "I have to do laundry today, so I'd better stay home. We're going to the burning station tomorrow. Right, David?"

I nodded. "I'll come over and load the truck at noon. We'll leave at one o'clock. Okay?"

Jenny nodded, "I haven't started the truck since I broke my collarbone. We'd better check the battery; it might need charging."

"Don't worry, I always carry a set of jumper cables. How about you, Meg? Can you meet me at the Shady Lake, cottage three?"

She raised an eyebrow and said, "Didn't the Nash family remodel those cottages last summer? I'd like to look at the interior of one of them. Yeah, I'll meet you there." Meg glanced at the grandfather clock. "It's twelve-thirty. I'll meet you at one o'clock."

"Would you like to see Mr. Whitmore, Mrs. Kincaid?" She looked a little flustered, but I didn't know why.

"No, David. I'm cleaning up the kitchen and throwing out things that should have been discarded years ago."

I commented, "Yes, I know that's a messy job, but someone has to do it." I got a good laugh from all the women. "See, I can be funny."

Pulling up to the Shady Lake Motel a few minutes early, I waited for Meg to park beside me. It was one minute after one when the jeep squeaked up next to my Subaru. We walked on pavers about fifteen yards to cottage three and I knocked on the door. No answer.

Megan remarked, "I think he's in there. I can hear the TV."

Megan's hearing was better than mine, but I concentrated and heard the faint noises. The sound didn't appear to be turned up. I knocked again, this time much louder so the door and the front windows rattled. He had to hear that racket. I looked at Meg and shook my head.

She said, "Try the door, David."

I did. The skimpy door wasn't locked, so I cracked the door a few inches and yelled inside, "Mr. Whitmore! It's David Drum and Megan Isaacs. We found two more stones." I purposely avoided mentioning diamonds. I didn't want to broadcast the discovery of the diamonds to everyone in the motel. There was no answer.

I pushed the door wide open and saw Whitmore sitting in a recliner watching TV. He hadn't looked toward Megan and me as we entered the cottage. I pretended to be sneaking over to scare him and Meg said, "Don't, David. You'll piss him off."

She was right, so I walked over to him from the side but a little in front so he could see me approaching. I shook his shoulder, thinking he was asleep, but there wasn't the slightest reaction. "Mr. Whitmore?"

Nothing. "Come here, Meg. Check his pulse." I began to tremble a bit.

Megan came swiftly and put her fingers on his neck to check his right carotid artery. After a few seconds she felt his forehead and stepped back. "David, he's cold and he's dead."

"I'll call Scott."

I picked up the motel phone and dialed nine to get an outside line and then nine-one-one. I had to wait a few seconds which gave me time to scan the interior of Whitmore's cottage living room. I saw an opened box of glazed doughnuts; three were missing.

"What is the nature of your emergency?" I recognized the voice; it was deputy Doureline.

"This is David Drum, Deputy. I'd like to report a death in cottage three at the Shady Lake Motel. I think the man had a heart attack and died. Megan Isaacs and I are there now."

"Don't touch anything, David. The sheriff will be right over. He's on his way. Go outside and wait." There was a short pause and then, "And don't touch anything."

"Okay." I heard a click on the phone and then the police siren a few seconds later as we moved toward the cottage door. Megan was about to pick up the remote and turn off the TV, but I blocked her hand, "Better not do that Meg, the deputy said not to touch anything. Dad is on his way. I think that's his siren."

She retracted her hand and stepped back from the corpse. We went outside and stood by Meg's jeep.

"David, you said dad instead of stepdad."

I grinned and said, "I was saying that for both of us."

Scott's cruiser with Sheriff painted on the sides in big capital letters pulled up behind Megan's jeep. Scott got out and said, "Are you guys all right?"

"Yeah, it's Mr. Whitmore, he's dead."

Megan added, "There's no pulse and he's cold. I think he's been dead for about twelve hours, maybe longer."

I couldn't help suggesting a reason for his death. "I think he died of the same thing Sheriff Howell did, an overdose of glazed doughnuts." Megan punched my shoulder and said, "This isn't a good time to be funny, David."

We watched as our dad pulled on a pair of rubber gloves and grabbed a finger printing kit from the back seat of his car. As he walked past us, he said, "Megan, please come in here and help with the prints."

I was a little surprised that Scott didn't ask me to help with the fingerprints, but maybe he thought that I would be uncomfortable working with the fingers of a dead man. Megan had more experience with death than I did, so I decided to forget about it. Megan was the best person for the job.

"David, go to the office and call Dr. Rennick. Tell him to bring the ambulance."

"Okay." I jogged to the motel office and found Mrs. Nash sitting at the admissions desk playing solitaire on the office computer.

The door had activated a two-tone sound. I waited a couple of seconds until she took a last look at the monitor before standing. "May I help you?"

"Yes. I'm the stepson of Sheriff Wilson. He wants me to call Dr. Rennick and have him bring the ambulance. Could you please call the hospital?"

"Did someone get injured?"

"No. The man in cottage three, Mr. Whitmore, is dead."

" W h a t ?   Y o u ' r e   k i d d i n g   m e . " "Nope, do you want to talk to the sheriff? He wants us to call the ambulance."

"But I didn't see or hear anything, so I don't know what I could add."

"Look, the music on your computer is too loud for you to hear anything outside. Are you going to call the hospital, or do you want me to do it?" I was almost ready to jump over the counter and get the phone if she didn't shut up and dial the hospital. I could see the number right in front of her on the emergency call sheet.

"Oh, all right." She sat back down, dialed the number and held out the phone so I could talk to the hospital.

"Suddenly Hospital, how may I direct your call?"

I recognized Nurse Berg's voice.

"This is David Drum. The sheriff asked me to call Dr. Rennick and have him bring the ambulance to Shady Lake Motel. There's a dead body in cottage three."

"Did the sheriff shoot somebody, David?" She joked.

"No, a fat guy had a heart attack last night. He died watching TV, eating doughnuts."

Nurse Berg replied, "Must not have liked the late movie?"

I was almost laughing, but I kept it together and got serious. "No, I think he overdid exercise yesterday and his heart gave out last night."

Serious again, she said, "So, it's not an emergency. Dr. Rennick is operating right now, taking out an appendix. I can drive the ambulance over. Would that be all right?"

"I don't see why not. Megan is here helping the sheriff with fingerprints right now. You don't need to hurry. You can park next to my light-green Subaru. That's the shortest distance to roll the gurney. I'll help you load the body; I've always wanted to push a body on a gurney." I couldn't help joking.

"Okay, David. I'll be there in ten minutes; I have to get someone else to handle the front counter admission services."

"Thanks, Mrs. Berg. I'll meet you where our cars are parked." She hung up and I returned the receiver to Mrs. Nash, thanked her and went back to cottage three. Scott and Megan were standing outside the cottage and looked expectantly when I came from behind our cars.

Scott asked, "Is the ambulance coming?"

"Yeah, but Dr. Rennick can't come. Nurse Berg is bringing the ambulance. She'll be here in a few minutes. How's Whitmore?"

Megan almost laughed but saw the serious look on her father's face, grinned and replied, "He's resting comfortably."

Chapter 16

I was trying to think of something funny to say, but after a few seconds, I decided being funny was not appropriate. I wondered why Scott had taken Mr. Whitmore's fingerprints. We knew who he was.

Nurse Berg didn't use the siren on the ambulance; a good choice, as there was no hurry to load the body and deliver it to the morgue. The vehicle rolled to a stop and Scott met Nurse Berg as she exited the vehicle.

"Thanks for coming, Mrs. Berg."

"No problem, it's been slow at the hospital today. Nothing like picking up a dead body to get out in the fresh air. Where is he, in bed?"

"No, he's in a recliner in cottage three, right here." Scott pointed his thumb at the small light-blue structure surrounded by eight-foot arborvitae and three-foot high boxwoods.

The nurse swung open the ambulance rear door and motioned for me to assist. After the gurney was expanded to waist height, Megan and I rolled it into the cottage. Nurse Berg stood in front of dead Mr. Whitmore, shook her head back and forth, and said, "Why are the ones I transport have to be grossly overweight?" She called out the front door, "Sheriff, we're going to need your help, this guy is well over two hundred pounds."

Nurse Berg gave us orders. "Megan, you and I are going to brace the gurney and the men will do the lifting. I hope rigor hasn't taken over yet." Nurse Berg unfolded a blue sheet and dropped it to the floor. She released a lever dropping the gurney to about a foot above floor level.

With everyone in position, the nurse said, "On three. One, two, three, lift! Megan, hold the gurney so it doesn't move."

Scott and I lifted Whitmore and swung him onto the gurney without much trouble. I straightened Whitmore's legs and folded his arms over his large belly. Nurse Berg covered him with the sheet and had us raise the gurney back to waist level. While she started pulled the loaded apparatus toward the door, we helped push and guide it outside to the ambulance.

I saw Mrs. Nash watching from the motel office building, her left hand at her right elbow and her right hand over her mouth. She looked concerned but didn't appear to want to see anything close up. I don't think she had ever seen a body removed from one of her cottages. I thought that she must have seen dead people at funerals, though.

With the body loaded, Nurse Berg slammed the cargo door shut and walked up to Scott. "Are you going to order an autopsy, Sheriff?"

"Yes. I need to know the cause of death so I can file the necessary paperwork. I'll have to inform his employer also. I'll let Dr. Rennick know what to do with the body in a day or two. Well, by Tuesday anyway. I might not get much done over the weekend; most agencies will be closed."

The nurse said, "I'll have Dr. Rennick call you so arrangements can be made. He's the acting coroner since Doc Lindsey retired last fall, but you know that." She climbed in the ambulance and pulled the door shut.

We all waved as Nurse Berg drove off with Whitmore in back. I wondered who would replace him. I hoped it would be a gentler, more appreciative person to deal with. I walked up to Scott and said, "Did Whitmore have a computer in there? I saw an Internet connection on the wall beside the TV set. I don't remember him saying he had talked with the insurance company office, but he said he was filing reports."

"I found an Apple laptop on the bureau beside his bed. I'm taking it down to the office. Deputy Doureline can check it out;

that'll give him something to do beside watching for non-existent speeders. I think he only wrote one ticket all last week. Few travelers have shown up, but the summer's still young."

Scott started for his cruiser, but I stopped him for a moment. "Dad, we found two more diamonds at the Kincaids' this morning. Megan and I came over here to tell Mr. Whitmore about them. I think you'd better put them in your office safe; I don't want to carry them around." I gave him the sealed envelope Mrs. Kincaid had given me for carrying the stones. It was a green Christmas card envelope that had been steamed open at some point and was now taped shut.

The sheriff tucked the envelope into his shirt pocket and said, "What did you touch inside the cottage when you found Whitmore's body?"

I thought for a moment, "I used the cottage phone to dial nine-one-one; that's all. I guess I should have used the office phone, huh?"

"Ideally, but don't worry, I don't expect any foul play here. I found a small container of nitroglycerine tablets in Whitmore's pocket. He was aware of heart problems; he just didn't get a chance to use the meds. He might have passed away in his sleep."

"How old do you think he was?"

"I would guess about mid-fifties but being obese robbed him of a normal life span. We have to stay in shape as we age, or medical problems arise." Scott reached into the back seat and picked up a roll of crime tape and we worked together sealing off the cottage doors and windows.

"I've got to get back to the office, David. Would you please tell Mrs. Nash the tape will be removed as soon as possible?"

"Okay. Talk to you at dinner."

Megan waved at Scott as he got in his cruiser, backed out of the motel parking area, and rolled off toward the downtown area. Megan was sitting in her jeep waiting for us to finish with the cottage.

I looked at my watch and noted the time, 1:52. She was due at the hospital in eight minutes. As I walked toward her, I said,

"Thanks, for coming with me, Megan. I was glad you confirmed that Whitmore was dead. If I'd been alone, I might have been even more shook-up. You were fantastic."

"No need to thank me, it was fun to be with you. We need to discover more dead bodies together. It's a real treat." She grinned, started the jeep, shifted into first without grinding the gears and slowly moved toward the hospital after yelling over the motor noise, "Mom is going to get excited about this when she and dad get back. See you after dinner."

I waved, "Bye, Meg."

As I climbed into the driver's seat, I wondered what Megan wanted to talk about after dinner. Could it be that she had already changed her mind about going out-of-state to college? Nah, it had to be something else; she didn't change her mind about anything that quickly. Maybe she wanted to discuss the event we had just experienced; I guess I'd find out soon enough.

Scott brought home pizzas so mom wouldn't have to cook anything, but she still made salad for a more balanced meal. Mom believed a meal full of fat, a small amount of protein, and lots carbohydrates didn't make a lot of sense. She made sure we had veggies. We didn't talk about Mr. Whitmore until we were having dessert.

Scott leaned back in his chair and said he wanted to bring us up to date about the deceased agent. "I sent Whitmore's prints into the fingerprint identification system and it turns out Mr. Whitmore was not Mr. Whitmore. His real name was Wilbur Ira Damon and he didn't work for any insurance company. He was a crook with a long rap sheet."

Shocked, Mom questioned, "So, how did he find out about the diamonds?"

"That's the big question. His last known haunt was St. Louis so I think he probably found out about the stones from someone there. After submitting his fingerprints, I was contacted by the FBI. They notified the company that originally shipped the diamonds back in nineteen ninety-seven. We expect an agent from Belgium to show up Monday or Tuesday."

"All the way from Belgium?"

"Yes, David. The diamond shipment originated in Antwerp and was insured by SABIC; that's South Africa-Belgium Insurance Company. SABIC is headquartered in Brussels."

I was stunned to find out Whitmore was a fake agent, a thief. How could I have known? I asked Scott, "Should I have been suspicious of Whitmore? Was there anything I should have been aware of; the way he acted, anything?"

"No. Remember, he was a career criminal. It was fortuitous that he showed up after you and Megan discovered the first diamond. I was fooled, too. He was a good actor and he seemed to have good credentials. Someone in St. Louis was his contact pretending to be his home office."

Mom said, "I thought he was legit, too. My professional experience with animals and trees wasn't enough to alert me to any subterfuge." She smiled. Her comment relieved the feelings that we had all failed to recognize Whitmore for what he was.

Scott grinned and said, "Maybe your woman's intuition was blunted by your pregnancy."

She laughed, "That's right, give me an excuse." We all laughed.

I watched Danny pull the B encyclopedia from the bookcase archive that was our dad's pride and joy, flop on the floor and start turning pages. "Here it is: Belgium is a tiny country with a population of about nine point five million. It's only about twelve thousand square miles in area." Then he got the M volume and said, "Montana has an area of about one hundred forty-seven thousand square miles and a population of less than a million."

Mom laughed, "I hope the real agent likes open spaces and few people. I wonder if he or she has ever been to the states."

I looked at Mom leaning back against the sofa pillows. She looked uncomfortable. "When do we expect the population of Montana to increase by one?"

Mom replied, "Next week is the due date, David. I hope you are around so you can take me to the hospital if Scott is busy."

Scott chimed in, "Maybe the baby will come over the weekend. Our main law enforcement officer will be available to ferry you to the delivery room."

Mom winked at Scott, "That could happen, I guess. The way the baby has been kicking recently, she wants out."

Scott sat on the sofa next to Mom's legs and put his left hand on her swollen stomach. He tapped on her belly like it was a watermelon, checking to see if was ripe.

"Hey, little fella, don't cause your mom any problems, I've got plenty of room for a wise guy at the jail."

We were all laughing when the doorbell rang. "It must be Megan, she said she was coming over tonight." I jumped up from the floor where I was scratching Spectrum's chest and stomach. He also got to his feet, tail wagging, and followed me. I slowly opened the door to prevent Spectrum from jumping up to greet Megan, but Meg wasn't there, it was Suzy and she barked when she saw Spectrum coming outside. I opened the door wider and looked for Megan; Suzy didn't know how to ring the doorbell.

"All right, Megan, where are you hiding?"

Laughing, she came out from behind the boxwoods where she had been crouching. When she grabbed my right hand and began yanking, I pulled the door shut and followed her over to the steps of her front porch. We sat down on the porch swing, legs dangling, holding hands. Her hands were soft and smooth, perfect for a nurse, even a volunteer one. She had something to tell me; I knew that, having dated for nearly a year and a half and knowing each other for our entire lives.

"Remember my ex-boyfriend, Rick Hadley? His mom called me late last night and told me how frustrated she and her husband were with Rick's lack of interest in his rehabilitation."

"How could I forget Rick. I remember when he dumped you. What happened, did his girlfriend dump him?"

"Kind of. She recovered from her motorcycle wreck and went

home. She told him he wasn't trying hard enough with his rehab. I guess he went into a slump and needs some encouragement."

"So, she wants you to help with Rick?"

"Yeah. His parents want to hire me to come to the ranch and assist with his therapy."

I didn't say anything. I just sat there thinking. Megan wouldn't be strong enough to support Rick if he attempts to walk. I would have some difficulty and I'm much bigger and stronger than she is. I don't want her to go out there alone. "Does he want to get back with you?"

"I don't know." She squeezed my hands. "Will you go with me?"

"When?"

"I told Mrs. Hadley I'd come out Monday at one o'clock."

I nodded, "I've got Monday free. Okay."

"Nothing planned with Jenny?"

"Come on, Megan. I'm still working for Mrs. Kincaid. I can't help seeing Jenny. We're taking a load of yard debris to the planned burn tomorrow."

Chapter 17

Ready to change the topic, I got up from the swing and said, "Do you want Suzy to stay with you again tonight?"

"Not really, but nothing has happened during the last few nights, except I have to let her out early to pee. She wakes me up so she can go, but she's a good companion. Did you know she can do several tricks?"

"Like what?"

"She can play dead, roll over, shake hands and bark on command. She's fun to play with."

"Do you think she'd bite prowlers?"

Meg grinned, "I doubt it, she's very low key; kind of like us."

I reached out to Megan's hands, pulled her to her feet and gave her a good night kiss. "Have a good night. Your parents will be back tomorrow, right?"

Megan laughed and said, "Yep. They should be home about three o'clock in the afternoon."

"You won't feel alone any longer."

"Funny, I haven't felt alone while they've been gone. Knowing you, my bio-dad and a police dog, my little protection squad, were just next door was a comforting feeling."

"One more year and all that will change, Meg."

"I know." She nodded, smiled briefly, turned to go inside, "Good night, David."

I waited for Megan to enter the house, turn off the porchlight and lock the door before I went to my garage to put a pitchfork, tarp, and some tie-downs in a pile on the floor. That was all I needed to take to the Kincaids' tomorrow. I thought the debris burning by the fire department would only take about an hour. Afterwards, Jenny and Mrs. Kincaid could tell me what else I needed to do for them. If they want me to paint the house, that would be the only big job I could do before finding some new clients.

I was going to miss seeing Jenny every day. She's smart and fun to be around, plus she is great eye candy. I had to admit I'd be jealous if Jenny finds a boyfriend this fall. I had two more summer months before that might happen. Hopefully I'd figure it out by football season, or I wouldn't be able to concentrate on the game. I decided I'd better go to bed; my thoughts were muddled like a bunch of tumbleweeds blowing across a barren field. I've never been so confused about girls, with no resolution in sight.

Scott didn't have to be at work until ten o'clock, so he took time to make breakfast. I like my bacon well done, so had him serve it last; it was really crispy, just like I wanted. I don't remember if my real dad was a good cook, but Scott is great. I can't believe the FBI has a cooking class; he must have learned somewhere else. I think mom is relieved when he takes over for her. We all are hoping the baby comes soon so we can resume somewhat normal lives. Mom is so miserable; I think this will be her last baby.

Scott left for the office where Ginny Gumble, his secretary, was coming in for paperwork concerning Whitmore's death. She didn't normally come in on Saturday, but she also had to make reservations for the real investigator en route.

I made enough lunch for two, loaded my equipment in the Subaru and started for the Kincaids'. I had only travelled two blocks when I saw George Chase, another football player, jogging down the road. He lived on the other side of town and I wondered why he was so far from home. I beeped my horn and pulled over to talk.

"Jesus, Drum, you scared the shit out of me."

"Sorry, Chaser, you getting your legs ready for football? Isn't it a little too soon?"

"I want to be a running back instead of wide receiver this year. I'm working on my legs in the morning and arms in the afternoon. The coach gave me some exercises and diet suggestions to help me build my strength and put on some muscle. Where are you headed?"

"Kincaids'. I've been helping Mrs. Kincaid and her granddaughter clean up the place."

"That's the new chick, Ginny?"

"Name's Jenny, not Ginny, Chaser."

"I heard she's prime real estate but broke her arm; kind of a klutz?"

"Broken collarbone; she fell off her porch; an accident. She's not clumsy. Better stay away from her, Chaser, she's a city girl and too smart for you." I grinned.

"You bone her yet?"

I frowned and said, "You kidding me? I just met her a few days ago and she's got a broken collarbone."

"You still with Megan?"

"Yeah. We discovered a dead man yesterday. It'll be in the paper. I've got to go. Keep up the strength work, we'll need a big running back this year. Gary graduated."

"Okay, Drum. Stay out of trouble with those women, okay?" He winked and wiggled his tongue.

I've always known he was a bit of a crude bastard. All he ever talks about is sex and football and I doubt if he's ever thought about going to college or any future after high school. That was a conversation I could have done without. "See yah, Chaser." I stepped on the gas and continued to the Kincaids'.

As I approached the property, I saw Jenny and Mrs. Kincaid raking weeds into small piles. Jenny was trying to use a rake with one hand. I doubted she had accomplished much, but she was trying, that's what counted. I parked behind the Kincaids' pickup, not far from Jenny.

"Hey, ladies, I can do that." I stepped out of the Subaru and walked over to Jenny. "Good morning."

She smiled and said, "Good morning, you're late."

"I don't think so." I glanced at my watch. I wasn't late.

Jenny laughed. "Got you!"

"You scared me for a second. I stopped and talked to a friend on the way over."

"Who was that, a girl?"

"Nope, a guy, named George Chase. Everybody calls him Chaser."

"Close friend?"

I shook my head. "No, more of an acquaintance than a friend. We play ball together."

"Someone I should get to know?"

"I can't recommend him, Jenny. At best, he's a C student and has two things on his mind; not at the same time, football and sex."

"Hm. Sounds like someone I should get to know." She smiled.

"I heard that, Jenny!" Mrs. Kincaid yelled.

"Just kidding, grandma." Jenny laughed.

I responded, "I hope so. There are several guys you should stay away from. I'll clue you in before classes start." I changed the subject, "Does the truck start?"

Jenny nodded, "I started it when I got up. I ran it for about ten minutes so it should be fine."

"When you got up? You mean thirty minutes ago? Did you come out here in your jammies?" I smiled, expecting her to throw something at me but she ignored my comment. I got the pitchfork out of my car and checked to see if the pickup bed was clear. It was. I noticed a spare tire was resting against the porch. She must have shoved it out of the pickup and rolled it over there; neither of them could have picked it up.

I started tossing clumps of weeds and grass toward the truck and when the piles were more than a few yards from the pickup, I asked, "Do you have the keys?"

"I left the key in the ignition. Can you drive a stick shift?"

I had to laugh. She knew I could drive just about anything. We had talked about that the first day I came out here. I climbed in, started the pickup and backed up about the length of the truck closer to the debris. The front yard wasn't very hard to clean up, but the back yard was the location of most of the downed grass, weeds, and small chunks of wood from dismantling the windmill. It was a real mess.

I inspected the path I was going to take to the backyard. No sense in puncturing a tire. I didn't see any more turtles or doves, so I drove the truck around back and parked in the middle of the yard, easy access to all the trash. Jenny had gotten in the front seat and she laughed when I drove the pickup, I'm not sure why.

"Why did you laugh when we drove around from the front?"

"When we first met, I had imagined going on a trip with you to see a fire lookout tower, so driving about thirty yards was not what I had been thinking. I just thought it was funny; you know, how things turn out differently."

"Don't worry, Jenny. We'll go to one of the towers before long; after your broken bone has healed. We'll hike in so you'll need both arms to keep your balance. Do you have a camera?"

"Not here in Suddenly but I can borrow grandma's. She has several cameras; one of them uses rolls of film, can you imagine that?"

I grinned, "That's really old time."

I spread the tarp on the ground near the largest pile of debris and forked the rubble onto it, transferred the material to the pickup and repeated the process half a dozen times until the bed was overflowing. I covered the loaded bed with the tarp and lashed it down so we wouldn't leave a trail of trash leading from the farmhouse to the burn site. No use in getting a citation from the sheriff for littering. That would be a little embarrassing.

Jenny watched from the cab and when I climbed back in the driver's seat, she asked, "Can we deliver this now? I'd like to get it over with."

I smiled and said, "What? You mean you don't like my company?"

"That's not what I meant." She giggled. "I just don't want to be hanging around a bunch of firemen watching trash burn. Isn't it about the same as watching paint dry?"

"So, what, you really mean that you want me all to yourself?" When that came out of my mouth, I realized my trap had opened before my brain had functioned. I tried to cover up. "I mean you don't like crowds when you have your arm in a sling; it causes too many questions, like who's the chick with the broken wing that's with David? Where's Megan?"

Jenny frowned, "Let's get this junk to the burn site. I'd like this over with."

"You don't need to come along. It's not very exciting; kind of like you said, watching paint dry." I grinned.

"David, please shut up and drive to the burn site."

"Okay, boss."

Chapter 18

I t took about ten minutes to get to the designated burn area. Located at the far edge of a gravel parking lot adjacent to the waterpark, we joined a queue of trucks and trailers, some with overflowing debris. There was a fire truck and a small CASE front-loader present with about half-a-dozen volunteer firemen helping to unload trash and direct traffic at the yearly event.

There were three small piles forming a triangle. One fireman motioned for me to back the pickup to the center heap. As soon as I cut the engine, a volunteer began untying the tarp while another walked toward the truck carrying a broom and pitchfork. I went to the back, dropped the tailgate and fished my pitchfork out of the rubble.

Two of us unloaded in less than five minutes. A guy with a broom tossed it to me and I swept out the truck bed.

I shook hands with the closest volunteer, got back in the cab, and drove away as another pickup loaded with tree branches and leaves took our place. I glanced at Jenny, grinned and said, "Want to stay for the burning? You'll love it. The fire is massive."

"Do you have marshmallows?"

I laughed and said. "No, but I brought my lunch. I didn't know how long this was going to take."

Jenny looked around the cab. "I don't see any lunch."

"It's under the seat, enough for two. I have an idea. Would you like to see one of the towers?"

She grabbed my right arm. "That sounds awesome. How far is

it? Will we have to hike in like you said?"

"Not the one I'm thinking of; the road leads right to it. It's about ten miles from here. There are just over forty steps to the top. Think you can do it, or do you even want to?"

She raised her eyebrows and grinned. "Yeah, I want'a go. We'll climb to the top and have the lunch you made. We can vomit from the top." That was the first display of enthusiasm Jenny had shown today. I think she was so used to being in a big city where there was always something to do, she had grown tired of helping grandma clean the house and watching me clean up the yard. The windmill crashing to the ground was the only excitement she had experienced in the last week and that was over in a few seconds. Jenny wanted to have some physical activity in spite of having to deal with her broken collarbone.

I thought I should tell Mom where we were going so, I drove home and left the truck idling in the driveway while I ran inside for about ten seconds.

When I returned to the truck, Jenny had my plastic lunch box in her lap. "Getting hungry?"

"Not yet. I was going to open it and see if it was still edible. I was curious to see if the bread had turned black or had green mold on it."

I laughed as I backed onto the street and turned the steering wheel counterclockwise. I snickered, "Don't worry, the sandwiches aren't more than a week old, besides a little mold never killed anyone."

Jenny smiled but didn't reply. I think she finally realized I was going to have a comeback to nearly anything she said to tease me. When we crossed the city limits, I announced, "Eight miles to our destination. It will appear on our left. Tower seventeen is thirty-four feet high with forty-eight steps to the observation level."

"You sound like a tour guide."

I grinned, "I do my best work in the forests."

I had forgotten to check the gas gauge before leaving town, luckily a quick glance showed we had plenty of fuel, over half a tank.

We were alone on the road and left a dust cloud behind us despite travelling only twenty-five miles per hour. Jenny lowered her window and stuck her head out and looked skyward.

"What are you doing?"

"Looking at the skyscrapers. This reminds me of narrow downtown city streets, but the buildings are made of wood and are all alive and green; it's beautiful! It smells so good!"

"It's even better after it rains. The colors are even brighter, and the odors are stronger; the forest has a clean smell, no garbage or exhaust fumes."

We drove on for another two miles before Jenny suddenly leaned forward toward the windshield and pointed. "What is that!"

Ahead of us a large bird had swooped down and grabbed a small animal, rose into the air, and disappeared high into the trees. It was carrying dinner in its talons.

"That was a small eagle or a large hawk carrying a squirrel or a baby rabbit; I couldn't tell what it was going to have for dinner."

"That's kind of gross, isn't it?"

"Not really; wait until you see the carcass of a deer that has been killed by a bear. You'll remember that for the rest of your life. It's the way of the wild. I imagine it's quite different than seeing someone shot in the streets."

Jenny sat back and remained silent for the last ten minutes of the drive. I couldn't imagine what she was thinking, but I was pretty sure she was disturbed with the idea of animals killing other animals for food. I slowed the truck as we came around the last bend where the tower jutted above the trees on our left. It was built on a rock outcropping and occupied the center of a relatively clear area about an acre in size.

As I coasted to a stop, Jenny exclaimed, "Oh, my gosh! Can we actually climb to the top?"

"Yes ma'am, that's the plan. Don't drop our lunch; the only thing up there to eat is probably peanut butter. Maybe I'd better carry it; you only have one arm for balance. Make sure to hold onto the railings."

We exited the cab and she handed me the lunch container. As we began walking toward the tower, I tried to pick our way so Jenny wouldn't trip or otherwise lose her balance. Fortunately, the path was fairly clear of debris except for a few small branches and pinecones. The going was relatively easy; we quickly reached the tower, Jenny clearly in awe of the imposing structure.

The first few tower steps had been replaced; the old steps at ground level had decayed and had become a problem. I remembered stepping over a rotted one the year before. Mom must have had the renovation squad out here last fall before the weather got nasty.

We climbed twenty-five steps and had only reached the third landing when I could hear Jenny breathing hard. I stopped to give her a chance to catch her breath and look around.

"What are you stopping for?"

I thought I was doing her a favor but when I looked at her, she had a frown on her pretty face. She seemed to be enjoying the challenge the climb offered.

"I thought you might need a breather."

"Hey, I'm no pansy; keep moving, we'll get a breather when we reach the top."

I smiled, turned and started up the third flight; Jenny stayed right on my heels two steps behind. When I reached the platform at the top, she had fallen two more steps behind. Smiling, she was using her right arm to pull on the railing. Her legs were getting tired, but I had to give her credit; she wasn't as out of shape as I thought. I wondered how sore she'd be when she got out of bed in the morning.

I didn't enter the cabin, instead I set the lunch container near the door and watched Jenny test the top railing with a little tug. Finding it solidly constructed, she leaned over the guardrail, looked straight down and took a deep breath.

"I love it!" She turned toward me and breathlessly exclaimed, "Thank you for bringing me here. This is awesome! It's much better than being on the roof of a four-story building in the city. It's so quiet! No horns, no noises from engines or garbage trucks, the el, or people yelling. I think I could let my imagination take complete control and sketch for hours without interruption. David, this is what heaven must be like."

She began touring the platform, looking at the trees and sky, ignoring the cabin and observation room. I let her complete the stroll alone to experience the solitude and the beauty of the forest in her own way, without my intervention. She rejoined me at the railing opposite the entrance door.

"Now, show me what's inside."

Assuming the interior was organized and clean, I was severely disappointed when I opened the door and stepped inside. The place was a total mess. I held my breath as I looked for the alidade but couldn't see it anywhere. Had someone taken the smoke sighting apparatus?

Jenny was right behind me and when her eyes adjusted, she exclaimed, "Oh, David! What happened?" She had never seen the interior before but recognized the destruction immediately.

The two beds were tossed sidewise and upside down with one of the legs missing. The alidade mounting table was tipped over and displaced against the east wall, its drawers removed and broken apart, making them useless. I stood there scratching my head in amazement; why would anyone do this?

I moved to the cupboards beside the gas stove and cautiously opened the wall cabinet in front of me. It was empty; the shelves missing. Bitch was spray painted in yellow across the windowless northern wall. It faced the nearby trees that jutted over the height of the tower.

"Son of a bitch! Someone has totaled this place. It was left in rent-ready condition last fall. Mom is really going to be pissed off."

"Maybe we can fix some of it. My grandpa's tools might help. Don't tell your mom, she'll get upset and with the baby coming, she doesn't need to know. In a couple of weeks, my arm will be useful again and I can help. I can remake the drawers and paint while you work on the tougher jobs. What do you think?"

"I don't know, Jen. This is really bad. It will take us all summer to do it and I have to earn money for college next year. And then there's the search for the diamonds. You've made the nicest offer, though. Thank you." I dropped to the floor and just sat there disappointed.

Jenny came over with the lunch container and sat down beside me. "Let's eat something and then straighten up a little. Okay?"

I couldn't say anything, but I looked at her and nodded. I popped open the plastic container, laid out a napkin for each of us, and let Jenny choose which of the four sandwiches she wanted. The food was sealed in plastic bags so she couldn't give them a smell test. She was clever though and carefully separated the slices of bread without opening the packages. She chose one that contained bologna and dill pickles. I watched her open the plastic bag and take a bite.

"Umm, I love dill pickles. It's been weeks since I had any."

I laughed and grabbed one for myself; the other two were peanut butter and jelly.

When we had eaten and wiped crumbs from our clothing, we got up and did a complete survey of all the damage. After I had gotten the few pieces of furniture righted and placed in normal positions, I began to open all the cabinets looking for the alidade. I found the pieces and reassembled it where it had been previously located. Jenny was sweeping up when I finally finished the repair. She put down the broom and asked, "How does that thing work, anyway?"

"Come over here, I'll show you."

I fixed the sighting mechanism and realigned the compass readings as best I could. The binoculars were missing, but there was a small telescope available that was not damaged.

I gave Jenny the scope and pointed to the tallest trees on a ridge about two to three miles almost directly south. "Focus on those trees sticking up on the horizon where I'm pointing. Pick the tallest one." I waited for a few seconds until she replied.

"Okay. Now what?"

"Now, crouch down and align the directional circle on that tree. You can use the telescope to find the tree if you need it."

She squinted and rotated the circle until the sight lined up. She stood up and said, "What's next?"

"Write down the compass reading from the circle and call in the smoke sighting."

"That's it? I mean is that all there is to it?" She put the telescope down on the alidade and said, "Where's the phone?"

"It's supposed to be over there inside the wall cabinet to the right of the stove. It's been pulled out of the wall here and tossed over in the corner. See the broken wires?" I pointed to the wires sticking out of the floor by the base of the alidade table.

"How do we report smoke, David? Look out there, a little to the right of those trees we were focusing on."

I picked up the scope and scanned the area she described. Sure enough, there was a thin trail of smoke rising from the trees about five degrees from the alidade's current position. I wished I had a cell phone, but the cost was prohibitive. Mom's cell was for her job, funded by the Rangers.

"Damn! We don't have a working phone. Hopefully the satellite images will show it and a crew will be sent out soon. I wish I had some tools; I could fix the phone. All I have is my pocketknife." I pulled it out of my pocket and laid it on the alidade table.

"What do you need? There's a tool kit in the glove compartment."

"A pair pf pliers would do."

"I've got pliers in my kit. Hurry. Go get them! Bring the whole kit!"

I was already out the door when she said pliers were in her truck. I took two steps at a time going down, being careful to avoid tripping. Making record time, I found the box and raced back up the tower. Jenny was aligning the alidade on the smoke and writing down the direction when I got back.

I got the phone and checked the wires dangling from the handset. The four colored small gauge wires were broken off at different lengths with the insulation stretched but curled away from the wires. My pocketknife allowed a clean cut to the wires so I could strip back the insulation and twist the exposed wires to their like colored mates from the floor connection. I didn't know how to dial the regional fire center; Mom had never told Danny or me how to do it.

"Jenny, do you see a number to dial anywhere?" We both searched the tops of all the surfaces but couldn't see anything that made sense. I stood there holding the phone up to my ear and heard a normal dial tone hum.

"Here's something, David!" Jenny had discovered a number on the wall next to the phone connection box to the outside wires. "Nine-nine-one-seven is scratched in the paint. Try it!"

Chapter 19

I punched in the numbers on the keypad and was surprised by an almost immediate answer.

"Bitterroot Regional Fire Center. What do you have, tower seventeen?"

"Smoke about five degrees east of due south; about two to three miles distant."

"Right. Who is reporting?"

"David Drum at tower seventeen. Just visiting today."

"Thanks David. We've got a drone in the area. We'll check it out. Tell your mother hello for me. This is Ranger Lyle Conner. Out."

I turned and looked at Jenny, "I guess that's it. We'd better get back to your house; your grandmother will be wondering where we are."

"I guess so, but I hate to leave this place in such a mess. I bet your mom would be shocked at the destruction." Glancing back at the tendril of smoke, she mused, who would have thought this would be so exciting?

We had only driven a mile or so toward Suddenly when Jenny had an idea, "Could we come out in the mornings and work on the lookout accommodations? Say from eight to twelve? You would still have afternoons for your job."

I pulled over and stopped the pickup, sat there for a moment looking at Jenny. "You're serious, aren't you?"

She nodded, "Uh-huh. Grandma never has anything for me to do in the mornings. She says it's too cold to work outside; we should wait 'til afternoon. I have the whole morning free, David, and I'd like to help. I didn't think I would like the forest, but I really enjoy being out here. It's like another world."

"I like your idea. Should we tell your grandmother what we're doing?"

"I don't see why not. She won't tell anyone, especially if we tell her we don't want your mom to know." Jenny grinned, "She's always saying that the people she used to know in Suddenly have either moved away or are six-feet under. That's why she wanted to meet your mom, to see someone new."

I was enthusiastic now that Jenny wanted to help me rebuild the interior of lookout seventeen.

"When we get to your house, let's make a list of things we'll need to start the tower repairs, if it's all right with your grandma. Do you go to church?"

"Nah, only if I attend weddings or funerals when they're held in a church.

Nobody in my family is very religious, but we are respectful of those that are."

"Same here, but that might change shortly; mom will want to have the baby baptized. After that, I don't know."

"You want it to be a boy, don't you?"

"Yeah, but I think mom wants a girl. She's outnumbered three to one."

"Has she said?"

I chuckled, "She hasn't said much but once referred to the baby as a she. And mom seems to like pink better than blue."

Mrs. Kincaid was sitting in her wicker rocker reading a book when we pulled into the driveway. She promptly stood, closed the book and tossed it in the chair. "Where did you go, girl? I thought you'd be back an hour ago."

I volunteered, "We drove out to one of the fire lookout towers and had lunch. Jenny noticed smoke and we called it in, but a situation came up. So, we have a question for you."

"What have you two gotten into, something questionable?"

Our delayed return seemed to have caused Mrs. Kincaid to become suspicious. I wondered if Jenny had gotten out of control when living with her parents in the city. I imagined she was about to ground Jenny for some rotten behavior, but how could coming home a little late generate a problem. Jenny had never confided in me about her city life. I couldn't believe she would do anything bad; she was too smart.

I looked at Jenny. "You want to tell her?"

She moved closer to her grandmother. "Someone trashed the inside of the lookout tower and we want to fix it. David and I want to work on it in the mornings next week, but I wanted to ask if it was all right with you. We'd need to use some of grandpa's tools."

Mrs. Kincaid relaxed a bit but stood there looking at us, finally asking, "David, doesn't the forest service have repair crews for that? Can't your mother call them in?"

I didn't have to think much to answer. "Well, the crews are involved in forest fire watch and fire fighting now. The repairmen that work on the towers do that stuff in the early fall before the bad weather. I really don't want to tell my mom about the vandalism; she doesn't need anything to worry about but have the baby. It shouldn't take more than a week or two to fix things."

"But look at her, she's only got one good arm. What can she do?"

"I know her handicap, but she can paint, make plans for the repairs, and boss me around." I glanced at Jenny and winked. "Also, she's stronger than you think."

"Well, it's okay with me, but I'm not getting up to cook for you, girl. You'll have to get your own breakfast."

Jenny gave her grandma a hug and said, "Thanks, Grandma. I'll help you in the afternoons."

"Thank you, Mrs. Kincaid. Remember, if you want the house painted, I'll do that as soon as we finish with the tower and I'll inspect your roof. You don't want any leaks during the winter months; if you recall, we get about three feet of snow here in December and January."

"Thank you, David. Give me a bill for the work you've already done, and I'll write you a check."

"I'll do that, but I won't charge you for the time I spent searching for diamonds. I'll get a finder's fee for those. That's enough."

Jenny walked me to my car, and I told her I'd see her at eight o'clock sharp Monday. She replied, "I really enjoyed our forest adventure. I'll be ready Monday. See ya." She turned back towards the house and I watched her walk away. Sighing, I slowly drove off.

When I got home, I found that mom hadn't just laid around reading while I was at tower seventeen. She had prepared a list of chores to keep me busy most of the afternoon. The jobs were mostly outside so I started at the top: mowing, weeding, fertilizing, and cleaning the garage. Danny joined me and we organized the garage together. Fortunately, we worked together with positive results; the cleanup took only a half-hour.

After dinner I went to my room to make a list of things Jenny and I would need Monday. I had hammers, saws, nails and a half-gallon of light-blue paint, but no brush. I remembered seeing paint brushes in her grandfather's tool drawers, so that was not a problem; I made some notes for items at her house I hoped she could use. Exhausted from the busy day, I went to bed early.

Sunday started slowly with a relaxed breakfast. Afterwards, mom and Scott went to the living room to read the paper and watch TV. About eleven o'clock, mom yelled at Scott, who was out in the backyard with Danny and me tossing a football around. We thought she wanted one of us to get her something. She had been lying down on the sofa reading, as usual, but Scott sensed her call was more urgent than usual. He went inside and a few seconds later, yelled at me to start the Subaru. I knew then we were going to the hospital.

By a quarter after two in the afternoon, I had a baby sister: eight pounds, six and one-half ounces.

When Scott came to the waiting room and informed us of the good news, we had a three-way hug. "Your mom and baby are doing fine. Why don't you guys go home and order pizza? I'll be by later. I'm going to stay with the ladies a bit longer."

Nurse Berg drifted into the waiting area and told us mom was going to stay overnight, just to make sure everything was stabilized. We could see her and the baby in the morning. Danny and I headed for the exit knowing pizza for dinner would ensure we wouldn't have any failed cooking experiments. Scott had asked us to pick him up about eight o'clock. He'd grab something to eat at the commissary.

As we pulled into the driveway, I saw Megan crossing our front lawn. She waited for me on the porch.

I walked across the grass to see what she had in mind and she said, "I think I know where you guys were; was it a boy or girl?"

"Yeah, we were at the hospital. Mom had the baby; about eight and a half pounds, twenty-one inches long."

"Well?"

"Well, what?"

"Geez, David. Is the baby a girl or a boy?"

"Oh!" I grinned, "It's a girl. You, Danny and I have a sister."

Megan chuckled. "That's awesome. Call me when you have to change her diapers. I'll show you how to change a girl."

"Come on, Meg. The pee and poop come out of the same places for boys and girls. I'm not that dumb."

"But there's a difference, David. Your mom will probably show you what to do."

Danny yelled that he was going in the back door and order pizza. Megan and I sat down on the cold concrete porch but quickly stood back up to avoid shivering.

"I came over was to ask about the baby and check about tomorrow. Will you be going with me to see Rick? You promised, you know."

"No problem, I'll be back here by noon."

"Back from where?"

"Jenny and I are working on a project in the mornings for the next couple of weeks."

"So, what's the project?" Megan gave me a frown that bothered me. I wanted to tell her, but if the nurses found out, anything unrelated to medicine would spread like the news of the sinking of the Titanic.

I grinned and pointed my right hand at her like I was holding a gun. "If I told you, I'd have to kill you."

"You don't trust me?"

"No, that's not it and it's not a secret. I don't trust the people you work with. Look, Meg, I need some time to solve a problem. I'll tell you about it in a couple of weeks; I'll even show you. Just let it go, okay?"

"Does Danny know about it?"

"Nope. Stop it Megan." I shook my head from side to side. "Look, it's not even a big deal to you. You'll be disappointed when you find out." I changed the subject, "Do your folks get home tonight?"

"Uh-huh. They called last night and said they would be back about seven o'clock, driving a new car."

"Really? What kind?"

"I can't tell you. Word would get around. You know how things like that spread throughout the whole town; probably overnight. People would start driving past our house to see the car and the sheriff would have to deal with traffic problems."

I started laughing. Megan smiled, and joined me with her regular giggle. Her trap had partly worked. "Did they really get a new car?"

"No. Before they left, Father mentioned that we'd probably get a new car next year. He's saving so he can pay cash. He's kind of funny that way, a banker that hates to pay interest on loans."

"He's a smart man, Meg. He lives within his means; something to remember. But think about it, if he pays for your college tuition, will there really be a new car? Maybe you can lessen the burden and earn some money by babysitting or something like that. Mom might need you for that and you're right next door."

Megan didn't say anything, but she checked her watch and looked at her house.

"I'd better go home and make sure everything is cleaned up. They'll be tired from travelling and will want to relax." She glanced back at me, "Tomorrow at one o'clock?"

"I'll be ready. I'm curious to see how Rick has progressed in the last year after that logging accident. I hope he hasn't wasted away." I've never been one of Rick's fans, but I can't deny being jealous when he was dating Megan. But now that he needs help to regain some of his former physical strength, I kind of felt sorry for him. I wonder why he hadn't developed the kind of mental toughness his father has.

I loaded the back of the Subaru before I went to bed, I hoping I hadn't forgotten anything. I'd see what tools Jenny had ready to load in the morning. I had a hard time falling asleep, thinking about all the work at the tower. I couldn't understand why anyone would trash the tower. I wished I had been there.

I got up at seven, dressed, ate a large breakfast, and pulled on a jacket. The thermometer outside the kitchen window read fifty-eight degrees. As I backed out into the street, I saw the Isaacs' car in their driveway. Meg's parents had returned. They must have arrived late after I had dozed off; I hadn't heard anything from next door last night and neither Suzy nor Spectrum had stirred. I was relieved that Meg wouldn't be home alone any longer.

Jenny was sitting in the rocker on the porch when I arrived at the Kincaids'. I could see a pile of tools and a few pieces of wood that looked as if they were enough to remake the kitchen drawers. She looked ready for work; a sweatshirt was stretched over her sling; the empty sleeve was rolled up and safety pinned at her shoulder. It reminded me to make sure she didn't overdo it.

"Right on time, David!" Jenny stood and waited for me to meet her on the porch.

"Shh! You'll wake your grandmother."

"Nope. She's in there snoring like a dead whale."

I started laughing, "That makes no sense."

Jenny grinned, "I know, but you get the idea." She looked at the things she had assembled and said, "Let's get this stuff loaded and get to the tower. I think the mornings are going to go very fast."

"Yes, ma'am." I noticed she had included a wide paint brush.

Ten minutes later we were on the dirt road to tower seventeen, a rooster tail of dust kicking up behind us; the light headwind assisting to disperse the churned-up particles into the air.

Chapter 20

I backed the Subaru as close to the tower as possible and opened the cargo door. Two toolboxes lugged me down and Jenny carried a canvas bag of lighter supplies we thought we could put to immediate use. The twenty-pound toolboxes were becoming a slight burden to my legs and lengthening my arms when we reached the bottom of the fourth flight of stairs, and I counted each step off to the top. I was grateful to set the boxes down next to the cabin door.

Jenny stepped ahead of me and entered the observation door. She gasped, "David! Someone has been here again." She was standing in the doorway but dropped the bag and backed away from the door so I could see. "There's more damage!"

I stepped inside and couldn't believe what I saw. "Shit!" The alidade table was tipped over and the direction circle was broken in half and tossed into the kitchen area. The gas stove was tipped over, but fortunately the gas line was still closed. Whoever had done the damage did not want to burn the tower to the ground and possibly start a forest fire. More spray painting was on the wall; it said GoTchA.

Jenny came in after me and put her hand on my shoulder. "What are we going to do?"

"I wish Scott had jurisdiction here, but this is under ranger control. The man in charge while mom is off duty is working with the fire control people this month. He won't come out here for this. We'll fix what we can this morning, and I'll stay here tonight. I'm going to catch whoever did this. Boy, I sure hope they come back."

"You can't stay here alone, David. If there are two of them, you'll be at a big disadvantage. What if they're armed?"

"Oh, I won't be here alone. Spectrum and Suzy will be with me and I'll have Scott come out at midnight to check on me. Someone is going to get a dog bite. A hammer can be a good weapon, too. If they don't come back tonight, I'll stay every night until they return." I thought the culprits probably were kids and they wouldn't have guns.

Jenny started cleaning up the place as we had done previously, and I brought in the toolboxes. I gradually cooled down from the disgust as we got to work. By the time we left, Jenny had painted the wall to hide the graffiti, and I had rebuilt three of the cabinet drawers and replaced all the wall cabinet shelves along the northern wall. We were originally going to leave the tools, but we were afraid they might be stolen or used to inflict further damage, so we took them with us. I had a much easier job carrying the boxes down the tower stairs than going up; gravity was helping out.

Jenny and I talked about my staying in the tower over night and I convinced her that there was no problem, even though I did have a slight concern for my safety. The person I would have to obtain clearance from was mom. I was pretty sure Scott would think my sleeping in the tower at night was not a problem, especially since I would be accompanied by the two dogs; Spectrum was trained to fight.

When I let Jenny off, she took her time getting out of the car, hesitating after she opened the door.

"I'll see you in the morning. Be careful; don't get hurt being dumb. Do you have a gun?"

"I've got a twenty-two, but I couldn't shoot anyone. I wouldn't be fearful of losing my life. I have to obey the law; the gun stays home. Bye, Jenny. See you at eight o'clock; don't be late," I grinned. She slammed the passenger door and laughed.

On the way home I considered having a slingshot with me for a long distance weapon, but I dismissed the idea. Mom would think I was worried and needed a weapon.

Danny and I had lunch together and I told him about the tower seventeen damage.

He was just as mad as I had been and said he would try to find out from his friends if they heard of anybody screwing around. I told him not to let anyone know what had happened and he swore to secrecy. He would be careful when investigating.

At ten 'til one, I went over to the Isaacs' and asked Meg's mom about their trip to St. Louis. She tried to sound enthusiastic, explaining how much she enjoyed the trip, but I didn't buy it, she seemed disappointed. Just as Megan joined us in the living room, Mrs. Isaacs said, "Bruce was very busy most of the time, but we enjoyed the concluding party Saturday evening. I got a little tipsy." She giggled and continued, "I'm happy Megan was being looked after while we were gone. Thank you."

"You're welcome, but it was quiet over here; Scott didn't have to break up a wild party." I grinned but stopped making more jokes. "She probably told you she had Suzy for company." I watched Megan and she nodded affirmatively and moved towards the door.

"Are you ready to go? Mom will talk your leg off if you let her."

"You guys go ahead; I've got things to do here. We're out of a lot of groceries." She got up and disappeared into the kitchen.

"Are we taking your jeep?"

"Why not? I can show you my driving skills. I've mastered the clutch."

I wasn't sure which of us was more nervous about seeing Rick; it had been over a year since the logging chain broke and mangled his legs. The last time I saw him he was sitting with his new girlfriend, Donna Givens, both in wheelchairs. That was a year ago. Recently, she had recovered from her motorcycle injuries and gone back to her family's ranch near Cheyenne.

Mrs. Hadley had called Megan and had brought her up to date on Donna's departure. Following five weeks of strength training after regaining her ability to walk on her own, she called her father and he came to pick her up, unbeknownst to the Hadleys.

Mrs. Hadley met us when we parked at the Hadley's residence, a large log cabin built from timber Mr. Hadley had harvested from their property.

"I'm so glad you came, Megan, and you too, David." She quickly embraced us in greeting. "It'll mean a lot to Rick having you here." She squeezed Megan's hands. "He's always been so fond of you. This will help him, I'm sure."

The three of us slowly went toward the house, Mrs. Hadley clearly wanting to quickly chat before Rick could hear voices. "I had never seen Rick cry since he was a little boy, but when Donna told Rick she was leaving, he stayed inside and sobbed. Donna told him he wasn't trying hard enough. It wasn't what they agreed to. He had to want it for himself, not for her. She said she was sorry. Good luck. Rick went to his room and didn't say goodbye."

In the house we were ushered into the living room. Rick was nowhere to be seen. "I was furious with her for abandoning him, but over the past few weeks, I've begun to understand. Depression after the accident has been crippling for him. Most mornings, when I wake up, I wonder if he survived another night." She looked out the window, but her eyes didn't seem to focus on anything.

"I'm glad you called us. We'll see what we can do." Megan gave me a weak smile.

Mrs. Hadley reached out, patted Megan's hand and almost whispered, "Rick doesn't know you're here. I'll get him." She left us and went down the long hallway. We could hear a door open and close. A minute passed, then two and the door opened. We heard Rick's angry voice.

"Tell them to go away. I don't want to see them!"

"But Rick, they just want to say hello."

The door closed and we heard footsteps approaching. Mrs. Hadley came back in sight and sat down with us. "Rick doesn't seem to be feeling well."

Megan leaned forward and touched Mrs. Hadley's hand. "We heard what he said but tell him I have something very important that I think he'll want to hear. I've been keeping something from him for a long time; more than a year. I need to tell him."

I looked at Megan quizzically and asked, "Some kind of secret? Something you never told me about?" Megan ignored me, staring at his mom. Apparently, she had been keeping something to herself ever since Rick was injured. Something she had never mentioned, and I had never imagined. I had to wait to find out what it was.

Megan asked, "Can I go to his door?"

Mrs. Hadley nodded, "You can try but he's very obstinate."

Megan turned to me and ordered, "You stay here." She got up and walked down the hallway. I heard a knock and then, "Rick, I need to tell you something. Come to the living room and talk to us. David doesn't even know what it is."

Mrs. Hadley and I heard nothing, and Megan returned. She sat down beside me, placed her hand on my knee, and said, "Rick's coming to talk."

"Oh! Thank you, Megan." Mrs. Hadley dabbed tears with a Kleenex. She confided quietly, "I didn't know how I was going to get him out of that room. He hasn't left but for a few minutes since Donna went home. I've been afraid he might hurt himself."

Rick rolled slowly into the room, stopped about six feet from us and grumbled, "All right, I'm here. What is this secret you're talking about? Something stupid, I'll bet."

Rick looked tired and he had lost a lot of weight, his arms seemed about normal, but his pants looked much too large for his small waist and spindly legs. I didn't know if he had used any leg muscles for months. That had to change, or he would have little chance of walking again. I knew that from being around kids with athletic injuries.

Megan turned directly toward Rick and began, "You know I've been working as a volunteer at the hospital since about the time of your accident. Well, I met an elderly man there named Mr. Ganz. We became friends and he was moved by your story when I told him of your accident. He told me to tell you he would loan you money for your college education. After you graduate, you can repay the loan interest free." She paused to let it sink in.

"I never told you this because I thought you and Donna wouldn't like me meddling in your affairs. But now I think you need something to look forward to and I would like to help. I think you should redouble your efforts to rehab your legs. We can set up a schedule where David and I can come out and make sure you exercise. I don't know if you know this, but rehab is as much mental as physical. You have to retrain your brain as well as your muscles."

We were watching Rick and at first, he had no reaction; nothing to say, no indication that he had even been listening to Megan. Finally, he replied, "I'll think about it." He spun his wheelchair around and rolled quickly down the hall. We heard his door open and then close a moment later.

Mrs. Hadley, a little embarrassed, stood and said, "Wow, what an amazing offer. Thank you so much. Who is Mr. Ganz, Megan?"

"He owns the hospital; he's not only rich, but very generous." Megan smiled, "He owns several hospitals and manufacturing companies in the states, so he can easily assist Rick. Rick no longer needs to have an athletic scholarship to attend college."

Mrs. Hadley escorted us to the door, obviously relieved by our visit. The concerned look had vanished from her face. She stepped outside thanking us for coming to see Rick and talking to her. It was now up to Rick if he wanted our help and the assistance from Mr. Ganz to work for a degree. I felt sorry for Mrs. Hadley. Watching her son waste away must be very tough. She was trying to help Rick but could only do so much. She didn't have but a few options left, maybe only one: calling Megan for help.

On the ride back home, I didn't say much, never having experienced such a defeatist attitude from Rick before. From my perspective, he had always been a leader, a tough guy, a powerful influence on our football team. Now he seemed so angry and broken, lacking the ability to regain even a part of his former stature. But I was comparing him to what I would be doing in his situation, busting my ass to learn to walk again.

"Thank you for coming with me, David. I'm worried about Rick; he was so sullen. I had no idea he was struggling so much. I hope he gets his mind out of the doldrums soon and reclaims his life."

We were about a block from Dairy Queen and I asked Megan, "Would you like a cone?"

"No, thank you. I'm not in a celebratory mood. I have such mixed feelings about what Rick is going through. I just hope he changes direction and asks us to come back, but I'm fearful he can't be helped, mentally, that is." Sighing, she asked, "Will you help me to get him up and walking if he lets us help?"

"Sure, Meg. We'll hope for the best."

The jeep's brakes squeaked when Megan parked in her driveway behind the Isaacs' family car.

"I wonder why my father is home at this hour; he isn't usually here until after four o'clock and that's only when everything at the bank has gone perfectly." Megan headed for the front door at a brisk pace and I started across our front yard.

Parked in our driveway were three cars, the Subaru, a police cruiser and another car I didn't recognize. I wondered if something was wrong. Danny met me at the front door.

"Hey, Mom's home with the baby and Scott's here, too. That other car belongs to two investigators: the real ones this time. They just showed up a few minutes ago. They're gonna stay in the garage apartment. Come on inside, you should meet them."

I followed Danny in the house and, having been forewarned, saw the two strangers on the sofa sitting side by side talking to Scott, who was in the recliner, but upright and leaning forward. I heard him say, "David, my stepson, will fill you in on how the diamonds were discovered." He saw me come in the front door and said, "Here he is now."

Chapter 21

The new, legitimate investigators stood up and Scott introduced us. After the introduction, we sat, and they filled us in on their background. Florinda Moyson and John Moresby met at an Interpol conference in Bern, Switzerland in 2007 and worked with others to break up a drug and diamond conspiracy. That was when they became aware of the decade earlier diamond theft. They worked together as police officers; she from Belgium and he a resident of South Africa. Two years later they married and now they work as insurance investigators.

They were an unlikely couple; Mr. Moresby was about five-eight, blond and wore his hair in a ponytail that hung down to his shoulders; his wife was nearly six-feet tall with an olive complexion and short reddish-brown hair. They both looked like they had gym memberships. I wondered how they were ever drawn to one another. I thought their different accents were interesting.

When Moresby shook hands with me, I felt the strength in his forearm and thought he must lift weights to have a grip that strong. I was guessing at his age, about forty-five, whereas his wife appeared to be about ten years younger. I was surprised to find out she was two years older than he was. I have always had difficulty estimating the age of a woman, and I decided some time ago that I'd better stop trying.

After shaking hands with Florinda, she said, "It's nice to meet you, David. We have many questions and would like to hear the story from the beginning."

I started with Megan's and my diamond find in the turtle and when I mentioned Whitmore, they were more interested in the reason Whitmore showed up in Suddenly than in the discovery of the diamonds. They listened with rapt attention to the events that led to finding the valuable stones. After I finished, Florinda turned to Scott and asked, "Did Mr. Whitmore have a computer with him?"

"Yes, I've got it locked in the safe at my office. Would you like to look at it today? I'll go get it."

John said, "We'll come with you, if that's all right. We'd like to get set up in an office. I assume you have direct access to the Internet."

Scott reacted quickly, "Yes, we have satellite service; it's very fast." He grinned and said, "We just got connected about three months ago. Up to that time we used smoke signals."

Florinda had a puzzled look and then laughed. "Oh! Are there many Native Americans in this area?"

Scott grinned and replied, "Oh, of course. They don't use bows and arrows anymore; they use guns like ours. The reservation tribes in western Montana are farther north, a couple of hundred miles from here." He noticed both guests were paying close attention to his words. He glanced at me, "Do you think they should be scared, David?"

I started laughing and said, "No, I think they should be more afraid of a person pictured on a wanted poster."

Scott resumed a straight face and continued, "We haven't had an uprising for over a hundred years, folks." He chuckled, "Native Americans are very nice people. I've been joking."

Mr. Moresby smiled and replied, "Sometime you and your family should visit South Africa. I'll show you some of our wildlife, many of which love to chew on human flesh."

Florina gave her husband a stern look, "Careful, John. If you tell them the truth, they might not come to see us."

We all had a good laugh and started toward the front door. Scott, Florinda, and John were leaving to get Whitmore's laptop and inspect all the recovered stones. Florinda wanted to see if Whitmore had any information on his hard drive or in emails about the diamonds.

I decided to stay home and visit with mom and see my baby sister for the first time. The bedroom door was shut, so I tapped gently. If the baby was asleep, I didn't want to wake her.

"Who is it?" Mom asked groggily.

"It's David, Mom. Can I see the baby? Also, I need to talk with you." I had decided to tell mom about tower seventeen and ask her if I could stay there tonight. I figured her permission would be imperative.

"Just a moment, I'm nursing."

I felt a little strange and wasn't sure what to do, so I waited in the hall.

"Okay, you can come in now."

I entered the bedroom slowly and saw mom in bed holding the baby in her arms.

I must have just stood there gawking 'cause mom said, "Come sit on the bed so you can see her tiny fingers and toes."

Her eyes were closed, but she was moving her little fingers making a fist. "She's beautiful, Mom. What's her name?"

"Scott and I named her Gwendolyn Anne Wilson. What do you think?"

"Gwendolyn? She won't be able to spell it until she's a teenager."

"Don't be silly; we'll call her Gwen."

"I think I'll call her Annie. It's crazy, but I'll be a sophomore in college before she'll know my name. I wonder what she'll call me?"

Mom laughed, "Mud?"

I smiled and decided to let her know about the tower. "I have to tell you something. Jenny and I rode out to tower seventeen. She wanted to see what a tower looked like, but I wasn't sure she could climb very many steps, so that was the best one; not very tall and not very far. She loved looking around at the forest. When we went inside the cabin, we found it had been vandalized. It was really torn up."

"Dammit!" She shook her head. "I wonder if any other towers are damaged. Was there any evidence who might have done it?"

"No. We worked on straightening it out, but it needs some carpentry work. Jenny and I want to fix it up and paint the interior. When we went out there this morning, someone had done it again."

"Do you think it was kids?"

I nodded. "That's what I want to talk to you about. I want to stay out there tonight and see if they show up again. I'll catch them in the act."

"I don't want you out there alone, David. Scott can't go out there with you; he's got other things to do here in town."

"I won't be alone, Mom. I want to take Suzy and Spectrum with me. Spectrum is trained to attack if I tell him. Suzy's snarl will slow anybody down. Maybe Scott could come out and check on me; it wouldn't take long."

Mom frowned as she looked at me and was thinking about my request. I was hoping for an affirmative answer when she said, "If you take the dogs and a sleeping bag, all right. You can also take my walkie-talkie so you can call Scott or the hospital."

I had been holding my breath and my lungs collapsed, air escaping through my mouth. Fortunately, I didn't whistle, or I would have scared little Annie. "Thank you, Mom. I want to catch who did the damage. I hope it's someone I know."

"Whoever it is, David, they probably know you. You can threaten them with community service: some form of detention. A ranger will back you up, as well as Scott, but he has no jurisdiction out there. But it's a good threat."

"I probably shouldn't ask you this, but could I take your handgun with me? I don't need any bullets. I couldn't shoot anyone anyway."

She sat there, kind of stunned, I thought. After about ten seconds, "I don't think you should have a firearm, David. The damage is not that sort of crime. A dog bite is probably a severe enough penalty. You don't need to overreact."

"Yeah, I guess you're right. I'll come home in the middle of the night if I catch someone, otherwise, I'll be home for breakfast. Okay?"

"Okay. Just use your common sense. I don't want you to get hurt."

"No problem. I'm gonna get some things ready for the dogs. I'll leave right after dinner." I turned to go, and she stopped me.

"Wait!"

I grabbed the door to stop my momentum and did an about face. "What?"

"There's a cluster of trees about thirty yards farther down the trail; on the right. Park the car behind the trees; no one will ever see it. They'll think the tower is vacant; you can scare them half to death."

"Hey, I like the way you think. Great idea!" I laughed and closed the bedroom door. She was on my side!

Mrs. Moresby volunteered to cook dinner, since mom was resting with baby Gwen and Scott had to talk to the city park committee. After dinner, our guests retired to the apartment over the garage. They balked at first, but Scott suggested they stay nearby to talk with me and have access to our drone surveillance system. They agreed.

I could tell Moresbys were tired from travelling; they were falling asleep at the dinner table. I waited for everyone to disperse before getting ready for my nighttime adventure. I didn't tell anyone where I was going, I left that up to mom.

Danny wasn't around to ask me questions; he was down the street at a friend's house playing a new video game. I packed the Subaru with my needs for the night, herded the dogs into the cargo area and drove to tower seventeen. There was no sign of anyone in the area, so I parked where mom had recommended and carried my gear to the tower top. Fortunately, the energetic dogs followed me, bounding up the flights of stairs.

Inside the cabin, I filled their bowls with food and water and unrolled my sleeping bag in the southwest corner where the floor was clear of debris. Anyone entering the cabin would not notice the sleeping bag until two or three steps into the observation area.

The valleys below were darkening and the temperature was dropping as the sun began to disappear below the far western tree line and the distant mountains. Both Suzy and Spectrum joined me on the sleeping bag, and I sat there petting Suzy with my left hand and Spectrum with my right. They both seemed comfortable, but I wished I had brought a roll of sponge rubber to place underneath the bag. I began hoping someone would show up soon, so I could return home to my comfortable bed for a good night's sleep. I didn't want to be surly in the morning when I met with Jenny.

I must have dozed off for about an hour. I jerked awake when Spectrum whined and got up. He was walking around the cabin; I could hear the clicking of his toenails on the wooden flooring. From the sounds of lapping water, I knew he had gone across the room to get a drink. I pressed the button on my watch and saw the red LED's light up with the time, 8:49. I listened to the forest sounds, but all I heard were some slight rustlings of the trees in the evening breeze.

I talked to the dogs for a few minutes; asking what they thought of the forest nights. They just adjusted their positions on the sleeping bag and curled up against my legs. I could probably sleep in that position; their body heat felt like my electric blanket set on low. I dozed off again but only for a few minutes. I was awakened by the dogs' movement and a slight shaking of the tower. I could hear footsteps; someone was climbing the stairs!

Spectrum began to growl, a low-pitched baritone rumble, as he crept next to the cabin door. Suzy sat up but didn't stand. I hissed, "Quiet!" Loud enough for the dogs to hear, but not with enough volume for the intruder outside to notice. As the footsteps came closer, I realized there were two people.

When they reached the platform, the footsteps halted. I heard a voice, "You and Timmy came up here at midnight?"

I recognized the voice; it was Chaser. "Turn on the light, bro. I can't see shit up here." A flashlight beam illuminated the tower observation windows. "On the deck, dimwit; I need to see where I'm going. You fall from here and you're a dead man."

Chaser's steps came closer to the door and then he hesitated. I had thought I would stick my flashlight in his back and say hands up, but suddenly changed my mind and put my foot out. He tripped as he entered the cabin and fell to the floor.

"Jesus, Gary! You left shit around to trip over."

I flipped the switch on my flashlight and pointed the beam in his face. He put his hands up to shield his eyes and yelled out, "Damn it, Gary, take the light out of my eyes!"

"It's not Gary, Chaser." I flipped the wall switch and the electric lights flooded the room with enough light to make us all squint. Chaser scrambled to his feet.

"Drum! What are you doing here?"

"Trying to find out who trashed the place the last two nights. Now that I caught you, my dad will be coming to see your parents. You'll probably get some form of detention; maybe you'll even have to raise the money for repairs, probably some kind of community service."

"You got the wrong dude, Drum. It was my idiot brother here and his stupid sidekick, Dennis Larush. I just found out about it today. I came up here with Gary to see the damage. I told them they were going to have to fix the place."

"That's being taken care of. Besides, I don't want either of them around, they'd waste my time. We'll let the sheriff decide on their punishment.

Chapter 22

"You gonna have to tell the sheriff?" Chaser was already trying to weasel out of the situation for his brother, and I nodded.

I looked directly at Gary, "You need to get your shit together and act responsibly. Tell your friend, Dennis, that he's in trouble too. Knock it off! You can't behave like this and get away with it. You're gonna end up in juvie court if you're not careful."

Gary hung his head and stepped toward me extending his fist. We bumped fists and he said, "Thanks, man. I'm sorry."

"Okay. I'll tell my mom and let my parents decide what to do." There is a major fine for destruction of state property. I think the minimum fine is five hundred dollars. You might be lucky this time. If it happens again, no way. I won't even try to help you."

Gary nodded and the brothers drifted to the door. Chaser thanked me for explaining things to his brother and motioned to Gary for the flashlight. I watched their backs as they started down the stairs, Chaser leading the way.

I could hear Chaser yelling at Gary as they worked their way back to the road where they had parked their truck. I heard the engine noise as they drove off and then nothing more. I decided to go home, so I left the sleeping bag but grabbed my flashlight and shut off the electric lights.

"Come on, guys, let's go home."

The dogs beat me to ground level without the flashlight illuminating the steps for them. Their night vision must be far superior to mine, I used the flashlight when descending the stairs. Suzy and Spectrum were waiting for me at the bottom and when I reached the ground, they took off running toward the car.

When we got home, I put the dogs on the back patio on their blankets and entered the kitchen by way of the slider. I tip-toed to my bedroom and as soon as I closed my eyes, I was asleep. It was near mid-night.

Danny woke me up in the morning. "Hey, David, what happened? Did anybody show up last night?"

I rolled over so I could see him, rubbed the sleepers from my eyes and blinked a few times before focusing on his Star Wars T-shirt.

"Yeah. Chaser's brother, Gary, and Denny Larush were the idiots that broke up the tower seventeen cabin. I'm going to ask Scott if he can make them do community service at Wilderness City Park for the rest of the summer. People leave trash and dog crap there all the time. The park is becoming a trash dump."

"Sounds like a good idea, David. That reminds me, I'm supposed to pick up our dogs' gifts in the backyard and the patio area."

"Remember to wash your hands after."

"You don't need to remind me, I'm not a little boy anymore. And you don't have to be the man anymore. Scott has that job." He gave me a dirty look as he exited my room.

I dressed quickly, grabbed some toast and downed a glass of milk. "I've got to meet with Jenny," I yelled to Danny as I ran to the Subaru. I was going to be a couple of minutes late picking her up; it was already seven fifty-five. I cringed at the razzing I was going to get from her. I was lucky Danny woke me; I had forgotten to set my alarm last night.

Jenny was sitting in the pickup waiting. I parked and jogged over to the passenger window.

She grinned, "Getting some beauty sleep today?"

I kind of gave a little snort and laughed. "I caught some criminals last night."

Then I walked around to the driver's side and got in. Jenny gave me a look that demanded an answer, but first, I started the pickup and backed out of the driveway.

She was still waiting for me to answer as I drove away from her property toward the tower.

"David! Tell me! You can't make me wait any longer. If you don't tell me what happened, you won't get any of the cookies I made last night."

"What kind of cookies?"

She sighed and looked straight ahead. "Oatmeal-raisin and peanut butter."

I decided I had tormented her enough, so I told her what had happened. When I explained the community service aspect, she began laughing.

"I hope they step in the dog poop and have trouble getting it off their shoes."

"My sentiments, too." I glanced at Jenny and grinned. "Now there should be no more damage to towers surrounding Suddenly. The word will get around and the delinquents will think twice before damaging any of the state property."

We arrived at the tower and I shut off the engine. The sun was illuminating the tower cabin and a hawk was perched on the roof. We stepped to the ground and moved to the bed to gather our tools for the morning's work. I observed Jenny having a problem of reaching her bag of tools and said, "Go ahead to the cabin. I'll get the tools. Just don't mash the cookies."

She stuck her tongue out and walked to the stairs.

We worked most of the morning, except for a ten-minute break for cookies. Major progress was made in the restoration. The cookies were very good, and I complimented Jenny on her baking skills.

"Grams helped me, but it was my idea."

"Well, tell your grandmother you both did a good job. Did I

tell you about the new investigators?"

"New investigators? No. When did they arrive? More than one?"

"They were at home when Megan and I got back from Rick's. They worked for Interpol at one time but now they're employed by an insurance company; they're married and they're staying in our apartment."

I told Jenny everything I knew about the couple, describing their physical appearance and that they were searching for clues on Whitmore's computer.

"I think they'll probably continue with the drone survey until Whitmore's x's are all checked out."

"Then what? If they don't find any more diamonds, what do you think they'll do?"

"Good question. I don't know."

I looked at my watch and said, "We've got about an hour left to work, what should we tackle next on our list?"

Jenny measured the pieces of wood we needed to fix the beds and I worked on repairing the phone system. After about ten minutes, Jenny grabbed the binoculars. We went out on the deck and focused as best we could on the area where we had reported the origin of the smoke two days before.

Jenny scanned the area and held out the glasses to me.

"I didn't see anything, do you?"

I swept the area with the glasses. "Nothing. The fire team must have gotten to it very quickly. It's pretty rare for a fire to burn itself out this time of year. I'll ask mom if she knows what happened." I put the binoculars down and checked the brown bag for cookies. There was one more. I broke it in half and tossed Jenny her chunk. She pretended to throw it back at me, but instead, stuffed it in her mouth. When she laughed, she sprayed cookie flack on the floor and into her hand when she tried to stop the explosive reaction.

I burst out laughing. "What a spaz!"

I turned away from her, picked up the jigsaw and suddenly felt a hand on my back. Jenny was wiping her messy hand on my shirt.

I shook my head, "Thanks a lot."

"You're welcome." She giggled but didn't spew food.

We packed up and headed home. Jenny became unusually quiet during the short drive. I could see her image in the rearview mirror and knew she wanted to ask me something. I waited until we were almost at her home, and as I turned into her driveway, I asked, "What do you want to ask me?"

She remained quiet until the pickup had stopped. We looked at each other.

"How did you know I wanted to ask you something?"

I chuckled, "My woman's intuition." I think she wished she could slug me, but her good arm was too far away. I opened my door and swung my left leg out of the cab.

"Wait! I want to ask you to do something for grandma and me."

When I had both feet on the ground, she said, "Oh, never mind. We'll tackle that when we're not so busy." She grinned, "It's a minor job anyway. It should only take a few minutes."

Now she had me wondering, but that was probably her intention. Our bantering was developing into a tit for tat relationship. I escorted her to the front porch, told her I'd see her tomorrow morning, and hustled for the Subaru.

The Moresbys' car was blocking the driveway when I got home, so I parked at the curb, walked to the back yard and crossed the patio. Mom and Danny were in the kitchen making sandwiches and soup when I came in through the slider. I said "Hi," and headed for the shower to clean dirt and sawdust from my hair and shoulders. After dressing, I joined Mr. Moresby in the living room where he was absorbed in reading through a stack of papers.

He looked up briefly, "I'm reviewing emails taken from Mr. Whitmore's computer."

I estimated there must have been at least a hundred pages

organized in three stacks. Moresby explained, "The biggest pile has yet to be read, the smallest is those I believe to be most important and the third stack is of little value. You can read through them if you like. They aren't in any specific order."

There were about ten pages in the smallest pile, so I began reading the text. The content, for the most part, was cryptic and made little sense to me. I frowned and asked, "Are these in some kind of code? I can't tell what they mean. They're written to and from someone called handsablur; who's that?"

"Flo is working on that right now at your father's office. She'll find out where he or she is located. Once we make contact, we'll determine if that person is Whitmore's accomplice." John found another message and added it to the cryptic pile. "Here's another."

I thumbed through the copies and found all the transmissions were made after nine o'clock in the evening; a few were time stamped after midnight, but only a few minutes past twelve o'clock. I couldn't remember Whitmore saying anything about staying up late, but he was not exactly talkative. I knew nothing of his contacts with anyone except phone calls to his home office. I thought he was talking to someone at an insurance company, but I guess it was all fake.

Scott and Florinda came home for lunch. I could tell she was excited as she leaned to John and began whispering. He exclaimed, "Really?" I couldn't hear what the exchange was all about, but John raised his voice and told us what Flo had discovered.

"It seems Mr. Whitmore was in contact with someone in St. Louis, Missouri, responding to the name handsablur."

"St. Louis? That's interesting, Jenny Kincaid left there for Wyoming not long ago." I watched the investigators exchange what I thought was a significant glance.

Chapter 23

Danny and I ate lunch on the patio at the picnic table. I filled him in on what I had learned about the St. Louis connection.

"So, you think the Kincaids are involved?"

"Not Jenny. She wasn't even born at the time of the robbery."

"Yeah, but her parents and the old bag were around then."

"Don't call Mrs. Kincaid an old bag. She's a very nice old lady. Her husband is dead and she's doing the best she can with that old house and supervising Jenny."

"Ah, Jenny. You like her, don't you?" He winked at me and I wanted to slug him.

"We're just friends, Danny. You know that, so don't start something that will mess up my relationship with Megan. If you cause problems, you'll regret it, big time!"

He shrugged, "Okay, don't get riled, but it's obvious you like her."

I was disturbed by his perceptiveness, but he had hit on something I was having difficulty with.

The Moresbys came outside and joined us at the picnic table.

Mr. Moresby asked, "Will you boys help us continue with the plan to inspect certain yards for ornamental clay items? We think that might provide some more positive results."

I looked at Danny. "What do you think? I'm willing to help." It just occurred to me we never got paid by Whitmore.

Danny quickly nodded, "Sure, I'll do it."

Danny surprised me by asking, "What if we don't find any more diamonds in lawn ornaments? What's the next step?" He was directing his question to the Moresbys, specifically, John.

But Florinda replied, "We'll have to make a trip to St. Louis and track down this handsablur person. We'll need to find out what his or her relationship was to Mr. Whitmore. We're very curious how Whitmore abruptly appeared after a diamond from the nineteen hundred ninety-seven theft was found in Suddenly. Had he taken part in the original heist? Perhaps he gained knowledge of the discovery from the jewelry trade, but he needed time to plan his insurance scam."

John added, "We have the map Whitmore marked and we'd like to finish the scanning of the specific properties targeted. Following that exercise, we will canvass the entire town with door-to-door interviews."

I was doing some mental exercises and commented, "There must be six or seven hundred families in Suddenly; how long would that take?"

"If Flo and I do the door-to-door, it would take about three weeks, but if we have a couple of helpers, about a week and a half." John was looking at Danny and me, grinning, waiting for our reaction.

I glanced at Danny, but he didn't look interested. I thought he didn't mind flying the drone but ringing doorbells and talking to strangers held no appeal. "Well, I have a job to earn money for college, but I might find some time to help."

"We'll compensate you for your time and if we find more diamonds, you'll get a reward from the insurance company."

"Huh, that's what Whitmore said, and it was a big fat lie. He said I would get a ten percent finder's fee. That was going to be fifty thousand dollars, enough to pay for at least two years of college. He also was supposed to pay for our time with the drone but that didn't happen. Maybe he would have paid us if he hadn't had that heart attack."

Florinda laughed, "Whitmore was giving you some bogus information, David. The diamonds stolen were valued at one million two hundred thousand United States' Dollars. The finder's fees would be a hundred twenty thousand. And we can guarantee payment."

I was speechless. My lawn maintenance days flashed through my mind. If what Mrs. Moresby was telling me was the truth, four years of college would be paid for if I could find the rest of the diamonds. "In that case, I'll help, plus I think I have a friend who will join us. Four of us will canvass the town. Are you going to put a note in the newspaper that will help?"

John responded, "Yes. Flo and I will buy a cheap cell phone and publish the number to call for anyone that has clay lawn ornaments. We will say that a Belgian family is looking for clay ornaments and is willing to purchase them if they meet certain requirements, but we will still go door-to-door."

I thought for a few seconds and mentioned Mr. Grinberg. "The jeweler at Leo's knows about finding the first diamond. We'd better have a talk with him, so he doesn't spoil our search. If people know of potentially finding diamonds in the ornaments, we might lose some of the stones."

Florinda agreed and said, "I'll have a talk with him. I think he'll be cooperative when he knows what's at stake."

About sixteen hundred miles east, Dexter Young was picking up a registered communication from the Avant Guard Designers, LLC to one of their clothing suppliers in downtown St. Louis. He parked his bicycle at the ground floor bike rack and padlocked a chain through the frame and both wheels. No wise ass was going to make off with his property.

He entered the ten-story glass and granite covered building, showed his pass to the guard just inside the door and continued to the elevators. Dex followed three suits into the first elevator that was going up, punched 8 and stepped back from the door. His presence wasn't acknowledged, but he liked it that way; he valued his anonymity. He had never been accosted on a delivery and was rarely spoken to. The OTIS moved abruptly and rapidly to floors 5 and 7, where the suits exited. He was now alone, ascending with his empty backpack to the eighth floor.

When the doors slid open, he was greeted by a trim young woman dressed in a purple suit. "You need to deliver this package." She handed him a nine by twelve Manila envelope and a ten-dollar bill. "Deliver it to Optimal Clothiers on States Avenue. It's only three blocks from here."

"Yes, I see the destination on the envelope. It should be there in about fifteen minutes." He had held the elevator door open with his right foot, stepped back into the box and pressed 1. The descending ride was rapid; no stops were made. Dex put the envelope in his pack and slid his arms through the straps. It had taken fifty-eight seconds to reach his bike from the eighth floor.

He unlocked the hardened steel chain and fifteen seconds later, was riding. Optimal was housed in an older four-story building that had recently had a facelift to bring it into the twenty-first century. The old stained white-brick facade had been replaced with yellow-stained concrete and large black letters O and C. He wondered how many people knew what the big plastic letters stood for; at least they were illuminated from behind at night. It was a big improvement.

He checked his watch. It had taken ten minutes, fifty-four seconds to arrive at the destination. It took him less than twenty seconds to carry the parcel to the main desk, obtain a signature, and leave the building. His next stop was the public library on Olive Street, a short ride from Optimal Clothiers.

Dex secured his bike to the nearly full rack and made his way to his usual spot in the computer access area. He liked the corner station where prying eyes were blocked from behind and to the right. He could also see everyone else online from this vantage point. He entered his gmail password and his email inbox popped up. A quick scan of the three new messages and they were deleted; nothing he was going to reply to had appeared.

Whitmore was now two days late with his update. While disconcerting, he followed orders and didn't send Whitmore an inquiry. The junk mail was just more garbage: sellers of pot looking for business, women from Russia looking for American husbands, and new diet aids were all deleted with a few clicks. Back to work.

The bike rack was slightly less crowded than when he arrived at the library, but two bikes were sandwiching Dex's wheels. Fortunately, being over six-feet tall, he was able to reach over the other bikes and had little trouble freeing his bike from between the mobile bookends. He felt like leaving a message about proper parking, but he decided against it. Another delivery from Jiffy Package Delivery and another ten bucks were probably waiting for him four blocks away.

He rolled into the parking garage adjacent to Jiffy Delivery, on 7th and Walnut, then walked his bike into the office area through a side door.

"Hey Dex, where've you been? You should've been back here thirty minutes ago. I've got another run for you; got the parcel right here: no pickup."

"I had to take a dump, Clyde, stomach problems. Where does the item go to?"

"It must be a book. Its address is the main post office on 16th and Market. You know where that is?"

"Yeah, it's nine blocks west of here."

"Well, it's to be insured, so better not lose it or you'll be out a full day's pay, including tips."

"Don't sweat it. Have I ever lost a package?"

"Not yet, and Dex . . ."

"What?"

"Comb your hair and make yourself more presentable. You're a reflection of the company."

"Shit, Clyde, no one pays attention to me. I'm just like the wind, invisible."

"Yeah. Okay, when you get back, I want you to give a new rider some of your brilliant delivery techniques. Be back by four o'clock. All right?"

"See you at four, Clyde. Bye-bye."

Clyde watched Dex push his wheels out the front door, swing his right leg over the seat and mount his bike. Dex was gone.

Dex glanced at his watch: 2:38. This delivery was going to be a snap; mailing a book from the main post office. He wondered what it was about; the return address was a professor, maybe it was a manuscript being sent to a publisher. It was being sent to Washington, D.C., Office of Academic Research. He'd check his email again on the return trip to see if Whitmore had finally gotten off his fat ass and made contact.

As he rode through downtown traffic, he got an idea. If Whitmore didn't send mail in the next forty-eight hours, he would take off for Montana. He was tired of the city and had been contemplating travel since quitting high school a year ago. He had saved nearly a thousand dollars in the last ten months. Maybe he could find a new girl and a new job, now that Marilyn had suddenly disappeared. He thought they were getting along swimmingly, but two months ago she dumped him without a word. Blindsided by the breakup, he was even more anxious to go somewhere new. He and Marilyn had made plans to go to California; Los Angeles to be specific, but the more he thought about it, the more appealing Montana was becoming.

It took Dex almost twenty minutes to deliver the package, so he had an hour to check his email and get back to the Jiffy Service center. He had plenty of time. As he made his way to the library, he hoped Whitmore had sent an email note about the diamonds. Dex checked his email, but there was nothing any different from his earlier monitoring, just two more items of junk mail.

Frustrated at Whitmore's lack of contact, he logged off the computer and headed outside to his wheels. He began to plan a bike trip to Montana as he rode to the Jiffy office. He hadn't looked at a map yet, but he guessed it must be over a thousand miles to Suddenly, Montana. He wondered if the little town was even shown on the old roadmap he had at home. He'd google it next time he was online. Clyde probably had a newer map at the office.

Jiffy Service had a bike rack outside at the curb where he chained his bike. He didn't worry about anyone stealing from the sidewalk in front of the office; high resolution cameras scanned the area continuously 24/7.

Dex entered the lobby and observed a young woman talking to Clyde. He wondered if one of the other two bikes parked at the curb belonged to the chick. She wasn't very big, but her defined legs looked like she had been exercising regularly. She carried a red and black checkered helmet, wore a yellow sweatshirt with SPEED written in black caps contrasting with her black biker shorts.

"Hey Dex, come here." Clyde wasn't issuing a request; it was an order. He moved over beside Clyde and got a good look at the confident girl. She was Hispanic, appeared to be in her early twenties, and had a left-eye shiner, black and purple; something she must have gotten in the last couple of days.

"This is Sylvia Montes. She's a new rider and needs a few tips about city traffic. I told her you are our best rider, so give her your best stuff. Sylvia, this is Dex."

The riders shook hands and sat down on the bench just inside the entrance. Dex talked for a minute, then asked, "Have any questions?"

"Yeah. Trucks intimidate me; what should I do about them?"

"Don't get behind trucks of any kind. They can't see you and you're asking for trouble. Do you know the downtown streets?"

There were a few seconds of silence and then she replied, "Most of them." She gave a weak grin.

"Okay, take home a city map and memorize everything. When you are delivering, you don't have time to look up where your destination is, just go. The faster, the better, but don't run reds and watch for fat ass slow pedestrians. Anything else?"

"No. Will I see you around?"

"Maybe. How'd you get that shiner? Bad boyfriend?"

"My brother hit me." She smiled, "We were boxing; I should've ducked."

Chapter 24

The Suddenly diamond hunters' group completed the drone scans of the properties marked by Whitmore. No more clay ornaments were discovered in five days, but we did find a small statue of cupid that had 3-M-W-X on the bottom. Since that marking didn't correspond to anything on the Moresbys' new list, we didn't break it open. Tomorrow, Tuesday, we are going to start knocking on doors. The Moresbys had gone over a back story with us to give residents so house-to-house inquiries would move along smoothly.

Jenny and I were nearly finished with the repairs in tower seventeen. We had some cleaning to do, and then I was going to install a padlock on the cabin door. Jenny and I thought we should be finished by ten o'clock, then start canvassing for diamonds.

Mrs. Kincaid was pleased Jenny and I had restored tower seventeen. Once the search for diamonds was complete, she wanted us to take her to the tower for a tour. I told her it would be about two weeks before we could complete the house to house enquiries. She said she didn't mind the delay; she was busy deciding on paint colors for the house's interior rooms. Swatches of sample colors were all over the walls. She was tired of everything being white and was scanning magazines for ideas but was having difficulty making decisions.

Jenny and I were talking over her grandmother's dilemma.

"Grandma is so funny about the paint colors. She decides to paint the living room a light green and the hallway a lilac hue, but when she sees the colors together on the computer, she decides against her choices."

"Tell her not to worry, start off with light tints and we can always paint over them with darker colors. It's just time and money and I think she has both. Do you have any preferences?"

Jenny nodded, "Uh-huh, but I think she just wants to prolong the decision until my collarbone has healed. She's hoping you and I will help with the job." She grinned, "She has an ulterior motive. She wants us to work together." Jenny looked at me and continued. "I think she's planning something for us. She thinks we're developing a very close friendship."

I thought about the implication for a moment, "I can't deny that I like working with you. For one very important reason, you laugh at my dumb jokes."

"Not all of your jokes are dumb, David. Some of them are funny."

We both laughed.

"What does Dr. Rennick say about your collarbone?"

"I'm supposed to see him for an x-ray tomorrow morning at ten thirty. Can you drive me?"

"Um, I'll have to check my busy schedule, but I think I can work you in."

Jenny smiled and said, "Good. That will force us to finish at the tower by ten o'clock."

"All right, tomorrow morning is planned. Shall we have lunch and start the house-to-house search this afternoon?"

"Grandma told me she would have lunch for us. She wants to feed you, so your mother can focus on the baby."

I rolled my eyes, "You know I can make my own lunch; I've done it for years. Danny does his too, but I appreciate your grandmother's concern. She obviously knows what it's like to have a new baby in the family."

I parked behind the pickup and we went in the Kincaids' home. Jenny excused herself, went to her room, and then I heard the shower water running in the bathroom.

I talked with Mrs. Kincaid for about ten minutes before Jenny reappeared. She had changed to a loose fitting summer dress for the afternoon visitations to residences. After eating, Jen and I left for my house so I could clean up; I was a little stinky from working at the tower. I quickly showered, put on jeans, a white T-shirt, and my brown school shoes. We said bye to mom and drove to the east edge of town to start our enquiries.

Chapter 25

Payday at Jiffy Delivery was Friday, two days away, so Dex decided that would be his last day at Jiffy. He wasn't giving any notice; he just wouldn't show up for work on Monday. Sylvia looked as if she was going to do a decent job. She had that fire in her eyes, was physically strong and was fairly tall.

Dex thought she might be reasonably attractive without the black eye, but he wouldn't be around to find out. Dex had four days to prepare for making his first long-distance ride. He ate dinner while watching the news and rummaged through his collection of state highway maps he had collected in recent years. Even though he could find maps on-line, he preferred hard copies that showed entire routes. Finding maps had become an obsession like stamps to collectors. Most of his road maps were less than two years old. They were something he had gathered from filling stations when he and Marilyn had started planning a journey to the west coast; now they were gathering dust. They were rubber-banded together and stuck under his sofa.

His card table, the third piece of furniture in his downstairs rental, was where he planned his trip. States from Missouri to Montana were scantily populated for the most part and after checking the Internet, the only problem would be Iowa and Nebraska. They didn't allow bikes on interstate highways. He didn't like the idea of taking backroads and having to travel round about to get to South Dakota; the detours would add an additional one hundred miles to his already long trip; another day or so of riding.

Dex slid back his fold-up chair, went to the kitchen and started brewing another eight cups of coffee. While pouring water into the Mr. Coffee reservoir, it struck him that he might be able to go through Iowa or Nebraska by water. He could travel by barge up the Missouri, at least to Yankton, South Dakota, before encountering another dam. From Yankton, it was about 100 miles to Interstate 90. It would be clear sailing on freeways to Butte, Montana.

So, Dex decided he would ride the interstate across Missouri and find a boat or barge that would carry him to Yankton. Now, he had to make a list of items necessary to carry with him. He had four days and no more than two-hundred-fifty dollars to spend. He would have to live on the rest of his savings once he reached Suddenly. Whitmore was going to be surprised, if not shocked, to see Dex so far from St. Louis. He wondered what excuse the fat man would give him for the silent treatment.

Dex smiled as he began jotting down items to buy in the next couple of days, leaving last-minute items for Sunday. Saturday would be his biggest shopping day, but he would pick up pocket items during Thursday and Friday between deliveries. Must have items would be two extra tubes and tires, an extra hand pump and a 6-inch crescent wrench. Maybe he would buy another pocketknife. No, on second thought, a Swiss Army knife from the army surplus supply store out on Cass Avenue would be better. He would keep the majority of his cash and the Army knife inside the tubing below his bike seat, a safe place. The crescent wrench would be clipped underneath his saddle.

Dex hit the streets early Thursday morning and visited the Bikes-4-All shop on the way to work. He had Al Burrell, his bike guru friend, set aside a bike rack and waterproof bike saddle bags to pick up on his way home around six o'clock. The tab was only forty-five bucks.

"Where you head'n with this stuff, Dex?"

"I thought I'd go west, take a little trip at the end of the summer."

"Kansas City?"

"Yeah. Never been there. Need a change of scenery."

"I might like to go with ya. Let me know when you're leaving; give me a few days head start."

"Okay. Let me know when you'll have some time off. How long will it take to get to KC?"

"Not long, about three days if no equipment problems. The second day is the toughest. Sore muscles, but we can rub each other down with liniment."

"What's in that stuff, Al?"

"Well, there's different kinds. The Chinese concoction has herbs with apricot and olive oil. It's strained and the liquid is used for relief of muscle and joint pain from strains. Another type has capsaicin in it, but I don't know about the biology."

Dex thought about the liniment, but he didn't want to buy it from Al and make him suspicious. "I'll get some before I leave the city. I've got to go to work. I'll be back by six."

"See ya, Dex."

Thursday and Friday passed rapidly and Dex's cash flow continued its exodus. He was buying a lot, but it wasn't more than he had budgeted. After work on Friday, Dex went to the bank, cashed his final paycheck and withdrew all the money from his savings, a total of $947.32. That evening, he put eight hundred dollars in twenties and hundreds into a roll, for secreting inside his bicycle. He brought his bike into his apartment to attach the rack and saddle bags, so he would have storage available for purchases picked up over the weekend.

He didn't have room for all his apparel, so he chose two extra changes of clothes and donated the remaining small amount to the Salvation Army. Sunday night he checked his email only to be frustrated again that Whitmore had not made contact. He closed his laptop, decided not to bother checking for any more emails. Whitmore's time was up, the SOB had lied to him. He was angry and itching to make things right. He sat looking at his computer, trying to decide whether to take it or not, but since it was the only thing he had of any value, he decided to take it on the trip. He could always trade it for food or other supplies.

He went to the nearest grocery store to purchase enough

carbohydrate and protein rich food for the next three days. He dumped the contents of his refrigerator, except for three bottles of water and a package of frozen pancakes, in a sack and disposed of it in the alley dumpster. With everything he owned packed in and on his bike, he went to bed.

He got up at five o'clock Monday, scrawled a brief note to his super, ate two eggs and popped the pancakes in the microwave. After breakfast, Dex took his last shower in the apartment, got dressed and was on the street by 6:10. He decided to get on the freeway early to avoid as many vacationers' cars as possible. However, relief to get outside the city limits and leave the metropolitan congestion behind didn't last for long. The steady increase in traffic as the sun rose reminded him of the clogged city streets he had left behind.

He settled into a steady pace after about five miles with only passing trucks' airstream affecting his balance. Frequently forced to the far right side of the shoulder by several close calls, he found himself having to watch for cars and avoiding riding off the road.

He was quickly adapting his usual awareness of city traffic to a hyper-awareness of vehicles speeding past him on the highway. In city traffic, he rode out front, but here, he was left far behind by speed demons. He wondered how long it would take to adapt; to really feel comfortable. Frustration mounted as he seemed to be going west at a snail's pace.

Dex felt he was finally making reasonable progress in his second hour of biking when he passed the sign for a rest stop at mile 198, already forty-three miles from St. Louis. Even though he felt like taking a break to hear a voice other than from his inner thoughts, he decided against it. He had water and didn't have to use the facilities; he had to press forward. If he stopped at every opportunity to rest, Whitmore would never get the surprise he deserved. It was a personal goal that Dex didn't want to lose sight of.

He mulled over what the pioneers must have thought when they yelled out "Westward ho!" He was undoubtedly experiencing a taste of the determination they had moving west in a wagon train going all the way to Oregon or California or just to gaze at the great Pacific Ocean.

As he continued his slow pace on I-70 west, he noticed the sign for the small town Warrenton. He had already gone fifty-two miles from home, and it wasn't even noon. Since it was too early for lunch, he kept on pedaling, gradually shaving off the distance to far-off Montana. He planned to stop for lunch, to rest his legs and brain. While reviewing a Missouri map he would finalize his route and decide where to stay the night.

With Warrenton out of sight from his rearview mirror, he came upon a wide shoulder area, large enough for a semi to pull over. He decided this was a perfect place to have some lunch and check for the distance to the next rest stop. He was fully engaged with a cheese, peanut butter and strawberry jelly sandwich when a state trooper pulled over, his blue lights flashing. Dex swallowed, followed with a swig of water and waited for the trooper to approach on foot to enable hearing each other talk over the traffic noise.

He smiled as he thought the trooper would ask for his ID and registration out of habit.

The trooper was about three inches under six feet, looked to be about fifty years old, clean shaven, and a tad overweight. His ID tag said Jorgensen. "You doing all right, son?"

"Yes sir. Just having some lunch and walking a bit."

"Can I see your ID?"

I put the rest of the sandwich between my teeth and pulled my wallet from my hip pocket and flipped it open.

"Where you goin', Dexter?"

That was easy to answer. I took a big bite and grabbed the remainder of the sandwich with my free hand. "Montana."

"On this bike?"

"Yes sir. How far is it to the next rest stop?"

Trooper Jorgensen replied, "About seventy-five miles. You up to getting' there today?"

Dex figured it was another three hours and then he would quit for the day. "I should be there by three this afternoon. That's as far as I'll go today."

"Well, you take care and don't get too much sun. I don't want anyone telling me they found you passed out along the road."

"I've got water and sun-block. I'll be fine sir." I looked at the sky and said, "Clouds are rolling in so I'm getting some shade."

"All right. Have a good trip. Know anybody in Montana?"

"Uh-huh. I have a friend in Suddenly."

"Suddenly? Never heard of it. Must be a small place."

"Yep. It's in the Bitterroot Mountains; almost to Idaho."

"Good luck Dexter."

"Thanks for stopping."

"No problem. Bye." The trooper waved, climbed in his cruiser and pulled back onto the Interstate and accelerated. Dex watched him disappear as trucks blocked his vision to the west. He had expected the trooper to give him some static, but the officer was respectful and seemed genuinely interested in his well-being. While the trooper had no reason to examine Dex's belongings or bust him, a search would have had negative results. He had never taken drugs, having made up his mind when twelve years old to avoid them at all costs.

His Grandma Young couldn't understand why a sane person would want to alter their mind to escape reality. As far as she was concerned, humans suffer the good and the bad, they have to face it. She always said, "Grow up!" She had been a strong influence on Dex until she died his sophomore year. His grandma had raised him after his parents were killed by a drunk driver when he was eight years old. Before she passed, she arranged for Dexter to be an emancipated minor. Dex was on his own. He floundered for nearly a year as he lived on the streets and then dropped out of school. He had to start earning a living, the small sum of money left to him by Grandma Young had run out.

He walked around stretching, circling the shoulder area twice, before getting back on his bike. He felt like a second wind had arrived when he began riding again. His legs felt fine, but he knew that before long, he would start feeling some stress and strain. He knew Al's prediction was going to hit him before long, which was the reason he bought an eight-ounce bottle of liniment. He planned on using it liberally tonight.

As he rode, he began a mental game cataloging vehicle horns. He was amused to hear some of the beeps from little foreign cars; he thought they sounded like horn farts. The semi horns were like someone blowing a tuba from a foot behind him and were trying to scare him off his bike. One loud blast almost succeeded.

A car with children in the back seat went by and the kids yelled and made faces. He was enjoying a laugh when all of a sudden, a semi blaring its horn scared the shit out of him. He hadn't heard the big truck coming from behind. After that incident, he began glancing back every ten seconds or so in order to prevent an unwelcome surprise.

It was 2:48 when the sign for the rest stop; Boonville: 17 miles, alerted him. He wasn't making as much speed as he had thought, although he hadn't felt his pace had slowed. It must have been a gradual process. A quick calculation and he figured he'd arrive at the stop around 3:30. His legs were starting to fade but Dex's lungs and pulse seemed in good shape. He bit off the end of a small box of raisins and spit out the cardboard. The raisins would give him an energy boost until he arrived at the rest stop.

He could see the rest area from a mile away. As Dex got closer, he noticed about a dozen cars and pickups parked near the facilities. Less than a quarter of the parking spaces were occupied, and three people were exercising their dogs in the large grassy central space in front of the restrooms. When he turned into the blacktop area, one of the dogs, a little white fuzzball, was barking at the other bigger dogs. The lady strained to hold the leash as she scolded it. Dex had to laugh.

When he got off his bike about thirty yards from the men's room, Dex suddenly had the urge to pee as he looked at the lavatory buildings. He had to secure the bike first.

"Hey! How much for your bike?"

The voice came from a few yards behind him. Dex twisted to see who was speaking and said, "Sorry, it's not for sale." Dex continued walking backwards towards the men's room. The man kept moving toward him and he noticed another guy following about ten feet behind but didn't know if they were together. The closer guy was about five-nine and looked as if he was about Dex's weight, one ninety-five. He wore a white T-shirt, a size too small, grease stained jeans, and black New Balance running shoes.

"Come on, man. I need the bike. I'll give you a hundred fifty bucks, cash."

"Look, it's not for sale, for any amount. I need the bike. I'm riding it to Montana."

Dex didn't see a place outside the building to chain his bike but there was a sapling about two inches in diameter twenty feet from the facilities. He quickly chained his bike to the small tree and went into the building. Fortunately, the guy that made the offer for the bike didn't follow him into the restroom. Taking care of business only required a couple of minutes and as he stepped aside to allow a youngster to come through the lavatory door, Dex heard a loud engine revving just outside the building.

A pickup had pulled the young tree and Dex's bicycle about ten yards from where the tree had been growing. The two men that had followed him to the restroom were lifting the tree and the bike into the pickup bed. Dex yelled, "What the hell are you doing?"

The idiot that had offered to buy the bike jumped down from the truck and motioned for Dex to come at him. The guy wanted a fight. Dex had no choice. An onlooker, an elderly man with a small dog said, "Is that your bike?"

Dex didn't glance his way, but said, "Yeah. Could you dial nine-one-one for me?"

The second man, tall and skinny, was getting in the driver's seat. Dex only had a few seconds to react. The thief that wanted to fight had pulled a knife and was crouching, waiting to dissect Dex with his six-inch blade. Darting in and out of traffic was a way of life for Dex and he could get around this guy with quick moves. He started straight for him and when within six feet Dex launched into the air and kicked the guy's head as hard as he could. The loud whack was evidence that he had hit his target. Dex landed a little off balance and turned to face his opponent. The guy was on the ground, face down, apparently unconscious. His knife had been dropped, so Dex gathered it up and headed for the driver.

On the running board, Dex reached into the cab and grabbed the skinny guy around the throat and growled, "Cut the engine or I'll slash your throat from ear to ear." The driver tried to pull away from the vise-like grip, but the strength of Dex's forearms and hands was too much for him. He relented, reached for the key and shut off the engine.

"Get out! Give me the key."

Dex had the tip of the knife blade at the driver's throat, ready to slice open his neck. The guy had no options, gave him the key and stepped out on the grass. The police siren was approaching, so Dex had the driver sit beside his unconscious friend and wait for the trooper to arrive.

The siren was deafening as the cruiser rolled across the lawn and skidded to a stop beside the pickup. There was a moment of brief silence before Dex heard, "Drop the knife! Hands up!"

Before twisting around to see the trooper, Dex tossed the knife about twenty feet from him and away from the two thieves. Dex turned to see who had arrived and saw it was Trooper Jorgenson, the officer that had stopped to talk with him near the Warrenton rest stop.

When he recognized Dex, he holstered his weapon and said, "What's going on here, Dexter?"

"These two tried to steal my bike. The short ugly guy pulled a knife on me and I kicked him in the head. I think he's unconscious, not dead. I whacked him pretty hard. The other guy was trying to drive away with my bike attached to that tree. They ripped the tree out of the ground."

The elderly gentleman with the little dog approached and began talking to the trooper.

"Those two on the ground jerked that tree out with the bicycle attached. This young man knocked one of them down, picked up the knife and got the driver to stop the truck. The bike belongs to the young man. I saw him park it to the tree and go into the rest room."

The kicked guy rolled over, moaned and rubbed the side of his head. His eyes were still closed. He asked, "Hey sticks, did you get him?"

"Nope. We're busted. A cop just got here."

"Aw, shit. I wanted that bike for my nephew's birthday. Why wouldn't he sell it?"

The trooper was getting an earful and pulled cuffs from his belt. He straddled the bike thief and applied the handcuffs, helped him up and guided him into the cruiser's back seat cage. Dex stood beside the man who had called nine-one-one and they watched "sticks" until the trooper returned and cuffed him. Trooper Jorgenson caged sticks and returned with his notebook and pencil in hand.

"What is the value of your bike, Dexter?"

Dex hesitated, he didn't want to reveal the eight hundred bucks hidden in the bike frame, so he just said, "The bike and contents are worth about eleven hundred dollars."

Jorgenson's eyebrows went up like rockets and he gave Dex a dirty look, as if the value had been inflated. Dex moved closer and almost whispered about the money hidden in the frame. He didn't want to broadcast the facts.

The trooper stepped back, "Got it. If you want to retrieve your belongs from the pickup, you are free to go." He motioned to the elderly gentleman and said, "Tell me what you saw, sir."

Dex climbed into the truck bed, undid the security chain from around the torn-out tree and got his bike back on the ground. He checked the frame and tires and gave a once-over to the saddlebags. Everything was okay except for some minor scratches. He was ready to hit the road. He figured he would make it to Kansas City by nightfall, but before he mounted the bike, he wheeled it over beside the older gentleman and thanked him for helping. They shook hands and he wished Dex good fortune. They were headed for different destinations and probably wouldn't meet again.

When the rest stop was out of sight and Dex was back to creeping toward Montana at about twenty-five miles per hour, he gave a big sigh and relaxed. He was never so glad to leave a rest stop in his rearview mirror. Overall, it had been a successful stop; he had a good pee and got his bike back from two thieves. The day hadn't gone so bad after all; his legs felt loose, and he was making mileage, but what was he going to do when he reached K.C.? Dex had to find a boat to carry him up the Missouri River to South Dakota. He could pay a fare or offer his muscles for a ride. He'd rather work and save his cash for getting setup in Suddenly, but that might take some doing. As he rode toward K.C., he decided to wait until morning to look for a ride upriver to Yankton.

Chapter 26

Around ten miles from the rest stop, Dex felt the first drops of rain hit his cheeks. A slight breeze was coming right at him and he was slowing noticeably. Flashes of lightning straight ahead on the western horizon were illuminating dark clouds hovering at ground level. Just what he needed, a tornado to highlight his first day on the road. Had he made a mistake? Should he have stayed at the rest stop for the night? The brick bathrooms looked as if they could weather a tornado. He had a vinyl rain slicker that offered some protection but sweat would be a problem causing him to overheat as he pushed into the wind. Maybe he would just ride in the rain or stop and sit out the storm at the side of the road. He thought sitting in a low spot was a good idea.

More drops were striking as he began pumping the pedals a little harder to maintain speed and momentum. He tried to sit, but was losing too much speed, so he had to stand and use his weight to force the pedals down. Shifting to low gear helped. Blinking lights from behind caused Dex to glance back. He expected to see a patrol car, but the lights were not blue, just a vehicle's headlights. It appeared to be a truck; the lights were higher above the ground than car headlights. The truck, a flat bed, pulled up beside him and the passenger window came down quickly.

"Hey! I'll give you a ride into K.C." The voice was that of an elderly man in dark clothes, maybe a farmer.

The rain was coming down harder and Dex's vision was distorted so he said, "Thanks, I'll take you up on that. There's a car behind us . . . better let it pass."

The truck pulled ahead, slowed, and turned onto the shoulder twenty yards ahead and stopped. As soon as Dex caught up, he lifted the bike onto the truck bed and laid it between two massive tires chained to the flat bed. He guessed they were from a tractor, but what did he know about tires from farm machinery?

The driver ordered, "Climb in front with me!" Dex clambered into the cab and shook some of the rain from his face and wiped his eyes with his shirt tail.

"I'm Ben Ackerman." He extended his right hand and we shook.

"Thanks for picking me up, Mr. Ackerman. I'm Dexter Young. This storm surprised me, came up all of a sudden."

"You live in the city?"

"No sir. I'm just passin' through. I'm headed to Montana."

"Big Sky Country. I went there once on the way to Idaho to pick up a plow. That was twelve-thirteen years ago. Still got that old plow. Works fine."

"Where's your farm?"

"A little south of Abilene. Got two sections."

"Wheat?" I looked at Ben. He was squinting, trying to see the road better through the downpouring rain. The windshield wipers were moving at top speed trying to clear the glass.

"Uh-huh. A little corn and about a dozen pigs, too. You ever need a job just drop on by."

"Thanks, but I think my future is in western Montana . . . Bitterroot diamonds."

"I could be wrong, son, but that area has been mined out for years. Copper, lead, silver and gold have all been taken, except for traces. I thought about mining one time, but you can't raise a family on pipe dreams."

"So, you have a family?"

"A daughter and a wife. My daughter is grown, a lawyer in New York City. My wife, Emmy, and I run the farm. Five more years 'til retirement. What are your plans after school?"

Dex didn't answer for a minute, but he figured he could tell the truth. He'd probably never see Ben again after tonight. "I dropped out after grade eleven. I was bored so I got a job." Dex didn't say he had to get a job to stay alive.

"And what is that?"

"I'm a messenger in St Louis."

"Any future in that?"

Dex thought again. "Not much, I guess. It's kind of like a paper route but delivering more important stuff, mostly business stuff. The pay's not bad though."

"My daughter makes three to four times what I make running a farm. She went to college and passed the bar exam. She worked hard but is a lot smarter than I am, that's for damn sure."

"Is she in criminal law?"

"No way. She works for rich people. Does wills, trusts, that sort of thing. She lives in a loft with two other women. One of them has a boyfriend they all like. He designs airplanes."

Dex had no idea what that was like, so he decided to keep quiet and not show his ignorance. Dex could see the lights of Kansas City reflecting off the low-lying gray-black clouds far ahead. It wouldn't be long before he was out in the rain again, but it had let up a bit. Ben had slowed the wipers and could see more clearly now, only a few drops were being cleared with each swing of the blade.

"Would it be possible to drop me off along the river where I could look for a ride tomorrow?"

"Not a problem. I'll drop you near a YMCA. It's only a short distance from there to the public boat ramp. Maybe in the morning you can find someone going upriver."

"That would be awesome."

True to his word, Ben dropped Dex off in front of a YMCA. The four story building was part of the old section of town that in recent years had been renovated to attract new investment money.

The streets had been widened and all the store fronts now met new building standards.

Dex thanked Mr. Ackerman for the ride, and they said goodbye. Dex squeezed through the glass door entrance into the YMCA lobby carrying his bike and registered. He got something to eat, surprisingly for less than twenty bucks. It was his only real meal of the day. He thought it was a bargain.

On his first day on the road, Dex had covered two-hundred fifty-three miles at less than ten cents per mile. At this rate, the money in his wallet would last for about a thousand miles before having to dig into his cache in his bike frame.

The room, 309, was much better than Dex had hoped for and was more than he needed or expected. He was able to take his bike in the elevator and parked it beside his bed against the outside wall. The TV had limited programming, but all he wanted was the news, not late-night porno. There had been one tornado that had briefly touched down and blown over an old barn fifty miles away in rural Kansas.

He stripped down to his briefs, brushed his teeth, retrieved the bottle of liniment from his saddlebags and began working over his legs. The muscles had started to tighten up while he rode with Ben. Tomorrow his legs were going to give him trouble, big trouble. He hoped the liniment would help ease the pain. When he capped the bottle, he absently wondered if the fumes from the bottle had some anesthetizing affect.

Dex woke with a start at the sound of a truck horn. He tried to stand and move to the window, but his legs wouldn't follow orders. Dex collapsed back onto the bed in near agony. The truck horn blast would have to be ignored. The pain in his legs had to be addressed first. The liniment was going to help but not until after he had taken a hot shower to help relax his aching muscles.

Dex could endure pain as well as anyone he knew, but his experience was only from high school athletics. He knew ice baths immediately after an injury were useful, but Dex had been off his bike for more than twelve hours. Heat was the solution now, along with massage. He eyed the liniment bottle and a thought crossed his mind that he might drink a little. He read the label and decided against attacking the muscle pains from the inside. A hot shower, stretching, and massage were his answer for the pain.

Chapter 27

Twenty minutes later, Dex's mobility had improved considerably. He dressed slowly, gathered his things and headed for the elevator with his bike, hoping as soon as he began riding again some of the muscle pain would relent. He turned in his room key, answered a three item questionnaire about his overnight stay, stuck a biscuit in his mouth, put an orange in his pocket and carried his bike through the entranceway to the curb. No activity was on the street except for a semi driving slowly past the YMCA.

Dex took a deep breath of humid air, unfolded a street map, and found his location. He saw that he was five blocks from the public dock area. It was time to ride. He mounted his bike a bit gingerly, pushed away from the curb, and was on his way to the waterfront.

At the dock, two boats were in the water and two others were being floated from their trailers. Dex walked his bike onto the pier and questioned the first person he encountered.

"Do you know of anyone going upriver?"

The young man, dressed in blue jeans, a red T-shirt and sandals, was only a few years older than Dex. He was untying a sleek looking outboard. It looked like a sixteen footer, built for speed. A girl, dressed in a light yellow uniform, her blonde hair in a ponytail, was sitting behind the wheel and looked a bit impatient.

"Come on, Dale. I have to be at work at ten o'clock."

Dale gave Dex a brief look and said, "Haven't a clue. Sorry. Ask that guy." He pointed at an older man sitting on a wooden bench near the end of the dock. Dex walked closer to the old fellow, who was watching the oil slick on the surface below him, flicking cigarette ashes into the water.

The bewhiskered smoker chuckled, "You gonna ride that bike across the river?"

Dex grinned, "Later today after the sun's been up awhile. Might you know of anyone going upriver today?"

"What time have you, son?"

"It's about nine-thirty."

"If you wait 'til ten, the Missouri Belle will take you as far as Yankton, South Dakota, but you'll have to work some."

"The Missouri Belle?"

"That's right. Captained by William Nicklem. He was on a destroyer in the Navy. Billy runs a tight ship."

Dex was growing a bit suspicious. "What kind of a ship is the Belle?"

"She's a recommissioned stern wheeler, starts north on Sunday and picks up garbage from small towns all the way to Yankton. Has to stop there; there's a dam a couple of miles upstream. But Billy unloads at Yankton so the garbage can be processed. The stuff picked up combines with coal for makin' electricity nearby. A big power plant for South Dakota is a mile outside Yankton. Don't know how it works."

Dex decided to wait for Captain Nicklem to see if he could hitch a ride.

Sunday in Suddenly was almost always a quiet day and this one was no different.

We were having a party of sorts, actually an after church barbeque. Mom and Scott had invited the Kincaids and the Moresbys to join the Isaacs and us at our house. It was a celebration of Gwen's baptism. I had no choice, and didn't really mind, I attended church and sat with Jenny and Megan which made the experience more than tolerable.

We were all sitting around stuffing our faces when Danny asked for an update on the search for lawn ornaments. There was a brief lull in the conversation, so I mentioned Jenny and I had visited fifty-seven homes in the past six days, but and hadn't turned up any new terra cotta ornaments. We found a small deer decoration, but it was made of metal and had been bought recently at the local hardware store.

Mr. Moresby cleared his throat, clutching a beer in his right fist, and said, "Flo and I spoke with seventy-one property owners and haven't found a thing. I'm beginning to think that we might be looking for the wrong things or the other diamonds are no longer in Suddenly. It has been two decades since the theft occurred; you know."

He looked around and I wondered if maybe he was right. But we had only covered about twenty percent of all the homes in town. I thought it was too early in our search to give up.

"Do you mean you're going to give up on the search?" I asked.

Florinda replied, "Oh, we're not giving up, but we're trying to think of other methods the thieves might have used to hide the stones. If it's all right with you, Mrs. Kincaid, we'd like to dig up your yard."

"Well, Jenny and I were going to plant some flowers and start a garden anyhow. I don't mind if you want to dig up the yard, but I want the dirt put back and leveled so we can have a lawn and garden."

Jenny raised her hand and Flo called on her. "Yes, Jenny. What is it?"

"When is the digging going to start and who will do it?"

"We think a professional landscaper should do it, but not until we have finished our door-to-door search. John and I think that will be completed a week from tomorrow."

Scott commented, "I know of only one landscaper that can do that kind of job and his business is about thirty miles away. You'd better call tomorrow to see if he'll even do the job. The headman is Burt Carlson in Dillon. Say I recommended him. He'll cut you a deal."

Dex thanked the grizzled old man and rode on the dock back to a bike rack. He chained his bike to the metal structure and sat on the grass watching the few boats moving up and down the river. He turned his back to the sun and unscrewed the cap on the liniment bottle. With his pant legs rolled up to expose his sore calf muscles, he began a vigorous massage.

Five minutes working on each leg coupled with the sun on his back made him feel like riding, but he had to wait for the Missouri Belle. It was going to the exact place he had planned. He heard a long, low pitched horn and looked a hundred yards downriver. Dex's big smile stretched from ear to ear when he saw the low-draft brilliant-orange boat approaching the launch area. That old-time looking craft was going to take him all the way to South Dakota where he could get back to riding towards his destination, the town of Suddenly. He smiled, Damn, Whitmore is going to get the surprise of his life. Dex put the cap on the liniment bottle, stored it in his saddlebag, unchained his bike and started back down the dock to meet Mr. Nicklem.

The captain didn't look much like a person in charge of a boat the size of the Belle, but the recommissioned boat was not meant to be a luxury craft. His white T-shirt was tucked under a belt that looked as if it came from a championship in the World Boxing Federation. The belt seemed to be keeping his middle from exceeding the opening of the door into the wheelhouse. His black trousers were a little too short and concealed most of his alligator hide cowboy boots. He was clean shaven, which struck Dex as surprising. Dex expected a long black beard.

Dex swung off his bike and asked, "Are you Captain Nicklem?"

"Who wants to know?"

Dex cleared his throat and said, "Dexter Young. I'd like a ride to Yankton. I'm willing to work for passage."

"Well, you got me at the right time, son. I'm in need of a skimmer. It's not a very interesting job, but someone has to do it, or I'll lose my license."

"License?"

"Yes sirree. The government wants the river to be as clean as possible. I have to agree. Come aboard and I'll show you what you'll be doin'."

Dex carried his bike and boarded the orange monster, which brought forth images of Chinese dragons; the kind that appeared in parades and celebrations. Dex followed Nicklem to the stern of the vessel where a small boat was stored adjacent to the big paddle wheel. There was a long pole with a net attached to one end lying on deck. Dex had seen such a rig for cleaning leaves from swimming pools. He knew what his new job was without any explanation.

Dex listened closely as the captain explained the job details: "There are fifteen pick-up stops. We don't handle large cities; they have a different service, away from the river. The Belle doesn't have the capacity to do the metropolitan trash."

"So, I pick up stuff that falls into the water from the barges?"

"Right. Actually, you'll follow the trash rafts in the skiff. Your boat will be towed behind the barges. You're the boat of last resort. You'll be responsible to grab anything that falls into the water from a barge."

"That's it?"

"Yep. I know it's a boring job, but it has to be done. Otherwise we're just another polluter."

"How long's a shift?"

"Sunup to sundown. It takes a little over three and a half days for one excursion; then we come back and start all over again. You willing to do it?"

"Sure. I have no other way to get to Yankton."

"Why are you going to Yankton?"

"From there I can ride to Interstate Ninety and take it to Butte."

Nicklem shook his head. "You're riding that bike to western Montana? Must be for a woman."

"No, Sir. It's for diamonds."

"Yah. That's all right. You don't have to share the truth with me, just do a good job while you're on my boat."

Dex didn't want to explain, he wanted to know where he could safely store his things. He realized that mentioning diamonds was a slip of his tongue. Whitmore would have punished him for saying the slightest thing about the stones. Dex, keep your damn mouth shut.

"I assume you'll get me in a trailing skiff after we pick up the first barge. Is that right?"

"You got it, Dexter. I'll show you where you can store your things. Don't you worry about anybody stealing your belongings. I don't tolerate thievery on my boat. I'll show you your bunk and introduce you to one of the other crewmen. Follow me."

There were four bunks. The captain's was closest to the head and elevated about a foot above the others. Dex was assigned a cot against the bulkhead and provided a thin mattress that smelled a little like bleach. The captain helped Dex suspend his bike from a metal ceiling hook.

Ronny Crow joined the men, carrying a book with his left index finger marking his place. Ronny was a college student from Northwestern. He was studying criminal law and worked for Nicklem during the summer months. Crow was stocky, blond, wore glasses and khaki shorts. They shook hands and he asked Dex, "Where do you attend college?"

Dex thought for a second and blurted out, "Montana School of Mines in Butte. I start this fall."

"So, you're going into engineering?"

"Uh-huh and a few business classes." Dex figured a criminal law student wouldn't know much about mining engineering or business, but he'd better not put his foot in his mouth. Dex didn't know much about those areas of study either.

"Okay. If you gentlemen are through blabbering, you'd better put on some gloves and get ready to work. Our first barge will be ready for us in about twenty minutes at Platte City. My youngest son, Leonard, will join us there. He's about your age, Dexter; a senior in high school."

The captain left Ronny and Dex and in a few seconds he called, "Dexter!"

Dex jumped to his feet and went on deck to see what he had done.

"Yes Sir?"

"Yell out, all aboard!"

Dex felt a little foolish, but he yelled as loud as he could, "All aboard!"

The Belle drifted slowly away from the dock and the stern wheel started rotating. Dex was on his way up the Missouri. His plans were moving forward but not quite as he had envisioned. He heard the captain's voice, "Good job!"

Dex returned to his bunk and sat down. Ronny was reading. He looked up and smiled, "I had to do that the first time I came on board, too. I guess he does that to everybody, kind of an initiation. He likes to joke around, but he takes care to not lose garbage."

Chapter 28

When the Missouri Belle docked at the Platte City transfer site, Dex was mildly surprised. He thought the trash would be in loose piles dumped from trucks onto a barge, but the barge was already loaded with a half dozen rectangular bricks the size of large refrigerators. The trash had been compacted and wrapped with Nylon straps. A front loader moved the large bricks from a flatbed truck to the flatboat.

Captain Nicklem went ashore, signed some papers, re-boarded the Belle and made his way to the stern. He motioned for Dex to join him and they launched the trailer rowboat. Dex climbed in cautiously. It was his first time in such a small boat, and he didn't want to go for a swim, he had never learned how.

The captain passed the skimmer pole to Dex and said, "Keep the water clean. Pretend the river is an expensive new swimming pool in your own back yard. Next stop is Craig. You'll get thirty minutes off." The captain walked toward the stairs which led to the second floor wheelhouse and began climbing.

Dex guided his craft alongside the barge and tied his tow rope to the stern of the large raft. Two loud blasts came from the big boat's horn and the Belle moved to the center of the river pulling a partly loaded barge and Dex in his skimmer craft. Dex sat in the middle of the skimmer boat and began watching for junk in the water. He didn't know that Craig was at least six hours away. In fact, Dex had never heard of Craig and didn't know the town was in Missouri.

The Belle's sluggish progress to the north seemed extremely slow to Dex. As he watched for refuse appearing in the water, he occasionally glanced at the water's edges and realized he was moving slower than if he were riding his bike.

There it was! His first item to skim from the water; a return envelope from a charity solicitation. The useful part of the torn envelope was there; a stamp was on it, uncancelled. Dex stuck the wet morsel in his pocket; the forever stamp was worth fifty-five cents. He would peal off the stamp after warming the piece of envelope using the heat from a toaster, probably after he found a place to stay in Suddenly. He would affix the postage when he wrote to Al at the bike shop in St. Louis to apologize for lying about when he would leave the city. Dex would also tell Al about using the liniment.

Nearly two hours had passed and Dex was getting drowsy. His grip had loosened on the skimming pole and as it began moving out of his hands, he snapped to and began shifting his back and arm muscles. He couldn't afford to fall asleep. Dex had pulled half a dozen items from the water in addition to the envelope in his pocket.

The sun was getting high in the sky and Dex realized he was going to be in trouble from the burning rays. His head and arms were bare and would be flaming red before the day was over. Self-recrimination was taking over his thinking. He looked in the nooks and crannies of the skiff but couldn't detect anything that would act as a shield from the sun. The sound of a small engine attracted his attention. He looked upriver, squinted, and saw a small boat approaching, but he assumed it would go on by, the boaters waving. He wanted something other than the backend of the barge and the river water to look at; the boat would divert his attention for a few seconds.

The craft drew closer and Dex saw only one person in the boat, a young guy, and he was aiming his boat right at Dex. They were on a collision course. Dex stood up and yelled, "You're going to hit me!"

"No, I'm not. I'm coming to visit." The little boat went by, turned around and caught up, pulled alongside and the boater hooked the boats together. The visitor shut off the little outboard engine and spoke at a normal level.

"I'm Leonard, the captain's son. I brought you something. Dad said you might need this stuff."

Dex dropped to his knees and caught a plastic bottle. He took a look at it and was relieved; it was a bottle of sun-screen lotion.

"Catch!" Next, Leonard tossed Dex a baseball cap with the KC Royals prominently written above the bill. Dex fumbled with it for a second and put it on. It would have been better if it had been a Cardinals' cap, but he couldn't be choosy. Then came the life changer, an umbrella.

"The umbrella slides into a tube that folds up from the bottom of the skiff. You can't miss it. There's one more item." Leonard pitched Dex a quart bottle of water.

"I'll be back in about two hours with your lunch. If you need to pee, dribble over the side; the river won't rise much." He laughed and uncoupled the boats, started the outboard, and slowly passed the barge.

Dex couldn't see around the partially loaded raft to observe the little lifeboat rejoin the Belle. He was happy to have gotten the items he so sorely needed. Worry about being fried to a crisp by the sun was no longer a problem, but he had forgotten to thank Leonard for the delivery. When lunch was brought, he would have a talk with the captain's son.

With the umbrella in place providing needed shade, the baseball cap shielding his head and eyes, and water to drink, Dex was able to relax, watch for junk falling from the barge, and think. During the next hour, he decided to quit lying, even if he would never see these people again. So far, they had been nice to him, their new recruit. He had a number of questions for Leonard, mostly about being a senior in high school. Dex began to seriously consider returning to school and graduating with seniors his own age.

If he waited much longer to finish school, he would be doing a GED or taking classes with younger kids. Where he finished high school didn't matter, maybe even in Suddenly.

A slight western wind began to ruffle the paper on the top of the bales and pieces were tearing off and dropping into the water. Using one of the oars at the bottom of the boat, Dex directed the skimmer to the eastern side of the river and began retrieving bits of newsprint and stationery, soaked, but floating.

"Damn wind!" he said. "I'm going to recommend that a tarp be thrown over the refuse on the barge. I wonder what the captain will say." Dex thought for a moment and said, "Maybe I'd better keep my trap closed or I'll be out of a job." Then he laughed when he realized he was talking to himself.

The wind kept picking up; Dex was nearly unable to keep up with the onslaught of scrap paper falling into the river. He was tired of retrieving things when he noticed Ronny and Leonard spreading a cover over the bales on the barge.

"Well, it's about damn time. I wonder if they heard me." He watched the guys give him a thumbs up when the tarp was in place. A few paper scraps continued to flutter into the water, but Dex gathered them easily.

Time seemed to pass quickly while Dex was wrestling with the skimmer pole. When Leonard reappeared with lunch, Dex's stomach was growling in hunger. He had been so eager to get to the boat ramp to find a ride; he hadn't eaten much. Prior to seeing Leonard approaching, Dex hadn't had the slightest thought about food. Now, all his thoughts were about badly needed calories.

"Hey, I've come to make a trade."

"What?" The comment took Dex off guard. Trade for what?

Leonard hooked the boats together as before and tossed Dex a metal lunch pail. It was fairly heavy, so must be full. He set it down and had to react quickly to catch a cardboard box big enough to contain all the wastepaper Dex had pulled from the Missouri. A pair of rubber gloves was in the box.

"Put on the gloves, load the box with that pile of wet crap and I'll get it out of your sight. Keep the gloves with you for next time."

Dex followed directions and after he passed the box back to Leonard, he said, "Your dad mentioned you'd be a senior next school year."

"Yeah, my last year of high school. I'm looking forward to graduation and college. I'm going to go to a JC for a couple of years. It's a lot cheaper than a university. How was your senior year?"

Dex looked away from Leonard. "I dropped out of school last year, only finished half of grade eleven." There, he had done it, admitted he had never graduated. It wasn't so hard, and he felt relieved; he hadn't told another lie. "I want to go back, but not in a big city school. I think I'd like some help from teachers in a smaller place."

"You have a hard time learning?"

"Maybe. I'm a visual learner, hands on instruction. Reading isn't my thing, but I always liked comics."

"Ronny told me you were going to college in Montana this fall. You sure pulled his chain. He believed you. We don't get along very well. He's kind of a jerk. I won't tell him what you said."

"Thanks, but it's not a big deal. After this trip, I'll never see him again."

"Well, I've got to get back; the Craig depot is coming up in about twenty minutes. I'll be running the loader today. Nice talking with you. Later."

"Thanks for everything. Thank your dad for me, too."

Leonard released the boats and pulled away. Dex opened the lunch box and found it packed with about twice as much as he normally had for lunch. He figured he would eat half and save the rest for an afternoon snack, or in this case, a second lunch.

The loading at Craig went without incident, much like the transfer at Platte City. Dex spent nearly twenty minutes ashore walking to get the kinks out of his legs. The inactivity of his sore legs, only working with his arms, and sitting for hours in the skimmer boat had made him restless. His legs felt like lead at first, but after a little exercise, he was limbering up and feeling much better. He wished he were back on the freeway riding towards Montana. Patience had never been one of Dex's virtues.

One blast of the Belle's horn brought him back to reality and he ran to the boat.

The captain, on the second level deck, motioned for Dex to come a little closer. "You're doing fine, Dex. Keep it up. We'll be making two more pick ups before we stop for the night; another six hours of work. We'll have dinner when we shut down for the day."

Dex replied, "Sounds good. I'll be glad to see my bunk. Thanks for the umbrella and the sunscreen lotion. I would have turned into a fried piece of bacon without help."

"No problem. You'd better get in the skimmer; we'll be departing in about five minutes."

Dex waved to the captain almost like a salute and headed for his little craft. The heavily laden barge was now slightly over half full of bales. He hadn't paid much attention to the loading procedure; he was too concerned with his stiff legs and tightening back muscles.

An hour elapsed before Dex saw anything to retrieve. He thought it had taken that long for a bit of paper to escape from a newly packed ton of refuse. He captured the wet piece of newsprint and dropped it in the bow of his boat. Then, he resumed scanning the river on both sides of the barge. His eyes moved like windshield wipers, back and forth.

Rotating his head from side to side and scanning the water's surface had become a habitual routine. Dex rarely saw anything other than all sizes and shapes of wet paper.

An occasional partly crushed plastic bottle floated among the papers and he quickly snared the synthetic item before it had a chance to submerge. Something different quickly changed his routine. At first, he thought it was a beaver or another aquatic rodent, but as he got a closer look, he realized it was a small dog in the middle of the river. It looked as if it wasn't accustomed to being in water and was having difficulty deciding how to get out of the river. It was thrashing around, first to the left and then the right, not knowing where to go.

Dex knew he only had a few seconds to get the dog before it went under, so he swung the skimmer pole toward the animal and hoped he could get it in the net. It worked! The pooch seemed to understand what was happening but continued to squirm. Dex lifted the little animal clear of the water and quickly slid the pole hand over hand to get the net and animal closer to his boat. With a final tug, he secured his shivering cargo.

Chapter 29

Mrs. Kincaid blurted out, "Steadman! That's the name I was trying to think of several days ago. Sheriff, when you said headman, I recalled the name Steadman. He was a friend of my husband, but we never exchanged cards with that man. He was a bachelor and lived in that old ramshackle of a house about two miles out to the north. His first name was Vernon. He kept to himself after Vietnam."

Julie remarked, "Scott, that's the flag lot near the Hadleys'. I think the city owns the property now. The house is a converted barn. Many years ago, the owners raised pigs, sheep, and a few cattle. I was out there once, but I don't remember why."

Mrs. Kincaid said, "That's all that remains of what was a homestead from the middle eighteen hundreds. The land out there was originally part of Barney Wigner's quarter section. It's all coming back to me now. I went out there with my husband about thirty years ago. The place was falling down then."

Jenny asked, "Gram, do you think there might be some lawn ornaments out there?"

"I wouldn't even hazard a guess, dear. I think Mr. Steadman suffered from what we now call PTSD, but he wouldn't see a doctor. He didn't trust anyone messing with his brain. Bob told me he had seen Vern Steadman a couple of times over the years and Vern was drinking heavily. Bob said he felt uneasy about being around Vern; he was so unstable, it made Bob nervous. Vern was such an expert with a rifle or a pistol."

Scott had been following the conversation and he asked, "What happened to Mr. Steadman?"

"I believe he died of liver failure about five, gosh, maybe ten years ago," said Mrs. Kincaid.

Jenny glanced at David and Megan and asked the obvious question, "Hey. Should we drive there and check out the place? Maybe we'll find some more lawn ornaments."

"I have an idea. Let's visit the Hadleys' and ask Rick to come with us. Maybe if we can get him out of the house, he'll think seriously about more therapy. What do you think, David?"

"Good idea, Meg. Jenny can come along to meet Rick and see the Hadley's ranch. Would you like to go?" I looked at Jenny and she nodded, "Sure."

Megan stood up and walked to the phone in the Wilsons' kitchen. "I'm gonna call Mrs. Hadley and tell her we're coming out to get info about the old Steadman place. I'm going to suggest involving Rick as well."

"Good thinking, Megan." Julie grinned, gave a brief glance at Sarah Isaac and said, "I think your daughter will make a good doctor, she can be a little sneaky."

Sarah reacted, "She's been getting worse since she started working at the hospital. The nurses have to be clever to encourage patients to help themselves."

Megan finished the call. "It's all set. Rick and his mom can talk to us this afternoon. Mrs. Hadley thinks it's a great idea to involve Rick. We just need to make sure the car is ready."

"On it," I volunteered and went outside, the girls following close behind. Five minutes later, I had removed most of the mowing equipment from the back of my car. Jenny and Megan were standing beside the Subaru talking about Rick's injuries and his depression especially following his recent breakup. I put away the gas can.

I returned from the garage and said, "Take a seat, ladies. Buckle up and we'll take a short trip to see Rick." Megan climbed in the front and Jenny slid into the seat behind me. I heard the two clicks, fastened my seatbelt, started the engine and backed from the driveway.

When we arrived at the edge of town, I instructed, "I'm taking the longest way I know of, so watch for a turnoff on the left that might lead to Steadman's. The road is probably overgrown with weeds."

Jenny was curious. "Will we be able to see the place from the road?"

Megan turned and said over her shoulder, "I've been out here many times and I've never seen what your grandmother described."

"Me either. I'll bet it's in a hollow or behind some trees on the Hadleys' property." There was no traffic, so I slowed to twenty miles per hour. I didn't think three pairs of eyes could miss seeing a side road.

But I was wrong; there was no sign of a road or pathway to follow to the Steadman structure. We'd have to ask Rick how to get there. I concluded our failure was a good omen; I had been thinking of what to say in a conversation with Rick. Fortunately, the girls would contribute; besides being great looking, they were smart.

Rick and his mom were on the front porch when we arrived. Mrs. Hadley waved as I parked. Megan released her belt and nearly jumped out of the front seat like she was sky diving. Jenny and I followed a couple of steps behind.

I was focused on Rick's face when Megan exited the car and noticed a slight smile, but it soon faded when he saw Jenny and me close behind. It was as if he was putting on an act and didn't want us to see that he had normal feelings beyond rage.

Megan gave Rick and his mom brief hugs, then I stepped up to Rick and extended my hand. I wasn't sure how he'd react, but he gave me a dead fish handshake. I introduced Jenny and she said, "I've heard a lot about you. I'm sorry you had that terrible accident. I recently had a bit of trouble myself. I fell off my front porch and broke my collarbone."

Mrs. Hadley shook hands with Jenny and said, "Thanks for coming. It's nice meeting you. David's mom told me all about you. She's right, you are very pretty."

Jenny said, "Thank you." She turned a complete circle and said, "You have a very beautiful place. I love your flowers. You must have a green thumb."

"I've tried to add some colors out here besides green and brown," she grinned.

Jenny didn't hesitate and inquired, "Mrs. Hadley, is there any chance you might remember a man named Steadman?" I was going to gradually work the name into our conversation, but Jenny didn't mess around, she got right into one of the reasons we came to see the Hadleys.

"Steadman?" Mrs. Hadley looked at Rick. He nodded and she said, "Yes, we know that name. He lived in that old barn of a house near the western edge of our property. Years ago, Rick used to visit with that old man until he got very sick. He was an alcoholic."

Rick spoke up, "We can tell them, Mom. I don't care anymore. It was a long time ago." Rick's response shocked all of us. What did he know of old man Steadman?

Megan was the first to react. "What is it? What happened?"

"I was nine years old. I went over to his place to see the animals. All we had around here was trees, but he had chickens, pigs, goats, and a couple of cows. They lived with him in that old barn, in the big part. He stayed in a couple of rooms on the side that he added.

"It was in the middle of the afternoon and as usual, he was drunk. He said, 'Come here, boy.' So, I walked over to see what he wanted. He smelled bad, like wet cow crap and booze. I think I made a face and didn't get too close. But he grabbed me and started pulling my pants down. I kicked and scratched and yelled as loud as I could, until he let me go. I ran like the devil was after me to get back home.

"I told Dad and he went to confront him. I never went over there again. For a long time, I though Dad had killed him. But after a year or so, I saw him walking across the field by the main road. He was carrying a shotgun. I think he was looking for pheasants. I was riding my bike and when I saw him, I turned around and rode back home as fast as I could go."

Jenny said, "That's something my father would have done; I

mean, killed him, and my dad hates violence."

Rick smiled, "I think it's a little different for a girl."

Megan decided to try the direct approach after what Jenny had done. "Rick, one of the reasons we came to see you is that we wanted you to show us where Steadman lived. We don't know how to get there. But, if you'd rather not take us, we understand."

Rick sat there for a few seconds with his eyes closed and then surprised us by saying, "I'll show you where the old building is, but you'll have to help me into David's car." He looked at me and said, "Do you think you can lift me, David?"

"How much does the chair weigh?" I smiled so he knew I was joking.

Rick backed the wheelchair about two feet, turned it ninety degrees, and headed for the ramp to get to street level. In ten seconds, he was at the front passenger side of my Subaru. I swung the door all the way open, picked him up from his mobile chair and set him down in the car seat. He reached for the belt and clicked it into position.

Megan collapsed his chair and the girls placed it in the cargo area. Jenny reached up, grabbed the hatch, and slammed it shut. Before I could get in the driver's seat, and start the car, the girls were in back and buckled up.

Rick lowered his window and yelled, "We'll be back in about an hour, Mom."

The girls waved at Mrs. Hadley as I started toward town. I had driven about two car lengths when Rick said, "David, you're going in the wrong direction. The access road to Steadman's is behind us."

I slowed to a stop and looked at Rick. "You mean it's farther out than your place?"

"You got it. We need to go about two hundred yards past my place and turn to the left at the first dirt road. It should be a little overgrown."

I let out a deep breath and made a U-turn in the middle of the road. "Damn, no wonder we didn't see a turnoff on the way to your place."

"It wasn't your fault, David. Grandma thought it was closer than the Hadleys'."

Rick couldn't turn to see Jenny in the back, so he talked into the windshield and raised his voice. "How is the work coming along at the Kincaids' mansion?"

We all started laughing when Rick said mansion. The Kincaids' house was anything but a mansion. I began to realize Rick had gotten some of his old humor back. I was thinking that Megan and I were going to be able to help him with rehabilitation after all.

"There it is David." Jenny poked me in the back at the same time I saw the bare spot in the weeds. I turned off the main road and started winding my way through the growth that nearly covered the access road. We could hear the tall weeds scraping the side panels and the undercarriage of the car. I saw the corner of an old barn-like building and knew that was the Steadman house. It was behind a clump of trees that shielded it from sight from the Hadleys'.

The ground was really rough, and I worried about punctures, so I drove slowly to about ten yards from the old unpainted building before stopping. The place was a wreck. Some of the windows were broken and there was an old wooden wheel, probably from a wheelbarrow or a small farm wagon, hanging at the corner of the old building.

I unlocked the doors and we got out. The girls wrestled the chair from the car and had it expanded in short order. Megan and Jenny were working well together. I lifted Rick from the car and got him into his chair without difficulty. The ground was too rough for Rick to move the wheelchair alone, so Megan grabbed the handholds and away we went. I checked with her and she shook her head; she didn't need or want any help.

"Are we going in there?" Jenny pointed at the door on the other side of a rusty metal fence.

"Sure," I answered. "We'll find some spiderwebs and a few birds, that's all." I was pretty sure I was right about the interior of the deteriorating farmhouse. It was made from an old barn, a chicken coop, and what looked like boards from an outhouse.

I entered the side door and heard the flutter of wings, but in a different room. Jenny was right behind me, her free hand holding onto one of my belt loops. I didn't think her reticence was real, but I guess it was. I felt her release her fingers and I turned to see if she was all right. She had picked up an old broom and, using her good hand and arm, was sweeping away spiderwebs hanging from the ceiling.

Megan pushed Rick into the room over a bump in the threshold and onto the uneven flooring planks.

"It's much smaller than I remember, but I was only nine the last time I was here. Back then the floor was just dirt. Steadman did some upgrading. Maybe he expected company." Rick grinned.

Megan stood behind Rick and said, "Upgrade? This looks like something from the nineteenth century, not the twenty-first."

Chapter 30

Jenny said, "I agree, and I thought our house was bad. There's no electricity, no running water, and no heat. How could Steadman have lived here?"

"Look, over in that corner, to the left." Rick pointed into the shadows. I saw what he was referring to. There was a small pot-bellied stove in the corner. So, there was a source of heat. The occupant could cook on it as well, but only with one small pan, most likely for pancakes and biscuits, and a couple of pieces of bacon, or an egg but not all at once. I don't think he drank coffee, he probably had alcohol for every meal, and for snacks.

Megan observed, "I don't think we'll find anything here unless we come back with shovels and flashlights. Let's get out of here; it's kind of creepy."

Jenny added, "Yeah, let's go. Steadman probably died in this room."

I asked Rick, "Do you remember when he passed away?"

"It was on my twelfth birthday. The ambulance came out and picked up the body. At first, I thought Dad had paid for the meat wagon to bring me a present, like a new bike; something big, but it didn't stop at the house. I think Dad went out to see him the day before and found him dead. That was seven years ago.

"I heard Mom and Dad talking about him right after he died. Dad said he looked like one of those Jewish prisoners the Germans worked to death at the prison camps; skin stretched over bones."

"Oh! I've seen some of those pictures. I'm gonna have bad dreams tonight." Jenny looked at David and said, "Can we leave? We can come back some other time and do a search."

Rick frowned and glanced at Jenny. "Search? What do you mean?"

"Let's get in the car and we'll tell him what we're looking for, if it's all right with you, David." Megan backed the wheelchair out of the small side room and pushed Rick over to the car.

Rick looked up at her, "All three of you guys are searching for something?"

"Uh-huh. I'll let David tell you what it's all about."

We got Rick back in the car and I backed out of the overgrown path from Steadman's to the highway as the girls watched for traffic. I drove back to Rick's house, parked as before and sat in the car while I told Rick what we were looking for. He promised he would keep his mouth closed, not even tell his parents. He hadn't helped with anything like this ever and thought it was a cool project. Rick wanted to know how he could assist.

Megan answered seriously, "We want you to let us help with your rehab. David and I think we can help you strengthen your legs. Wouldn't you like to be able to at least get around with crutches?"

"I'll tell you what, I'll think about it, Give me a week or so and call me."

I said, "Okay. We'll be back in a week. We'll call ahead. No more surprise visits."

When I was helping Rick back into his chair, he said, "Thanks for coming out, David. That was fun going out there again. I didn't see any ghosts of Steadman, but I wouldn't have been surprised if I had."

I needed to ask him one more question. "What happened to the pigs, chickens, goats, and cows Steadman had?"

Rick started laughing. "I wondered if you would think to ask about them. We ate 'em. We had lots of bacon the year after he passed. When the city came out to remove the animals from Steadman's property, they didn't find any. We claimed ignorance and the city trucks left. Steadman had taken better care of his livestock than he did of himself."

On the way back home, Megan remarked about how much Rick had changed since she and I last saw him. We agreed that his attitude had been completely altered. He was much more talkative and animated than previously; it was like the chip on his shoulder had vanished. We felt good about involving him today and hoped he would cooperate and let us help him rehab his legs.

I realized the pot-bellied stove in the little room we had just investigated had no chimney, so Steadman must not have ever used it. Jenny suggested it might have been outside in the past. We still had to check the barn portion of the structure. I expected it to be very crude and the floor would probably be covered with cow poop.

Megan remarked, "I'm going to wear boots next time we go out there."

"I think all the poop would be dried out now."

"But what about the bird poop?" She had a point; the barn had several openings to the outside.

One last comment was made by Jenny as I pulled into my driveway, "I thought that old farmhouse would really stink but it smelled like dirt. That was another first for me; I'd never been in a farm building before. It was interesting and fun. Thanks, you guys. Oh, I thought of something that would explain the stove. I believe there was another building out there at one time. When it was taken down, the boards were used on the floor of the room we were in and the stove from the other building was put in that room. Therefore, no chimney."

I said, "Pretty smart for a city girl. So, detective, where are the rest of the diamonds?"

We all laughed when she said, "Give me a few minutes and I'll tell you." She pretended to conjure up an image.

As we exited the car, I thought if we didn't find any more diamonds in town, Steadman's old barn would be a prime place to search.

It was nearly five o'clock when Dex got the dog out of the net and on the floor of the rowboat. He'd missed a couple of pieces of paper, but he thought it was more important to save the animal. When he'd extricated the dog from the skimmer net, it collapsed in exhaustion on the bottom of the boat. It tried to shake off the water, but it was too tired to stand up, so it lay there looking at Dex, sides heaving as it tried to catch its breath.

"Hey, little guy, what were you doing out there? You're a poor little Yorkie. Let me dry you off."

Dex took off his T-shirt and started drying the tiny dog. He could feel the bones and theorized the dog had been on its own for some time. But Dex thought he had a cure for a hungry dog, the remains of his big lunch were untouched. But what human food would be all right for the miniature?

He guessed chicken would be all right, so he extracted the chicken from a sandwich, rinsed it free from mayonnaise and broke it into small doggie sized bits. The bread was too slimy with salad dressing, so Dex ate the flavored bread. He cut the small apple into skinny slices and then even smaller bits for his new friend.

Dex continued to watch the water for junk falling from the barge as he shared the rest of his lunch with the Yorkie. There was a chocolate chip cookie at the bottom of the lunch box, but Dex knew chocolate was not good for dogs, so he treated himself to the whole thing.

At the Rockport loading site, Dex inquired how long they would be stopped. After the captain saw the dog, he knew what Dex had in mind.

"If you want to go into town and buy some dog food, we'll wait for you. Try not to take too long; we've got one more stop before we tie up for the night. That's about two more hours on the water."

Rockport was only about a mile east of the river, so Dex hopped on his bike and took off for the little town. The captain volunteered to look after the Yorkie while Dex was gone. A supermarket was at the edge of town closest to the river. Dex chained his bike to a rack outside and went in where he was met with stares and a checker near the door said, "Put on a shirt or you'll have to leave."

"I just need a few cans of dog food."

"Sorry, you have to leave the store, or I dial nine-one-one."

Dex looked down at his bare chest and stealing three cans of food entered his mind, but the cashier was a big guy, really big. Dex didn't want to waste time arguing or starting a fight he would probably lose. He went out to his bike.

He opened the left saddle bag and dug out his red T-shirt, sniffed it, and put it on. Dex thought it might smell mildewed, but it was all right. When he re-entered the store, the big guy smiled, "Good job."

The pet food section was marked with an overhead sign so was easy to find. Dex picked four tuna fish shaped cans from the shelf and walked to the register.

"Is there anything else for you?"

"Nope. That's all I need."

"We have some cheaper dry dog food available in large bags on aisle five."

"No thanks, I'm in a hurry."

"Your total with tax is seven fifty-seven."

Dex gave the clerk a five and three ones. "Keep the change." He grabbed the four small cans and darted out the door. He heard the clerk say, "Would you like a bag and receipt?"

The words were still hanging in the air as Dex unchained his bike and headed for the Missouri Belle. Dex had been away from the stern wheeler for fifteen minutes. Captain Nicklem was standing on the top deck holding the tiny dog to his chest like he might carry a baby. Dex stowed his bike and climbed to the second story.

"What are you going to call him, Dexter?"

"I thought about that when I bought the dog food. I think I'll call him Skimmer."

"Not bad. That'll remind you of your short-time job and all the fun you had." The captain threw back his head and laughed. "We'll be leaving in a few minutes. Want to take him with you in the skimmer boat? I'll wrap him in a big soft bath towel."

"That would be great, Captain. Thank you."

Dex stuffed two cans of Canine Comfort in his pockets, climbed to the second floor deck and got Skimmer from the captain. When he was back in the rowboat trailing the near fully loaded barge, Dex opened a food container and emptied it onto a piece of scrap paper that had dried out during the stopover. He unwrapped Skimmer and placed his new friend next to the food. Skimmer wagged his tail, sniffed the new diet and began to attack it. When Skimmer had consumed about half the amount, Dex returned the remainder to the can. "That's enough for now, little buddy. More later."

The last leg of the day's journey up the Missouri went rapidly. Dex had one eye on Skimmer and one eye on skimming. Fortunately, neither required much effort. His little buddy was asleep, curled up on the bath towel and very few things fell from the barge. When the Belle arrived at the Hamburg site, it was getting too dark to proceed.

The captain made an announcement, "We'll lay over here and load up in the morning. Mess in fifteen on the quarterdeck. Bring your friends."

Dex wasn't sure where the quarterdeck was but he would soon find out. No one had friends, so the captain meant Dex could bring Skimmer with him. The captain must have felt some attachment to the little dog and wanted to see how Skimmer was doing.

Darkness on the river brought humidity and bugs. Dex avoided eating any flying critters. Captain Nicklem had a bug repelling device, but it wasn't highly successful. Dex thought it was sure better than nothing. After eating, all hands helped with clean up and then retired to their bunks.

With his roadmap spread out on his mattress, Dex knelt and calculated they had covered one hundred thirty-one miles on the Belle. While on his knees, he extended his fingers along the river and assumed they would arrive at Sioux City in twenty-four hours.

"You praying, Dex?" Ronny had put down his book and watching Dex hovering over the road map. His smirk was quickly erased when Dex answered back, "Yeah. I'm praying you'll fall off the boat and drown. You'd be doing me a favor."

"Don't get testy, Dexter. Wouldn't you try to save me with the skimmer pole?"

"Well, if you were about to go under, I'd give you an assist and push you under.

Look, I'm tired. Leave me alone."

Ronny decided to take Dex's advice and went back to reading his book. Dex calculated the distance to Yankton from Sioux City and figured it would be another five hours on the Belle. That would make a short day and he would then be on the road riding north to Interstate 90. Three more hours and he would call it a day. Early Wednesday morning he would start west on the interstate.

Dex folded the map and lay on his bunk next to Skimmer, who was curled up on his pillow. Skimmer moved up against Dex and licked Dex's chin. Dex covered his shoulders and Skimmer with the bath towel and went to sleep. It was too warm to need any blankets.

Chapter 31

Tuesday evening, following his second day of skimming, Dex began adapting his righthand saddlebag so Skimmer could ride in comfort. With holes for fresh air and a rectangular window opening cut out of the leather bag, the Yorkie could sleep on Dex's clothes or watch the countryside as Dex peddled along the interstate.

There were only two stops Wednesday morning, with the second barge almost full. Off loading began at one o'clock and Dex had nothing to do but watch. He asked Captain Nicklem if there was anything for him to finish before leaving.

"No, son. You can be on your way. You did a good job for me. Good luck to you for the remainder of your trip to the Bitterroots. Remember to have Skimmer checked by a vet when you reach your destination."

"Thank you, sir. I'll take care of Skimmer as if he is my baby. He'll be fine. If I'm ever this way again, I'll look you up."

The two men shook hands and said goodbye. Dex mounted his bike, with Skimmer close at hand and secure, they began travelling north on South Dakota route 81. Only one can of dog food remained, so Dex was determined to stop and shop as soon as possible.

Around three o'clock Dex saw a sign for Freeman, population 1,304. It was a small town slightly west of the highway. A sign advertised Uecker Supermarket: Easy Access from route 81. It sounded ideal for Dex to buy food for both travelers. He didn't want to waste any time riding around on city streets.

The sign was correct. Dex was in and out in less than twenty minutes and back on the road with a chocolate doughnut between his teeth and another one in reserve in his shirt pocket. He had drooled when in the bakery section and wanted to load up on calories for the next hour's ride to Interstate 90.

He spent over twelve dollars at the supermarket; over half for Skimmer, but now he had six more cans of food for the little guy. Dex expected Skimmer's food would last until they arrived in Rapid City, located in the far western part of the state. According to the mileage on the map, Dex expected the trip to Rapid City would take two days.

But first things first. He had to take Skimmer out of his lair for some exercise and a bathroom break whether they were at a rest stop or not. Interstate traffic was going to be much heavier than the state two-lane highway he was on, so he decided to stop now. The map didn't show a rest stop until Chamberlain, damn near a hundred miles, his next break. Dex spotted a turnoff on the right. It looked like it led to a farm a quarter mile away. Maybe they sold produce. He should pay the people a visit, plus there wouldn't be any traffic to worry about.

"Okay, Skimmer, we're going on a short detour."

Dex made a right turn and headed down a dirt and gravel single lane road. A sign about twenty yards from the turnoff said, "Witheralls' Retirement Community." Dex frowned, but continued on, wondering what he would find at the end of the road.

A small ranch-style home, white with dark-blue trim, sat facing west. Awnings in light-blue and gray shielded the windows from the afternoon sun. Dex parked his bike by leaning it against a fence post and walked to the door. He knocked twice and waited.

The door opened and a chubby lady in a floral print dress said, "Can I help you?"

"Would it be all right for my dog to get some exercise on your lawn? I'll pick up any deposits." Dex grinned and pulled a plastic bag from his jean's pocket.

"Why, sure, young man, but I don't see any dog." She pushed

the screen door out about six inches, peered around her yard, and looked at my bike.

"He's in my saddle bag; a Yorkie. He's real little."

"You go ahead and get him out. He might need to relieve some pressure. I'll be right out to talk to you. I'll get my husband."

"Okay. Thanks."

Dex sat down on the grass beside Skimmer as the little guy got used to the grass and deposited a small pile of fertilizer. Dex collected the poop in a plastic bag and walked to the side of the house where two garbage cans were sitting, one for recyclables, the other for household waste. Skimmer had followed his dad and was eying a small tree that looked as if it had been planted recently. Dex escorted his buddy to the tree and watched the water flow.

The lady and her husband appeared from the back of the house. He was holding another larger Yorkie, apparently well fed while living on the small farm. Skimmer saw the dog, scampered to Dex and tried to hide behind his legs. Dex picked Skimmer up and the men moved toward each other so the dogs could get acquainted.

"I'm Charles Witherall. Call me Chuck. You've met my wife, Sharon."

"Dexter Young, and my dog is Skimmer. Glad to meet you. We're on our way to Butte, Montana." Dex shook hands with Charles as the dogs sniffed each other.

"This little girl is Thelma. She runs the place. Sharon and I just work for her."

"You have guests? I noticed your sign."

Sharon came closer and said, "That's just for laughs, Dexter. Chuck has a strange sense of humor." Sharon had a wide smile and Chuck raised his hand to his mouth and chuckled. They appeared to be a well adjusted happy couple. Chuck wore tan trousers and a light-yellow long sleeved shirt with the sleeves rolled up. He was about five-nine. Sharon was all of five-four and outweighed her husband by at least fifty pounds.

Chuck walked over to let Thelma down, "You said you were on your way to Butte?"

"Yes sir. I started from St Louis four days ago. The map says I've got about nine hundred miles to go."

"Yep. Last time we went to Butte we drove about eight hundred ninety miles."

"So, you've driven there before?"

Chuck nodded and Sharon said, "We're going to Butte tomorrow. Chuck's writing a book about one of the ghost towns out there and I'm going to look for some nuggets. Chuck calls me a gold digger." She had a hearty laugh, louder than her husbands, and Dex joined in. He was enjoying their company.

Chuck asked, "If you'd like to share gas expenses, we can give you a ride. We'll spend a day and a half on the road. It's a working vacation for us, but you'll get there much faster than riding your bike."

Sharon added, "And your dog will have a Yorkie friend, too."

Dex did a quick calculation and realized he had struck it rich. He could shave almost three days of heavy riding off his road time. He had lost a day on the Missouri Belle, and was eager to make up time. He had a surprise visit to keep. The two dogs were on the ground and running around in the yard playing. Dex couldn't say no.

"Thanks for the offer. I'll do it but only if you have room for my bike."

"Not a problem. We take bikes with us on the front and back of our gas eater. I'll show you."

Dex followed Chuck to the other side of the garage to a Grand View motor home.

It was too large for their garage and Dex wondered what kind of gas mileage it got on the highway.

"How much does it cost to drive to Butte?"

"A couple hundred dollars, minimum. Can you afford a third?" Chuck was serious when asking Dex to cough up more than sixty bucks.

Dex was thinking that four and a half days on the road would cost at least fifteen to twenty bucks a day so he could afford it. He dug out his wallet and counted the paper money left. He had forty-seven bucks, so he was short. He'd have to adjust the seat on his bike and slip out forty or fifty bucks from his stash. He'd then have enough extra for the trip from Butte to Suddenly without having to take anything more from his bike frame.

Dex counted out three tens and handed the cash to Chuck. "I've got the rest in my saddlebags. I've got to make an adjustment to my seat that I'd like to make off road and after that, I'll get you another forty bucks."

"You can pay as we go if you'd rather."

"No, that's okay. I'd have to keep track then. I'd rather pay up front if you don't mind."

"It's fine with me." Sharon had joined them carrying the two dogs. She gave Skimmer to Dex and took the money from Chuck.

"I'm the banker for our trip. That's so we don't go overboard." She grinned, folded the money and stuck it in her breast pocket. "Let me show you our guest room. You'll stay there tonight. We eat at six tonight and six in the morning. Get what you need from your bike."

Chuck leaned toward Dex and whispered, "She runs a tight ship. We'll be on the road at seven o'clock, sharp."

Dex went to his bike and fiddled enough to get the extra money without causing suspicion. He didn't want anyone to know where his money was hidden, no matter who they were. Three twenties were taken from his roll and the seat was replaced in the same position he used for a comfortable ride. He met with Sharon and handed her forty dollars.

Dex was invited to dinner and answered their questions about how he arrived at the Witheralls' home. He had many questions of his own.

Dex discovered Chuck and Sharon were retirees. They had

worked for the electric power station for twenty years. Chuck, as an engineer, monitored the output dials at the station and Sharon had been a bookkeeper. Now, they were having fun, looking for precious stones and writing about early history of the western states. Chuck had developed a strong interest in ghost towns and abandoned miners' claims from the middle eighteen hundreds. Sharon had become a whiz at finding all types of metal objects buried near the earth's surface by scanning with metal detectors.

By nine o'clock, Dex and the Witheralls were in bed, having exhausted their inquisitive nature and anticipating the trip to western Montana. Dex had brought his saddlebags in and locked his bedroom door. A little suspicious, he wedged a chair against the doorknob for a touch of added security.

Just as Chuck had anticipated, they were on the road toward the interstate at seven o'clock the next morning, full of biscuits, bacon, and coffee. Chuck drove at a consistent speed of fifty-five miles per hour for optimum gas mileage. Nearly every vehicle moving west passed them, but Chuck and Sharon didn't deviate from their routine. Dex sat behind Chuck and carried on conversations with Sharon and occasional grunts from her husband. Skimmer seemed happy to be secured in a small pet carrier belted to the seat beside Dex.

Sharon was copilot and kept a watch on the computer screen to anticipate rest stops and gasoline stations. She said they rarely used the GPS system. The Witheralls liked following up-to-date road maps marked with a yellow felt tip pen. Thelma was free to roam the vehicle but slept most of the time.

Following Interstate 90 all the way to Butte was very simple. The motor home was well stocked with food and they never stopped at a restaurant during the two days on the road. Only four stops were needed along the way so all travelers could stretch their legs, eat, and use rest stop facilities. As their owners watched, the Yorkies were allowed to run on the grassy plots adjacent to parked cars and trucks.

Once in Butte, Dex and Skimmer parted company with the Witheralls. Dex was extremely grateful he had met the congenial couple. A hug and a handshake, followed by best wishes, were given all around. He told the couple how much he enjoyed the trip and wished them good luck with their retirement activities. He then followed signs to an on ramp and set out for Interstate 15. Dex and Skimmer were headed south to Dillon, population a bit over four thousand, only thirty miles from Suddenly.

Dex began to think of what he would say when he surprised Whitmore.

He smiled when he decided he would say, "How's my old man?" Dex anticipated Whitmore would ask, "How in hell did you get way out here?" The imagined exchange of words with Cyrus Whitmore came to a halt when he saw two people on the roadside busily engaged with repairs to a bicycle. As the distance diminished to about ten yards, he saw it was a man and woman. Both were wearing headgear and discussing something. The petite woman was pointing at something.

Dex rolled up to them and said, "Looks like you've got a problem; blown tire?"

"Yeah." There was a bit of anger in his voice. "We won't make Dillon tonight. I've got the spare on, but no way to inflate it. We forgot to bring a pump."

"Well, don't worry. I've got a hand pump. I can help you out. I'm headed to Dillon, too." Dex straddled his bike and the twenty something young man stood and extended his hand. "I'm Devin Springs. This is my wife Clair." Dex shook hands and glanced at the young lady. She quickly stepped over and said, "Hi. What's your name?"

"Dex. My buddy is Skimmer."

Devin laughed, "Okay. We're travelling with Harvey, a six-foot invisible rabbit."

Dex smiled and put down his kickstand, stepped to the back saddlebag, and opened it so Skimmer could get out. Skimmer stuck his head out and Dex picked him up.

"This is Skimmer."

Chapter 32

"Oh my gosh! He is so cute." Clair came closer and asked, "Can I hold him?"

"Sure. He won't bite. He's very affectionate; loves people."

"Here, hold him while I get a pump. I don't want him to get on the road."

Dex pulled a small hand pump from the bottom of his other saddlebag and tossed it to Devin.

While Devin put air in his tire, Dex talked with Clair. Clair divided her time between talking with Dex and talking to Skimmer. Devin and Clair were newlyweds and decided to spend their honeymoon in the Bitterroot Forest renting a tower formerly used for detecting forest fires. They planned on staying for one month but would leave sooner if they didn't like it. Dex said he was going to surprise a friend from St. Louis, but he didn't elaborate.

"Where is this tower located? Whitmore had never mentioned anything like renting an observation tower. Dex didn't know it could be done; he was a city boy.

"It's a few miles outside of a little town called Suddenly. It isn't on our map." Clair frowned and continued petting Skimmer.

"I know where it is; that's where I'm going. Where are you guys from?"

"Helena. We came from there today. We wanted to get to Dillon and take a break; stay overnight in a motel. We'll have a soft bed for one more night before we rough it. We plan to leave for Suddenly in the morning after getting directions."

"If you don't mind, Skimmer and I will ride with you to Suddenly. We'd like the company; this is the farthest west I've ever been. The state of Montana is new to me, and probably new to Skimmer, too."

"I'd better give him back to you; he's starting to squirm. I think he wants his daddy."

Dex laughed, "I think he wants to pee." He took Skimmer about ten yards off the highway, located a shrub and set his buddy down. Sure enough, bush irrigation followed. Dex was surprised by the amount of water Skimmer had been storing in his little body.

Devin finished inflating his tire and called to Dex, "We're ready to move on. You coming with us?"

"One second, I've got to put Skimmer back in his bedroom." When Dex got close to his bike, Skimmer squirmed and barked. He jumped in his traveling motel room and curled up. Dex fastened the straps on the bag and they were off toward Dillon.

An hour later, the bikers rolled into Dillon, a few minutes before seven o'clock. They could see motel signs from the highway, so the honeymooners decided to take the nearest one. It was a Super 8 hotel with their room costing over a hundred dollars. Dex told them he would see them in the morning. Dex didn't want to spend the cash to stay there. He then asked the management if they could recommend a camping site nearby. The woman behind the desk said, "Check with the Shell station at the end of the block. They might know of something."

"Thanks, I'll do that."

Ten minutes later, Dex parked next to the service door and asked for the boss. The wiry guy with glasses, a smear of grease on his left cheek, and short cropped gray hair asked, "What can I do for you?" He wiped his hands on a soiled rag. Carl was embroidered on the pocket of his gray work shirt.

"I'm looking for a place to stay overnight. I'm on my way to Suddenly, but I'd like something cheap, not a motel room; just for me and my dog."

The man pushed his glasses back with a dirty right index finger and glanced at Dex's wheels. "You're riding that? Where's the mut?"

"I nodded, he's in my right saddle bag."

Dex guessed the guy wanted to see if his visitor was lying. Dex opened the ventilated bag and lifted Skimmer out.

"Oh! You've got a Yorkie. Me and my wife have two of 'um. They're great pets."

The man-in-charge said, "Let me show you what I can let you use for ten bucks a night."

He started walking around the side of the station. "Watch your feet, it's startin' to get a little dark out here; sun's goin' down."

Dex followed with Skimmer at his chest, tail vibrating against Dex's ribs.

"Here we are."

It was a small damaged trailer. It had been in a wreck and one side was partly caved in, but it looked weather tight.

"It was left here about a week ago. The owners said they'd come and get it in a couple of days, but they never showed. I can't store stuff like this very long, so I'm gonna make a few bucks while it's here. If they don't show in a week, I'm gonna sell it as junk."

Dex reached in his pocket and pulled out ten bucks. "I'll take it for tonight."

"Well, it's got a mattress, but no bedding stuff. I can supply a pillow."

Dex replied, "That's all right, I'll curl up with my dog. He'll keep me warm."

Dex smiled and Carl laughed, "Yeah, blanket coverage." Carl walked back to the front of the station talking, "I'll get you the key."

Dex secured his bike to the trailer's hitch and waited for Carl.

Dex woke up with the sound of a truck's squeaking brakes as it stopped at the station at 6:07, Saturday morning. Dex gathered his things, repacked his saddlebags, except for Skimmer, and let his buddy out to water the landscape. Dex slipped on his light jacket to keep from shivering and muttered, "Damn, it's chilly in the morning here." Skimmer followed Dex as he moved to the front of the station. Carl was talking to the truck driver as he filled his customer's tank with diesel. The oversize city dump truck was loaded with gravel. Dex put Skimmer in his mobile room and tossed the trailer key to Carl.

"Thanks, man. When I get a car, I'll stop and say hello."

Carl waved, grinned, and said, "Hope you enjoyed the classy accommodations. Write us a good review."

"Just what I wanted. I'll do that. Take care." Dex waved, pointed his bike at the Super 8, and rode to meet with Clair and Devin.

The Springs were almost ready to leave the hotel when Dex arrived a few minutes before seven o'clock. Clair had opened the door to room 111 and was attempting to roll her bike outside, but the door was trying to close on her.

"Damn! Devin, please hold the door open."

Devin pushed the door wide open, put his foot against it and saw Dex. Clair struggled for a second until she got free of the door. "Thank you!" She put on her helmet and adjusted the strap.

Devin said, "Hey, Dex, catch." Dex caught an orange with one hand and stuck it in his pocket because Devin was tossing him some biscuits. He needed at least one hand loose to catch the free breakfast. Had he been able to park his bike, the catches would have been much easier using both hands, but he didn't drop anything.

Devin joined Clair and Dex and asked, "Which way do we go."

"We stay on fifteen for about twenty-five miles and turn west at the sign for Suddenly. It's uphill most of the way, but there's some coasting. Should be fun."

Traffic was light in the early morning and Dex found eating as he rode to be an easy task, even in low gear. He was glad to have the orange and biscuits to fuel up. He stopped occasionally for a few seconds and slipped Skimmer pieces of the biscuits, then caught up to the Springs. He followed the Springs' lead closely as they gradually climbed in elevation. Devin slowed and stopped when they reached the Suddenly turnoff. Dex had heard Clair yell to her husband that her legs needed a rest.

Dex was relieved to stop, too. He needed a bathroom break and Skimmer needed to eat some dog breakfast. He thought that after all the inactivity while driving with the Witheralls, his legs would be aching, but they felt fine. He was strong physically and he began looking forward to confronting Whitmore and finding out why the guy hadn't kept up with the bargained emails. According to Dex's map it was only seven more miles to Suddenly, with an increase in elevation of only a hundred feet.

The first road sign for Suddenly, other than a mileage marker, appeared three miles from the city limits; a four by eight foot piece of plywood was painted white with maroon letters giving the population, area, and elevation of the municipality. The sign was on the other side of a fence, apparently on private property. Dex's pulse rate was climbing, not significantly as a result of pedaling, but in anticipation of his meeting with Whitmore.

Clair was leading and Dex was trailing ten yards behind Devin. Devin looked back and yelled, "Sharp curve to the left, pavement narrows."

Dex didn't have much time to react when a truck came around the bend and skidded in the recently oiled gravel and dirt road. He saw Devin escape the sideswiping, but he had to steer off the road into an eight-foot deep gully. Dex's bike slid, but he fought to keep it from slamming down on the right side. Skimmer would probably suffer grievous injury if that happened. He knew this crash could be bad. Dex heard the crunch of his left ankle and felt pain so intense it overcame all his other senses.

Laying on his left side with the bike still between his legs, dust settling, he heard from above, "Are you all right?" He thought he had made it off the bike, but he hadn't been able to overcome the physics of the moving bike, elevated rider, and steep incline.

Overcoming the pain, Dex cried out, "I think I sprained or broke my left ankle, my foot caught on something coming down. I don't think I can ride any farther."

Devin looked down and said, "Clair and I will go into town and get some help. I don't think we can get you out of that hole without more muscle. Sit tight for about fifteen minutes. We'll be back A-S-A-P."

"Okay, I'm not going anywhere."

Dex couldn't reach his saddle bags to let Skimmer out without experiencing almost unbearable pain, so he decided to lay there and wait. He had no choice. All he could do was cuss the truck driver who had negotiated the curve too rapidly. He couldn't believe the guy didn't stop to help.

Skimmer was trying to get out of his bedroom and was able to poke his head through the porthole Dex had cut in the bag. Skimmer whined and Dex could only hope the little guy wasn't hurt. The bike looked all right except for a thin layer of dust that dulled the paint. That would easily wash off.

Dex surveyed the surroundings, but he could see only tree branches and directly above, blue sky. He grimaced but forced a smile when he thought Paul Bunyan could help right now. Babe would scare Skimmer, however. Dex thought he heard a siren, but it had to be too soon for an ambulance to be on its way.

Skimmer whined again and Dex tried to sooth the stressed pup, "I'll get you out in a few minutes, hang tough, buddy." He heard it again. It was a siren! The sound was being filtered by the trees, but the noise couldn't have been just a memory from St. Louis where the wail of ambulances occurred daily at all hours.

The siren got louder and then was abruptly silenced. Dex heard a car door slam and a familiar voice, "We're back, Dex, with an ambulance and a sheriff. Four of us will get you out of there in a minute.

"Can you get down there, David?"

"No problem."

Dex watched a young man about his age slide down the incline to the bottom and survey the situation.

"My name is David. Hang on just a little longer and we'll get you out of here."

Dex laid back in relief. "Will you check my right saddlebag for my pup and make sure he's okay?"

"Sure, I'll check."

David yelled, "Nurse Berg, slide a backboard down to me, and Scott, toss me a rope. You can pull up the bike first."

"No! You've got to get my dog out of the right saddlebag. He wants out and I don't want him injured. He won't bite."

"Okay, take it easy, I'll get him out. I've got two dogs myself."

"Not like this one, I'll bet."

David untied the bag and lifted Skimmer out. Skimmer licked his hand. "Scott, you're going to have to help me with the bike. It's in a crappy position with the rider's leg." David looked at the rider and said, "What's your name?"

"Dexter."

"Okay, Dexter, my stepdad's the sheriff. He's coming down to help. Can you lift your right leg?"

Dex was able to raise his leg about a foot but not enough to slide the bike out without dragging on his injury. David grabbed Dex's right foot and lifted until Dex groaned. Scott was able to slide the bike away from Dex's left leg and tie the rope around the frame below the seat. "Can you pull the bike up, Megan?" She immediately began pulling on her end of the rope with Devin and Clair helping.

David gave Skimmer a quick check for injuries. The dog seemed fine after being freed from the saddlebag.

Chapter 33

I held the little dog and began climbing up the steep grade, but needed both hands for balance, so I released the dog and it scampered up to Megan. Clair and Devin were hauling the bike the last few feet to the road.

"David!" Scott got my attention.

"What do you need?"

"Get the shovel from my trunk. I'm going to cut some steps into the dirt so we can climb out of here with the biker on the backboard."

Scott chopped and shoveled dirt until the incline looked like it had been part of an old stairway that had experienced some severe erosion. With Dexter strapped to the board, we started up to the roadway. Clair and Devin had the front of the board, Scott and I took the rear corners. With intense effort, we took one step at a time and after several minutes reached the ambulance. Nurse Berg helped us fasten the patient in place and shut the door. Dexter yelled, "Hey, where's my dog and my bike?"

Scott leaned in the open passenger side window, "We'll take your dog and bike to my residence. They'll be safe there."

Megan slid into the passenger seat and Nurse Berg backed the ambulance onto the road, completed an awkward turn around, and sped off to the hospital. She didn't use the siren. Scott and I put Dexter's bike in the trunk of the cruiser and tied the lid down with a piece of rope. With Clair and Devin in the back seat, we followed the ambulance. Dexter's dog curled up on my lap and looked like he was asleep. No trauma for him. He was the friendliest dog I had ever seen.

Scott and I arrived at the hospital a few minutes after the ambulance. The hospital wagon was empty, so Dexter was probably in one of the emergency rooms. Scott glanced at me, "I'm going back home. I'll file a report with the state troopers. Can you get a ride with Megan?"

"Sure, not a problem. She should be off before long."

It was almost time for lunch, and I had planned to take Meg to the Dairy Queen for a burger. I checked ER1 and it was empty, but I heard voices from ER2. I took a look.

Nurse Berg had rolled up Dexter's left trouser leg and was inspecting his ankle. Megan was holding his left shoe. She said, "Should I page doctor Rennick?"

Mrs. Berg smiled, "Don't bother, I'm sure it's just a bad sprain but we'll check with an x-ray. We can handle it."

Dexter was looking at Megan and I knew what he was thinking. "What's your name?" he asked. He was making a move, and I wanted to hear how Meg handled him.

This was going to be fun.

"Megan." She let his shoe fall to the floor. "Are you called Dex or Dexter?"

"Dex, usually. Say, this is a pretty small town. Would you know a guy named Whitmore? He's an insurance investigator."

Megan froze for a second and then looked at me. I nodded and she said, "Yes, I found him in a motel room. He had died of a heart attack."

"Are you sure? This guy is overweight, bald, and bossy."

"That's the guy. Sorry."

I stepped into the ER room and said, "The sheriff will want to talk to you about Whitmore. He was involved in a mystery."

Dex looked at me and frowned, "You're David, right?"

"Uh-huh. I was with Megan when we found your friend."

"Well, he wasn't really a friend. We met in a library where I was using a computer after the battery on mine died. He told me that if I would pose as his son, he would give me fifty bucks. After that, he wanted to keep in touch by email. He was emailing me some information and the contact suddenly stopped. I decided to find out why. I guess I found out."

"You're from St. Louis? You rode a bike all the way out here? That's about sixteen hundred miles."

"Yep. I had some help. Some nice people gave me rides. They cut a two week trip in half."

"David, you'll have to step aside for a few minutes. I've got to take an x-ray of the patient's ankle." Nurse Berg had given me marching orders. I motioned to Megan to come out in the hall to talk.

She joined me and I said, "I don't think Dex can be arrested unless he's an accessory to some theft or fraud, but Scott has to figure that out. We need to find out more about what he knows from acting as Whitmore's son. Can you get him to ride with us to my place? Moresbys will want to talk to him. Maybe he holds clues to finding the other diamonds."

"Good idea, I was trying to think of something to get more info about Whitmore, but I wasn't coming up with anything. I'll invite him to have lunch with us. That'll give him more opportunities to hit on me."

"Better watch out, he's from a big city."

"Yeah, but I'm a big girl." She grinned, poked me in the ribs, and kissed my nose. "Why not wait in the parking lot. Nurse Berg will probably wrap his ankle and give him a pair of crutches. Should be fifteen or twenty minutes."

I sat in Megan's jeep and waited, pondering what Dexter might know. Something was absent in our quest for the rest of the diamonds. Three quarters of the heist was still missing, and we had run out of clues and ideas. After a week of searching town we were no closer to answers. A million and a half dollars' worth of diamonds was still missing, and I was beginning to wonder if the stones were even in Suddenly.

Megan came out of the hospital entrance beside Dexter, who was on crutches. They were moving slowly and when they reached the turn in the sidewalk, she pointed to the jeep where I sat waiting. I moved to the back seat, Dexter handed me the crutches, and he plopped down beside Megan. I helped him latch the belt while Meg started the engine and shifted to reverse.

She turned onto the paved street and we headed home for the inquisition. Dexter had no idea what he was in for, but right now he was checking out Megan.

"Do you have a boyfriend?"

"Sure do."

"So, if I asked you out, you'd turn me down?"

"That's right, I don't even know you."

Dex grinned, "But you've seen my bare left foot."

"Yeah, that was real exciting, made my day." Megan looked straight ahead at the road.

"Do you know where your boyfriend is right now?"

"I do."

"Where is he?"

"He's sitting behind me."

He tried to look back at me, but he wasn't able to see my grin. Meg drove past her house and turned into my next-door driveway.

Mom came out holding baby Gwen and I introduced her to Dexter. Behind Mom and the baby were Scott and the Moresbys. Scott had changed clothes, these were clean. The Moresbys hadn't heard about Dexter yet, but they were going to get an earful in a few minutes following introductions. Dexter had quickly adapted to the crutches and shaking hands was no problem. We all moved into the back yard.

The picnic table had been moved farther from the house to allow more chairs to be placed on the patio. I was surprised at the amount of food present. Sandwiches were encased in a large transparent cake container I had seen at Kincaids. At least it looked the same.

I asked Mom, "Are the Kincaids coming for lunch?"

"Yes, they should be here any minute. Jenny wants to talk to you about something at her house. She didn't say what it was."

"Oh. I think I know. She wants to see what's in their attic. She needs a narrow ladder. I told her I'd help after we completed canvasing the town for lawn ornaments."

"Why don't you help Dexter find a seat near the picnic table so he can go back for seconds without crutches?"

I ushered Dexter to the end of the table where there was one chair within an arm's length of the buffet area. The Moresbys hadn't been informed of Dex's knowledge of Cyrus Whitmore yet, but I was sure the item would pop up with all the questioning that Dex was going to get during lunch. He was the only outsider present.

Mr. and Mrs. Isaacs arrived with Megan and she introduced her parents to Dexter. He didn't try to stand. If I had been in his situation, I wouldn't have either.

Dexter leaned toward Megan and said something. She came over to me and said, "Dexter's looking for his dog."

I pointed at his bike, leaning against our garage. "Skimmer is in his saddlebag bedroom. He seems to like the security there." I whispered to Meg, "It's warm and comfy in the leather bag." She laughed at my whispering and walked toward the bike.

I heard the purring engine of Jenny's pickup and made my way to the front yard. She had parked blocking our mailbox, but I didn't care. We hardly ever got mail on Saturday until late in the afternoon. Everyone would have cleared out by then.

"Hi, Jenny, Mrs. Kincaid. Everyone is congregating out back. We have a visitor I want you to meet." Jenny had removed her sling and was wearing a bright yellow dress fit for an Easter parade. She looked gorgeous. She had cut her hair even shorter than it had been the day before when we ended our search for clay lawn decorations.

We talked as we moved up the driveway toward the patio area. She mentioned the attic problem, so I told her, "I'll come out in the morning and we'll check it out."

When Jenny caught sight of Megan sitting beside and talking with Dexter, she grabbed my arm and pulled me back toward the front yard. She raised her right hand to her mouth and said, "Oh, my God!"

All I could say was, "What?" I had no idea why she had reacted that way.

"That guy talking to Megan, he's from St Louis. He's the boyfriend my parents didn't want me to be seeing. That's why I'm staying with Grams. He knows me as Marilyn."

"Jesus, Jenny. What do you want to do? Don't you want to see him?"

"I don't know. I can't hide, can I?" Jen had grabbed my left arm.

I had to think fast. Jenny had short dark brown hair now, not blonde, and she was wearing a new dress, not jeans and a sweatshirt. She had a name he wouldn't recognize. But her voice; that was going to be a problem. I told her what I had just thought, she grinned, and said, "You'll say I can't talk because of an allergy. My vocal cords are shot. I'll whisper to Gram. She'll understand, I hope. Oh, let me borrow your sunglasses." We started back towards the patio, but Jen stopped abruptly and said, "Have Gram come talk to me."

I left Jen standing there and found Mrs. Kincaid talking to mom and cooing to the baby. "What a beautiful little girl. She is just gorgeous."

I tapped on Mrs. Kincaid's shoulder. She turned slowly and asked, "What is it, dear?"

"Jenny needs to talk to you. She's waiting in the driveway. It's sort of an emergency."

Mrs. Kincaid turned back to Mom and said, "It's always so nice to see you and Gwen. I'd better go see what Jenny needs." She began walking to the driveway where Jenny anxiously paced.

I watched at a distance while the women put their heads together and had a short discussion. Mrs. Kincaid nodded, reached out to Jenny, patted her on the shoulder, touched Jen's cheek and returned to the patio. When Jen saw me, she gave me a thumbs up and grinned. Gram was in on the ruse. I didn't quite understand why Jenny didn't want to acknowledge Dexter or talk with him. I guess I'll find out later.

Mom announced it was time to eat. Everyone lined up and began helping themselves to a plate of food. Scott had joined the throng from the kitchen area where I had seen him through the slider talking on the phone. Someone from the office had probably called, maybe Deputy Doureline. Scott drifted over to Dexter and supported the disabled bike rider as he worked his way along the picnic table and back to his chair. Scott motioned to the Moresbys to join him next to Dexter.

I walked with Jenny to Dexter and introduced her. Jenny pointed at her neck and I explained why she couldn't speak. Dexter seemed to go for it. Jen turned away, started spooning potato salad on her plate, stabbed a couple of dill pickles with a fork and sat down across the patio away from Dexter. He looked at her for a moment and said, "Jeez, David are all the girls here as good looking as Megan and Jenny?"

Apparently, he didn't recognize Jenny, just what she wanted. But looks can be deceiving. I decided to get a seat close to Dexter to listen to his conversation with Scott and the Moresbys. There was only one place I could go, and it was also next to Megan.

Chapter 34

As we stuffed our faces, John Moresby asked Dexter why he had come to Suddenly. Was he on some kind of vacation?

"I was getting tired of the day-to-day hustle in St. Louis and wanted to find a friend of mine visiting here. I hadn't gotten an email from him in several weeks and I wanted to surprise him."

"My wife and I have talked with half the residents of Suddenly, maybe we know of him."

"I doubt that you've talked with him. I just learned today that he passed away a short time ago."

"Oh, I'm sorry. How did you find out? Would that be Mr. Whitmore?"

"Yeah, that's him. I helped him get some information about the location of some stolen diamonds. We were trying to get a recovery reward. He told me we would split fifty grand. It sounded good to me; all I had to do was act as his son."

Mrs. Moresby asked, "By any chance, is your email name handsablur?"

"Whoa, you guys are freaking me out."

"We have Whitmore's computer and checked who he has been emailing."

"So, you've taken Whitmore's position with the insurance company?"

"Mr. Whitmore didn't work for an insurance company; he was a thief."

Dexter looked mildly shocked and said, "Really? But he had

papers. He showed me."

The Moresbys replied in unison, "Forgeries."

Scott had the next obvious question. "What did you do as Whitmore's son?"

Dexter froze for a second and then asked, "Do I need a lawyer?" He stared between the agents and the sheriff and then looked directly at Scott.

"If you think you committed a crime, maybe. But I don't think so. We've all been working to recover the diamonds and we're still searching for more than half of them. What can you tell us?" Scott and Moresby pulled out little notepads and pencils. "Start from the beginning."

"Okay. Whitmore and I went to Lutheran Mercy Hospital and talked with a guy that was really sick. He had some letter disease and pneumonia. He was on oxygen, had this plastic thing in his nose."

"Letter disease?"

"Yeah. You know, like P-T-S-D, but it started with C."

"C-O-P-D?"

"Yeah. That's what it was, C-O-P-D and pneumonia. He looked like he was in bad shape, kinda pasty." Dex glanced around and noticed everyone was watching. "Mr. Whitmore asked him if he had any info about the nineteen ninety-seven diamond robbery. He nodded and stopped talking for about ten seconds, to breathe oxygen. Finally, he said a guy named Corporal Owens told him the diamonds were cleverly hidden in clay lawn ornaments and some homes in a little town called Suddenly, Montana."

John Moresby double checked, "You heard him say ornaments and homes?"

"Yes sir, but his voice was pretty weak and kind of gravelly. Whitmore told me the next day the old guy had passed away a few hours after we talked to him." Dexter shrugged his shoulders and said, "We couldn't go back and talk to him again, so Whitmore left St. Louis for Montana. He was flying to Butte. That's all I can tell you." He held out his plate, "Could I please have more potato salad?"

Scott tossed Dexter's paper plate in the garbage and dropped a big serving of salad on a clean ceramic plate. It was passed to the famished quest who dug in with his red plastic fork like he hadn't eaten in a week.

Megan leaned over to me and said, "Ornaments and homes, why not houses?"

"Hmm. Would that make a difference?"

Megan smiled, "I don't know, just thought I'd ask."

Danny walked over to me, stomach bulging. I think he, like Dexter had devoured more than one helping of potato salad. He got my undivided attention when he said, "That guy that was in the hospital in St. Louis . . . what if he didn't say homes, what if he said gnomes? There might be clay gnomes lurking underground. Isn't that where gnomes live?"

Danny is known to rhyme words and twist their meaning as jokes, so I thought he was on to something. "Tell them what you just told me. I think it might be important."

I watched him run his idea past Scott, Dexter, and the Moresbys. They all seemed to agree that was a distinct possibility. Then, Scott and the Moresbys went over to Mrs. Kincaid. Jenny joined the discussion, so all I needed to do was wait for a minute. She would tell me what was going on.

The group dispersed and Jenny gestured for me to come to her. I think she wanted me to get some separation from Dexter, who was still shoveling in salad. I expect he's going to suffer gas pains before long and I didn't want to be near him anyway.

She pulled me out of Dexter's sight and growled, "They're going to dig up our yard starting Monday. I want you to be there."

"Thanks for the info and the invitation. I'll be there." I grinned and teased, "How are your allergies?"

She slugged me in the gut, "Remember, we have a date to look in grandma's attic. Bring a skinny ladder that will reach ten feet."

I rubbed my stomach. "Damn, you pack a wicked right hook. Next time I'll block it." I was faking the pain from her punch. She didn't hit that hard; it was more like one of Meg's love taps. That got me thinking about her avoidance of Dexter. I had hoped to get details of their relationship when we were alone. Now I wonder if she's focusing her sights on me. Something else to think about. But first, we have hidden diamonds to find.

Jenny told me she was going to take her grandma home and whimpered, "Could you please escort Grams to my pickup? I don't want to be around Dex any more than I have to. Promise me that you'll come out Monday morning."

"I promise and I'll have the ladder. However, you get to go in the attic first. I hope there's nothing up there that will bite. You might not know this, but around here, a raccoon might get into an attic and make a home. They are known to attack pretty girls invading their space."

"You're kidding me again! I'll wear gloves."

"Okay, as long as you don't expect me to protect you!" I laughed and went to get Mrs. Kincaid.

Five minutes later, I returned to the patio and sat down with Dexter. He was loosening his belt one notch and massaging his stomach.

He glanced at me and said, "I think I overdid it. I might have to get some Pepto."

I laughed, "Where are you going to stay tonight? My Dad might let you have a cell for the night, maybe two nights of lock-up luxury." I winked at him. "There's plenty of room, no cost or roommates. You'd have to sleep on a bunk. You'd have a blanket."

"Stay in a jail cell? I don't know. How about my dog?"

"No extra charge. You'd have to clean up."

"Okay. Let me talk to your father."

I corrected, "My stepfather."

"Oh. I thought you called him dad."

"Sometimes I do. It was either that, sheriff, or use his first name. He's a good guy and deserves the respect."

I motioned to Scott to come over to talk. Dexter asked him, "David said I might be able to stay in a jail cell for a couple of nights until I can find a place that would be more permanent. Could I do that?"

Scott looked at me curiously before answering, "Sure. I suppose so, don't see why not. We wouldn't lock you in a cell. You'd have freedom to roam the area and use the facilities, but for only two nights. You'd have to be out on Monday."

"Sounds good to me. Where would I find a list of rentals?"

"In the same building as the jail, second floor. Follow the signs. Anything else I can help you with?"

Dexter chuckled, "I'll need a ride to the jail. I'll pay for the gas."

I volunteered, "I'll take you. Your bike will fit in my car. When do you want to go?"

Dexter sighed, "How about now? I need a nap, so does Skimmer."

"Okay. I'll load your bike. We'll drive around town a bit and you can see the sights of Suddenly. It'll only take a few minutes."

"Yeah, can you show me where Whitmore died?"

Sunday was one of those dismal days of gray skies, light rain, and brief gusts from the north. The Moresbys hadn't had a day off since arriving in Suddenly, so when Megan came over, the Moresbys joined us for a long game of Monopoly. Mrs. Moresby was easily the winner, the rest of us couldn't accumulate any money or hotels.

In the late afternoon, I escorted Megan home, a mere twenty yards, but she gave me a kiss. I figured it had been gratitude for not teasing her about being the least wealthy player in our game, but that hadn't come to mind. I remembered what it felt like when I had lost miserably to Danny in the past, but it was just a game.

The weekend had seemed too short but the Moresbys were up early and had been working with Scott in the kitchen early Monday. They were early risers and were anxious to get out to the Kincaids' to observe the digging. Mrs. Moresby had made Belgian waffles and the aroma contributed to my waking, but I wasn't ready to drive over to Jenny's until eight o'clock.

I tied a twelve-foot ladder to the top of my car to access the attic. Jenny ran out to greet us when I pulled in, parking behind a large flatbed from Dillon. The name of the excavation company was painted, unprofessionally, across the driver's door. We could hear noises from equipment working in the backyard.

"How long have they been digging, Jen?"

"About an hour. I see you didn't forget the ladder," she observed.

"I couldn't have forgotten. Exploring is all I've thought about. I've concluded that since thieves usually do the opposite of what you'd expect, we might find diamonds in your attic, not underground. Let's see if I'm right."

I had Jenny take the lighter end and I lifted the beefier part of the ladder. We worked our way through the living room without knocking over any antique furniture. In the hallway, the twelve-foot ladder just fit from floor to ceiling, inclined at a good angle for climbing.

I glanced at Jen, "Where's your flashlight?"

"Oh! Just a sec, it's in my bedroom." Jen disappeared for a few seconds and I looked up at the door to the attic, wondering what we would find above the joists, if anything, besides spiderwebs and dust.

She nudged me aside and started up the ladder with her little red flashlight clutched in her left hand. She was sling-free and climbing the rungs like a pro. I followed a couple of steps behind, trying to avoid her flying feet. When she reached the top, she stopped and looked back at me, then pushed on the access door over our heads. It was seated solidly and at first didn't give, but a crunching noise sounded, and the hinged wooden cover popped open several inches.

Dust dropped like sifted flour, but it wasn't enough to stop Jenny from sticking her head through the opening to further raise the trapdoor. She directed the beam from the portable light into the volume below the shingles.

"Oh, God! Rats!" Jen screamed, pulling her head back. The trapdoor slammed shut, she let go of the flashlight, then almost fell off the ladder. I was able to latch onto her right arm and pull her into a stable position one rung ahead of me. She was out of breath and with her eyebrows raised, her eyes enormous. She was scared shitless, no doubt about it. She turned her torso halfway around and threw her right arm around my neck.

"I've got you. Let's back down the ladder. Turn your feet around and sit on one of the steps."

We worked our way to the bottom of the ladder and sat on the floor. I didn't know what she saw, but she still hung on to me. I didn't mind one bit, she smelled like fresh lilacs.

"What did you see, Jen?"

"Sets of eyes, about a dozen. They were focused on me, ready to attack."

Now she had me worried. Jenny had great powers of observation as evident by the many sketches she had made. But the more I thought about a pack of rats being in the attic, the more doubt I had. If there were rats up there, someone would have heard their footsteps on the ceiling. It was time for me to take a look. I stepped into the living room and got my big flashlight. It could double as a weapon.

"I'm gonna take a look. Why not go in the kitchen and watch around the corner. Grab a broom and hit whatever comes down, except me, of course." I smiled, torn between believing her and thinking she must be wrong.

"Don't worry, I won't hit you with a broom, it'll be my fist."

From that comment, I felt she had returned to normal, so I started up the ladder, but slowed as I neared the top. I lifted the door a finger width and directed my flashlight beam through the opening. I saw the eyes, but they didn't move one millimeter. I increased the opening and got sufficient light up there to see about eight or more little figures staring back at me. They were gnomes, painted like Snow White's dwarfs. Whoever had painted them had apparently painted the characters with fluorescent eyes. Jen's flashlight hadn't provided enough light to see their shapes.

Excitedly, I grabbed one of the little figures, stuck it under my shirt, and quickly went down the rungs. When I reached the floor, Jen came into the hall holding a broom with both hands.

"Did you see the rats?"

Chapter 35

I wanted to laugh but I didn't want to poke fun, so I solemnly said, "Yes. They're all dead."

Jenn dropped the broom and approached hesitantly. "All dead? Like a bunch of skeletons?"

I began to unbutton my shirt and said, "Let me show you what we've found. I have one of them. There are seven more up there."

She backed a few feet away, "Don't throw it at me, that would be gross. I hate rats, even their skeletons."

"Don't worry, come a little closer." I had the little figure in my right hand, but she couldn't see what I was clutching. It was only six inches tall and behind my wrist. I turned my hand, raised it up and held out the gnome so Jen could see clearly what I had.

"That's not a rat! That's a clay figure of a little bent over gnome! God! Is this what we've been after all along?"

"Maybe. Let me show you what you saw with your flashlight." I turned my light on and pointed it at the face of the clay creature. The eyes lit up like a cat's at night when car lights made them glow.

"Let me see it, David." She reached out and I gave her the ceramic figure. She flipped it over, what I had forgotten to do, and exclaimed, "Numbers! David, we've found the rest of the diamonds! I have to tell Gram she can stop the digging."

I watched Jen disappear into the kitchen. I heard her steps as she ran toward the backdoor where Mrs. Kincaid was watching the equipment from Dillon systematically tear up her backyard. I climbed back to the attic, gathered four more figures, stuffed them in my shirt and descended the ladder. I put the clay creatures on the sofa, then climbed up for the last three little figures to get them all together.

There was a knock at the front door, so I went to see who was there. The Moresbys, expectant looks on their faces, wanted to see if Jenny and I had found anything in the attic. It wasn't my home, but I ushered them into the living room anyhow. I didn't say anything. I pointed at the sofa.

They rushed to the occupied cushions and immediately flipped the figures over, looking for numbers. Every gnome had numerical markings. The Moresbys started checking their list. Flo called out the scratched figures and John drew lines through the items on the printout.

Jenny and Mrs. Kincaid joined us just as John finished checking things off.

Mrs. Kincaid was most curious. "Is that all the diamonds? I'd like to get those men and their machines out of my yard. I don't know how much longer I can put up with all that noise."

"Well, Mrs. Kincaid, all but two of the diamonds are accounted for, if we can believe the markings on the figurines. Why not let the excavation people continue searching the grounds?"

Florinda suggested, "Maybe David could take you to his house until later this afternoon. The contractor says they will be finished about two o'clock, for sure before three." She looked at me, and I expected the question. "Could Mrs. Kincaid visit until then, David?"

"Sure. Mom won't mind and we have plenty of beds for naps."

Mrs. Kincaid reacted sharply, "I will not need a nap, young man."

"You can watch TV if you want or sit outside on the patio and drink lemonade."

I saw Jenny make a zipping motion across her lips. She wanted me to shut up. I took the hint.

John Moresby cleared his throat and asked, "Might I have a bag for the figurines?"

Jen went to the kitchen and returned with a plastic sack. Mrs.

Kincaid murmured tersely, "I'll get my purse. Jenny will drive me."

I wondered if Mrs. Kincaid was mad about me saying she could take a nap. She seemed a little put out, but maybe she was upset about having to vacate because of all the noise. I hoped that was the case. She started shooing us out the front door and Jen shrugged her shoulders.

The Moresbys got in my backseat and were jabbering excitedly when I got in to chauffeur them, I assumed to the Sheriff's office. As we pulled away from the Kincaids', John asked, "Could you please deliver us to the jewelry shop? We'll need some better tools than we possess to extract the diamonds and remove the fine clay particles. Once everything is clean, we'll conduct an accurate accounting of the recovery with the Sheriff.

"Okay. Mr. Grinberg, at Leo's Jewelry, will be glad to help. He identified the first stone Megan and I found. When you're finished there, Scott will give you a ride home. I imagine it will take most of the afternoon to recover all the diamonds and clean them up. Call the Sheriff's Office when you're ready to leave Leo's."

When I got home, Jenny was sitting in the overstuffed chair holding the baby in her lap. They were having a smiling contest. Mom was talking to Mrs. Kincaid out in the kitchen while preparing a bottle for Gwen.

The wall phone rang, scaring Mrs. Kincaid, so she moved away from it and sat in a dining room chair. I answered on the third ring. It was Stafford Realty wanting to talk to David Drum. I frowned, wondering why they would be asking for me.

"This is David."

"This is Arlene at Stafford Realty. Do you know a gentleman named Dexter Young?"

"Yes, I met him Saturday morning. The sheriff and I helped him out of a ditch. He sprained his ankle."

"He says he's from St. Louis. Can you verify that?"

"Yes, that's true. I can give you the name of a witness. May I ask why you are calling me?" I was confused about the call.

"Mr. Young has put a cash down payment on the Steadman property and has used you as a reference on his loan application. Do you know where the old farmhouse is located?"

"Yes, it's adjacent to the Hadleys', but it's very run down. I was just out there a few days ago. Has he seen it?"

Arlene cleared her throat, "Yes, I showed the property to him earlier today. He said he'd like to make it livable again, but he doesn't have a job. He wants to open a bicycle repair shop at the location."

I thought for a second. I needed to talk with Jenny about her ex-boyfriend.

"Can you give me a few minutes? I'll call you back. Okay?"

"All right." She hung up.

Jenny was still with baby Gwen, sunk into the cushions of that big chair mom was considering donating to The Salvation Army. It was like living room quicksand. Once a person sat in that chair, it was difficult to get out. I dropped to my knees beside the chair.

"Jen, that was Stafford Realty. Dexter wants to buy Steadman's barn out by Hadleys'. He says he wants to open a bike shop out there. Do you think he can run a small business with any chance of success?"

"Gosh, I thought he was only here temporarily. I had no idea he was going to stay. He'll figure out who I am before long, but I don't want to date him anymore. I want to finish high school, get in design school, and work as a fashion designer. I want to do what I love. Why did he have to show up here? Dammit!"

"Does he have any money? Can he make payments on the Steadman building?"

"He had a savings account, but I don't know how much was in it."

"Did he ever ask you for money, or have you pay for anything?"

"Nope. He wouldn't let me pay for anything. After dating for a couple of months, I realized he was honest and hard working. Then my parents intervened."

"That's all I need to know. Thanks, Jen."

I called Arlene Stafford back and told her what I knew about Dexter. She thanked me and said she would go ahead with the contract. She told me to let her know if any other people were looking for properties. Interest rates were at a low point and she would make some good deals.

After baby Gwen was down for the afternoon, Jenny and I started talking about Dexter. While we were gabbing, Mrs. Kincaid joined us and wanted to know more about Jenny's St. Louis connection with Dexter. We hadn't gotten far into the conversation when Jen's grandmother suggested, "We have all those tools, Jenney. Don't you think it would be a nice gesture to loan them to your friend?"

I kept my trap shut, anything I said might put me in mortal danger from Jenny.

Jen was quiet for several seconds, then came back to life, "I guess I should tell him who I am, but I wouldn't want him to get the wrong idea. I've changed in the last couple of months. I don't know if he still thinks we will go to California. I need to finish school here in Suddenly."

I was pleased to hear those words from her; I had been hoping she would be around during my senior year, but I wasn't sure she had decided. I wanted to support what Mrs. Kincaid had suggested.

I offered, "We could go out there, see what his plans are, and mention the tools. If I'm with you, he wouldn't try anything."

"Oh, I'm not worried about that. If he tries to kiss me, I'll kick his sore ankle or something higher up." She laughed and Gram said, "Thatta girl."

After we had lunch, we got another phone call. This one was from the Dillon excavation company that dug up the Kincaids' entire yard. The guy wanted to inform Mrs. Kincaid the soil upheaval was complete, and nothing but dirt and a few good sized river rocks were found. I was told the bill and was a bit surprised at the total. The company would send a bill. I didn't bother to have Mrs. Kincaid come to the phone; I relayed the information to her.

"Oh dear, I don't think I can pay for that in one check. I had no idea it would be so much. I'll have to make several payments."

Scott had brought the Moresbys back from the jewelry store before lunchtime. They stated that all but two of the diamonds were accounted for. Mr. Moresby jumped in, "Don't you even think about making payments, Mrs. Kincaid; the insurance company will foot the bill. The procedure won't cost you one penny. In fact, since the majority of the diamonds have been found on your property, some of the recovery money will be coming your way." The couple excused themselves to go for a walk and think about where to find the last two stones.

Mom looked beat, so I asked Mrs. Kincaid if she would like to see the Steadman place.

With the Moresbys gone and the Kincaids with me, mom would have some quiet time before Gwen came back to life.

I whispered to Jenny, "If Dexter is there, we can offer him the use of some tools. I can even volunteer to give him some help. I have an ulterior motive: I want to recruit him for football. He'd make a great wide receiver."

Jenny said, "That's pretty sneaky. If I didn't know better, I'd swear you were part city boy. Let's drive out there and I'll tell him who I really am, if he hasn't figured it out already."

"Will we go in the pickup?" Mrs. Kincaid asked.

"I thought I'd take my car, it's more comfortable, more room."

"All right. I'd like to see the place."

With Mrs. Kincaid in the front and Jenny directly behind me, we drove directly to the Steadman barn. As we pulled up to the metal gate, I noticed Dexter's bike leaning against the entrance door to the small side room. Mrs. Kincaid commented, "This looks like something from the eighteen nineties. Is Dexter going to live here?"

"That's his idea. That's what the realtor said."

Jenny saw the bike and leaned toward me almost whispering, "I think he's here."

I nodded, "I think so, too. Let's see if he's inside."

"Do you want to stay here, Mrs. Kincaid? It's pretty dirty around here."

She didn't answer immediately. After several seconds she said, "I'll stay here, you youngsters go ahead."

The gate made a racket, but we didn't try to conceal our presence. Dexter called out, "Is that you Mrs. Stafford?"

Jenny moved toward the door and said loudly, "No, it's Marilyn Gorton from St. Louis. Come out here and talk to us. David Drum is with me."

Skimmer shot out the barn side-door with his tail wagging like a spastic metronome. He made a beeline to Jenny and she picked him up. He tried to lick her face, but she held him at arm's length to avoid wet doggie kisses.

Dexter emerged from the shack; his pants covered with dust from the pockets down. He was clapping his hands together causing a small cloud of dust to surround his chest and arms. He sneezed and then squinted at Jenny.

"You're Marilyn? You don't look like her, but you sound like her. Your hair isn't blonde?" He began looking more closely, scanning her face from slightly different angles. I guess you do look a lot like her. Let me see your eyes."

He put his hands behind his back and came closer to Jenny and looked at her eyes. "Same eyes, hazel. How have you been? Have you been in this little town very long?"

"About two months. I'm living with my grandmother. You met her Saturday at the sheriff's home at lunchtime."

"You were introduced as Jennifer, weren't you?"

"Yes. My real name is Jennifer Kincaid. I go by Jenny."

"But you were Marilyn Gorton in St. Louis. I don't get it. Why all the lies?"

Chapter 36

"I'm sorry, Dexter. My parents had me use a fictitious name until I knew more about you. They were afraid you would start asking me for money. My parents are very well off and have been very cautious about who I date. I have no other support, so I had to go along with them. I'm staying with my grandmother now and my dad provides a monthly allowance, but it's not that much."

"You had me fooled Saturday, but I thought of you when David introduced us, you looked so different, I decided you weren't the same girl." Dex smiled and commented, "Skimmer really likes you, same as me. After I get this place fixed up, could I take you to dinner?"

"Let me think about it, Dex. My goals have completely changed since coming to Suddenly. I'll be going back to school in the fall."

"That's awesome! I'm going to do that, too."

"David wants to talk to you about that. I'll let him ask you some questions."

I had been listening to them talk and Jenny provided a segue.

"Two things, Dexter. I would like to know if you would turn out for football this fall. I think you would make a great wide receiver and we need someone for that position. Can you catch a football?"

"I can catch when I'm standing still but I don't know about receiving while running. Bring a football out here sometime and we'll experiment. I'd like to try out. I used to run the hundred and two-hundred meter dashes in track. What's the other thing?"

"Jen and I wanted to offer you the use of some tools. I've got some and Jen's grandfather had a room full, just waiting to be put to use."

Dexter started laughing, "I could have used a good hammer and some nails about an hour ago."

Jenny frowned, "What happened?"

"It was kind of funny. Skimmer and I were exploring in the barn and we found a porcupine, Skimmer did, actually. It scared him and he hid under the floor in this side room." Dex pointed where he had just exited. "I poked at the critter in the barn and it waddled away across the field to that clump of trees out back."

"I called Skimmer, but he wouldn't come out, even when I offered him some food. I pulled up one of the floorboards, but he still wouldn't come out, so I pulled up two more planks so I could see him. He was between two rocks and I pulled him out and put him in my saddlebag for a while.

"As I was trying to fit the boards back into position on the floor, I realized what I thought were rocks weren't really rocks, so I pulled them out. I now have three dogs."

"What do you mean, three dogs? You found two stuffed dogs? Steadman stuffed two dogs and hid them under his floor?"

Dex started laughing, "No, they're made out of clay, like figures someone might put on their porch."

I was getting excited and so was Jenny. She grabbed my arm and was squeezing the blood out. Her grip was really tight.

"Where are the dogs, Dex? Can we take a look?"

"Sure. I'll show you. One's a little bugger like Skimmer and the other is a St. Bernard puppy. At least that's what I think they are. They're kind of crudely made. Just a minute, I'll get them from the barn."

Dex went into the side room and Jenny let go of my arm. There was a mark where she had tightened her grip. I'm glad she didn't have her hands around my neck.

He returned holding a clay figure in each hand. Jenny and I each grabbed a dog and flipped it over. Jenny spit on the St. Barnard's feet and wiped them clean. There were no numbers. I wiped the feet of the Yorkie and didn't see any markings either.

I shook my head and Jenny showed her disappointment, too, "Damn! I thought we had discovered some more diamonds!"

Dex said, "What are you talking about? Are you still looking for the diamonds Whitmore was trying to find? I thought they were all found."

I answered, "Two big ones are unaccounted for."

Jenny looked at the bottom of the St Bernard again and started giggling. Dex and I glanced at her. I thought she might need a psych evaluation.

"Look, David, there's a number on the dog's scrotum. Check your dog's berry bag."

I joined in the laughter when I found a tiny number one on the Yorkie's family jewel's sack. Jen's dog had number two. I had to ask her, "What made you look there?"

"When you said two big ones are not accounted for, I thought, could those three little words be another clue? Mr. Steadman might have had a sense of humor mixed with his alcohol dependency. I couldn't help laughing."

Dex's smile faded and he said, "So you think Steadman was one of the thieves and when he found out the diamonds were marked with laser ID numbers, he got so depressed he started drinking heavily?"

I thought that was as good a guess as any, "Could be, Dex. You'll be getting a reward for finding these doggie's diamonds. We'll turn the dogs over to the Moresbys."

"I figured you guys would get the reward; I didn't know enough to realize there were expensive stones inside the clay dogs."

Jenny and I hadn't talked it over, but she didn't object when I told Dex he would be receiving some reward money. We wouldn't know what our rewards would be for finding a major part of the diamonds in the gnomes until the Moresbys submitted a detailed report to the parent company. Megan would get some money and Mrs. Kincaid, too. I was guessing, but I estimated that the last two diamonds in the dogs were about twenty-five percent of the total value.

Dex was looking at me, "What do you think I'll get? Will it be enough to make a dent in fixing up this place? I don't want to freeze out here in the winter."

Jenny ventured a guess, "I think it will be at least a couple thousand, don't you, David?"

"At least. Maybe as much as five or six." I asked Dex again, "What about the tools, Dex?"

"I'd like to borrow some, thanks. I can't carry much on my bike, though."

I thought that would be a problem. "Come with us and we'll get what you need and bring the stuff out here."

When Mrs. Kincaid beeped the horn at us, we all jumped. She was getting bored and anxious to get back home. We piled into my car after getting Skimmer from Dex's saddlebag and went to the Kincaids' to select some tools. I foolishly volunteered to help Dex with his renovations. So did Jenny. With more than two months before school started in the fall, we were going to renovate a barn. I still had my lawn service; I couldn't depend entirely on diamond finder's fees for college tuition.